ARTHUR

M000203346

THE COAST OF CORAL

Arthur C. Clarke is the world-renowned author of such science fiction classics as *2001: A Space Odyssey*, for which he
shared an Oscar nomination with director Stanley Kubrick,
and its popular sequels, *2010: Odyssey Two*, *2061: Odyssey
Three*, and *3001: Final Odyssey*; the highly acclaimed *The
Songs of Distant Earth*; the bestselling collection of original short stories, *The Sentinel*; and over two dozen other
books of fiction and non-fiction. He received the Marconi
International Fellowship in 1982. He resides in Sri Lanka,
where he continues to write and consult on issues of science, technology, and the future.

ibooks titles by Arthur C. Clarke
The Sentinel
Tales from Planet Earth

ALSO AVAILABLE

Eclipse: Voyage to Darkness and Light
by David H. Levy

Horizon's Ancient Rome
by Robert Payne

Horizon's Ancient Greece
by William Harlan Hale

Scientific American Guide to Science on the Internet
by Edward Renahan

Scientific American's The Big Idea
David H. Levy, Editor

Space: The Next Business Frontier
by Lou Dobbs with HP Newquist

Starry Night: How to Skywatch in the 21st Century
by John Mosley

The Ultimate Dinosaur
Robert Silverberg, Editor

THE COAST OF CORAL

THE FIRST VOLUME IN
THE BLUE PLANET TRILOGY

ARTHUR C. CLARKE

WITH PHOTOGRAPHS BY
MIKE WILSON AND ARTHUR C. CLARKE

ibooks
new york
www.ibooksinc.com

To our new friends in the oldest continent
A.C.C.
M.W.

An Original Publication of ibooks, inc.

An ibooks, inc. Book

Distributed by Simon & Schuster, Inc.
1230 Avenue of the Americas, New York, NY 10020

ibooks, inc.
24 West 25th Street
New York, NY 10010

The ibooks World Wide Web Site Address is:
http://www.ibooksinc.com

ISBN 0-7434-3507-9
First ibooks, inc. printing February 2002
10 9 8 7 6 5 4 3 2 1

Cover photograph copyright © 2001
by Australian Picture Library/CORBIS

Cover design by carrie monaco

Printed in the U.S.A.

Contents

Introduction   ix

1. The Road to the Reef   3
2. Fair Dinkum, Etc.   11
3. White Water   18
4. Death of a Spearman   29
5. Enter the Cops   40
6. How to Call on an Octopus   45
7. In the Wet   59
8. Out to the Reef   71
9. Heron Island   80
10. The Stone Jungle   87
11. Rendezvous with Sharks   95
12. Devil on the Reef   105
13. The Wolf Pack   113
14. "Spike"   121
15. North to the Sun   128
16. Through the Torres Straits   143
17. Drifting for Shell   156
18. Pearls and Politics   171
19. Of Perilous Seas   183
20. A Chapter of Accidents   204
21. The Turtle Hunt   212
22. Aladdin's Cave   227
23. The Last Dive   238
24. A Walk in the Dark   249
25. The Reef is Waiting   255

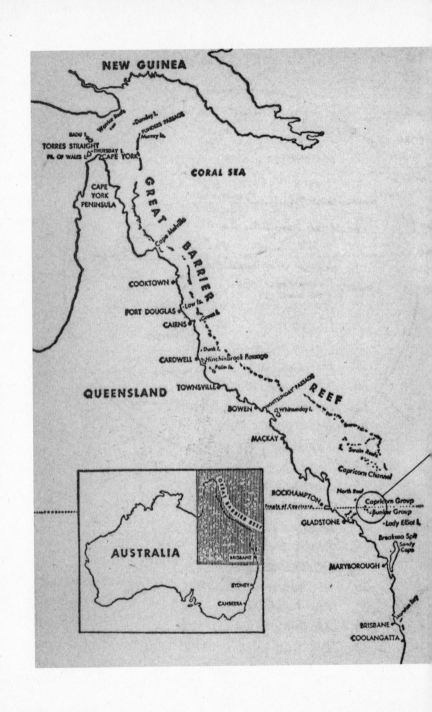

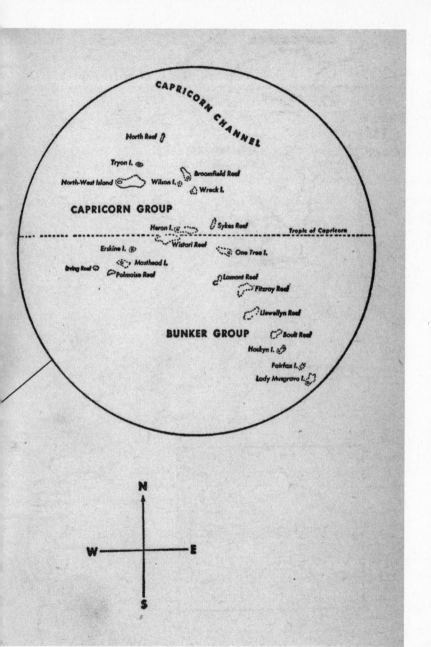

The Coast of Coral

An Introduction by Arthur C. Clarke

Though I cheerfully toss astronomical periods of time around in my fiction, I find it hard to believe that it will soon be half a century since the 37-year-old Arthur Clarke sailed from wintry England for an underwater expedition. This move was quite a surprise to my friends, because a few years earlier I had published *The Exploration of Space*, and they wondered why my interests had made a hundred and eighty degree turn. The answer was simple: I realised that underwater, I could experience something very close to weightlessness—which I was unlikely to enjoy in any other way.

Looking into *The Coast of Coral* again after several decades, it now seems a message from another age. I am sure that much of the Australia I described has vanished without trace. In the hope of recalling it, I have left the text completely unchanged. However, a few comments are in order.

I am slightly embarrassed by my frequent reference to spear guns—which I've since done my best to get outlawed. But, if you have to catch your fast-moving dinner on a remote coral reef, their use is justified.

I am more embarrassed by my advice about walking on exposed coral reefs—DON'T DO IT! Far too many of the world's corals have now been destroyed by legions of tourists trampling over them: the anchors of glass-bottomed boats have also made a major contribution. Fringing reefs can be much more comfortably and harmlessly viewed from walkways constructed a few feet above the high water line.

Advances in underwater technology over the last half century make the equipment Mike Wilson and I used seem incredibly primitive—flash bulbs indeed! Anybody remember them? We had to carry sacks-full to the reef and I am sure the roofs of some underwater caves still have specimens bobbing about. What an incredible difference electronic flash has made: now, of course, digital cameras have triggered another revolution. How I wish we could have seen our pictures immediately after we had taken them! I hope the primitive techniques mentioned in Chapter 25 may arouse amusement—and perhaps sympathy amongst today's photographers.

And as for underwater movies, the revolution is even greater. We carried a 16mm camera to the reef—and the cassettes held only about 3 minutes of film! Once they had been exposed, they had to be shipped back to the mainland and it was often weeks before we knew what results, if any, we have obtained.

Today's SCUBA divers will find it incredible that we were able to operate on a remote island without the aid of an air compressor. Portable units capable of charging air bottles were simply not available then—so we had to carry dozens of cylinders, and send them back to the mainland to be replenished. No wonder that we conserved air as much as possible, and relied largely on free diving!

Chapter 6 describes my encounter with Dr. Woolley, who later became Astronomer Royal. On his arrival in England,

just one year after our meeting, he became famous for say-
ing that "Space travel is utter bilge." The very next year—
1957—the Space Age opened with the launch of Sputnik 1,
and poor Woolley was never able to live down his gaffe.

In Chapter 13, I referred to the free diving 'record' of
128 feet. I can no longer keep track of developments in this
field—but I believe the record is now more than twice that!

What I did not know, when I completed writing *The
Coast of Coral*, was that my underwater odyssey would
completely change my life. On my way to Australia in the
P&O liner *Himalaya*, I was able to spend one afternoon in
Colombo, and met the assistant director of the Colombo
Zoo, Rodney Jonklaas. He had introduced Skin Diving into
the island and said: "Why don't you come back when you
finish with the Great Barrier Reef and see what you can
find under the Indian Ocean?" Well, Mike and I did just
that, with results you can read in *The Reefs of Taprobane*.

For a few decades I had fantasies of returning to Heron
Island but I never did so, and now it is far too late. I salute
across the years the memories of my many friends in Australia, now all departed, who helped me on the first great
adventure of my life.

Arthur C. Clarke
Colombo, Sri Lanka
9 May 2001

THE COAST
OF CORAL

I

The Road to the Reef

Some words hold magic, so that when they are uttered the mind loses itself in mists of enchanted reverie. "Gold," perhaps, is the most potent of all such verbal talismans; and the names of many jewels, as they slip from the tongue, can also set the imagination afire. Opal, amethyst, emerald—these are words that sparkle in the mind, words that are a universe removed from the drab labels of everyday life.

Such a word of wonder is "coral." It has a power of evocation challenging that of any name in the jeweler's vocabulary. Indeed, coral is a jewel in its own right; it has been used down the centuries for ornamentation, though almost all its beauty dies when it is wrenched from its natural element.

And therein lies the special magic of coral. Unlike the jewels of the land, which were born amid fire and inconceivable pressure far down below the surface of the earth, coral is the product of life, growing only in the sundrenched shallows of the tropic seas. It is a creation of the organic world, and, remote though its kinship may be, it is less alien to us than the glittering minerals that have known nothing of life.

Linked inseparably with the name "coral" is the word "reef," with all its implication of danger and romance. Not all corals are reef-builders, but the reef is their supreme achievement. Nowhere else in the animal kingdom is there a greater disparity in size between a creature and its works.

Of all coral reefs, the mightiest is that stretching for more than a thousand miles along the eastern seaboard of Australia—virtually the whole length of the state of Queensland. The Great Barrier Reef is not, however, a single unbroken wall of coral, but a complex labyrinth of islands and reefs that has challenged cartographers for almost two hundred years. If its entire length could be observed from the air, and the Pacific waters were drained away to reveal the configuration of the ocean bed, the Great Barrier Reef would appear as a gently sloping shelf extending out from the Australian mainland. In places it would be as little as ten miles wide, but sometimes it would stretch for more than a hundred miles before dropping off suddenly into the abyss.

This slightly tilted plateau would be broken by innumerable small hills, some isolated, others forming extensive chains. These would be the reefs proper, most of which appear to the cautious navigator as low islands, or else reveal themselves only by the foaming breakers which their presence causes.

The larger islands—those which are always well above the water line—are covered with vegetation and often support myriads of sea birds. Only a very few have human inhabitants, for life on a tropical island may be picturesque but has certain drawbacks—as anyone who has tried to exist for a few weeks without bread, milk, newspapers, mail, fresh meat, hot running water, and the other amenities of civilization will testify. Those islands which are conveniently accessible to the ports of northern Queensland, or which have flying-boat bases, are visited by thousands of tourists every year, and are becoming increasingly popular as holiday resorts. But these partly occupied islands number less than a dozen—and there are more than six hundred in the Reef which are large enough to have their existence acknowledged by the State Lands Department. No one can estimate how many thousands of smaller islet and temporarily exposed rocks there are in the vast area enclosed by the Reef.

Nine tenths of the Great Barrier Reef is never visited except by pearling boats or fishing trawlers, whose crew are too busy and too concerned with their own safety in what are among the world's most dangerous waters to give much thought to the wonders over which they are sailing. The Outer Reef, in particular, is seldom visited; a small boat caught here during the cyclone season, which extends from January to March, would need a good deal of luck to survive. Every year the Reef takes its toll of life and property, but to the holiday-maker visiting the resort islands the seasonal storms are merely a nuisance, not a danger. He can regard with equanimity the perils which the professional sailors must face—and after all, no reef would be complete without its wreck.

Two of the greatest navigators of all times—Captain Cook and Bligh of the *Bounty*—were the first European explorers of the Reef, and for all their skill they were lucky to escape from its dangers alive. Many later voyagers were not so fortunate, and the charts still record the resting places of their ships.

In the early days, the perils of the sea were matched by the dangers of the land. Savage natives, not a few of them cannibals, lived on the mainland and on some of the adjoining islands. On many occasions, shipwrecked sailors escaped from the sea only to be massacred when they imagined that they had reached safety.

The Reef has a bloodstained history, but it also has a romantic one, for its northern third is the home of the pearl oyster. In all probability, there has never been a more dangerous occupation that that of pearl diver, yet men have always been willing to risk their lives for the sake of fortunes. And many fortunes have been found, as well as lost, in the waters of the Reef.

Only its remoteness from the western world, and from the great trade routes of the maritime nations, has prevented the Barrier Reef from becoming as legendary and as glamorous as the Spanish Main. Australasia was not opened up until late in history; treasure-laden galleons never plied its waters, and the occasional pirates it knew were hardly in the same class as Sir Henry Morgan. And so the world has been slow to realize the existence of one of its greatest marvels; outside Australia, indeed, the Great Barrier Reef is scarcely more than a name.

It would take a lifetime to visit all the islands of the Reef and to sail through all its channels. Even then, one would have come to know only a single aspect of it. The sea has two faces—that which it shows to the sailor looking down upon the waves, and that which the diver sees as it rolls restlessly above his head. It is the same with the Reef;

none can really claim to know it until they have gone down into its depths. Otherwise they are in the same position as visitors from space would be if they were compelled to survey Earth from beyond the borders of the atmosphere, and could not venture down into the busy, teeming world they saw below them.

This book records the adventures and mishaps, the successes and failures, of a rather small Underwater Expedition to the Great Barrier Reef during eighteen months in 1954 and 1955. The expedition consisted of exactly two people—Mike Wilson, diver and ex-paratrooper, and myself, author and ex-astronaut (armchair variety). We had previously tried our hands at underwater exploring and photography in various parts of the world, and had agreed that we would never be content until we had sampled the submarine attractions of the Barrier Reef. We knew nothing about the place, but we were certain that it was unique, that it would one day be the Mecca of underwater tourism— and that we wanted to be among the first to take a good fish's-eye view of it.

Mike left England on a preliminary reconnaissance, taking two Aqualungs with him, early in 1954. By the time I caught up with him at the end of the year, he had traveled over most of Australia, all the way in to Alice Springs; had worked as a pearl diver, rising rapidly from number three to number one position as the result of the death and maiming of his colleagues; had avoided their fates through the fortunate circumstance that his lugger was so badly damaged in a cyclone that it had to return to port; had trained native divers in the use of a revolutionary new type of breathing equipment; had written a few radio scripts; had joined a circus as part of a frogman act, working with an excitable partner who is now being boarded at state expense after a disagreement with the police in which much lead was thrown in both directions; and had left at least one fractured heart in every major Australian city. When I joined him just before Christmas, 1954, bringing with me another Aqualung and five underwater cameras, he had gathered a good general knowledge of the Reef, knew the problems we would be facing, and had made innumerable contacts with underwater experts, manufacturers of diving gear, and radio and newspaper personalities, whose assistance or advice would be valuable to us.

It would be impossible to list all those who helped us during our often erratic wanderings along the eastern Australian seaboard. Some will be mentioned as they appear on the scene, but we would now like to pay special tribute to the following who helped to smooth our path and often performed services beyond the call of duty:

E. Bennett-Bremner, Chief Public Relations Officer, QANTAS Empire Airways, and his secretary Eileen McKenzie, for looking after our publicity as well.

Alan S. Brown, Secretary of the Prime Minister's Department, Canberra, for valuable introductions to key officials.

John Cooper, Managing Director of *Reader's Digest* (Australia), for hospitality and encouragement.

Kodak (Australasia) Pty. Ltd., for photographic assistance.

The State Government Tourist Bureau, Brisbane, and its director, Edgar Ferguson, for arranging our introduction to the Reef.

The Commercial Bank of Australia, for acting as postman.

The Great Barrier Reef Committee, Brisbane, for the hospitality of its Marine Biology Research Station on Heron Island.

The Oxley Memorial Library, Brisbane, for permission to examine Mary Watson's diary.

Ted Eldred and Bob Wallace Mitchell, for the loan of three "Porpoise" compressed-air diving sets.

Charlie Mustchin, for giving us the run of his brand-new apartment in Coolangatta.

Don and Lois Linklater, for the opportunity of seeing Bondi from unusual angles.

Lyle Davis, for the last word in rubber-powered spear guns, and quantities of compressed air.

The Kingsburys, for inviting us for the weekend and waving good-by two months later.

Eric Robinson, of Robinson's Sports Stores, Brisbane, for helping us with equipment problems.

The Criminal Investigation Branch, Sydney, for not making a lot of fuss about a certain .45.

Ron Johnson, for keeping AEK942 on the road, and helping us in a hundred other ways above and below the water.

John Lawson, for fixing camera cases.

The Commonwealth Scientific and Industrial Research Organization, for making available the Fisheries Research Vessel *Gahleru*.

George and Jean Hales, for making us at home on Thursday Island.

Scott Meredith, for acting as supply sergeant for the expedition.

Eric, Glyn, and the rest of the Swiss Family Hasting, for the help they gave us during our first visit to Heron Island.

Bob, Cynthia, Jimmy, and Mum for assistance during the second.

And particularly—Don and Dawn Campbell, for looking after our affairs while we were on the Reef, and for giving us a home in Brisbane.

II

Fair Dinkum, Etc.

On a misty December morning the *Himalaya*, which had brought us from London in comfort which would have astonished the first Australian settlers, steamed round the Heads into Sydney harbor. The immense steel bow of the bridge reared before us, dominating the skyline and looking as if it were built for eternity. Surely no city in the world can have a more dramatic approach; the great bridge which spans the Golden Gate may be more beautiful, and more daring, but it lacks the massive grandeur of Sydney's metal rainbow. The harbor bridge belongs to that small class of artifacts which includes the Pyramids and Boulder Dam; one feels that they will pass down the centuries together, still arousing awe even in ages which will know far greater feats of engineering.

There is a moment, as you steam beneath the bridge and the ship's mast seems inexorably fated to snap against that sky-spanning parapet, when you would swear that the whole titanic arch was about to turn and topple into the harbor. Anyone who has stared up the face of a skyscraper, when a few fleecy clouds are hurrying before the wind, will have experienced the same sensation. The feeling of vertigo lasts only a moment; then you are through the bridge, like a traveler of old passing under the portcullis of some castle at the end of his journey.

One seldom has any lasting memories of one's first few days in a few country. There are too many arrangements to be made, and the problem of finding a place to live is considerably aggravated when, as in our case, you are traveling with large quantities of heavy and valuable equipment. (The first hurdle, the Australian customs, we passed with no trouble at all. They weren't interested in our numerous cameras, an example which I heartily commend to customs departments elsewhere.) Luckily we were able to find an excellent home with a pleasant—though as it turned out somewhat high-strung—family on the north side of the harbor, commanding a beautiful view of the city. This was to be our base for the next month, while we made the final arrangements for our expedition and Mike introduced me to the numerous contacts he had made among spear fishers and underwater explorers.

It is very dangerous to make sweeping generalizations about any country, particularly when one hopes someday to return to it. I will therefore refrain from discussing What Is Wrong with Australia (though many Australians told me) or What Is Right with Australia (though still more Australians told me that). In any case, one feels that a present-day assessment, however accurate, is of little importance. Here is a country still at the beginning of its history, with a future as vast and unforeseeable as was that of the United States a hundred years ago. It is a country as big as the

United States, but with less than ten million inhabitants, most of them living in a relatively narrow coastal belt. There are no inland cities, with the sole exception of the deliberately planned commonwealth capital, Canberra.

Unlike Canada or South Africa, Australia was colonized almost exclusively from Britain, and no matter how many generations they may be removed from the northern hemisphere, to most Australians the United Kingdom is still "home." Only since the Second World War has there been a large influx of European migrants, and today the population increase from immigration almost equals that from the birth rate. These "New Australians"—particularly those speaking with outlandish accents—are often regarded with some suspicion by those of English or Scots origin. Yet the factors which gave the United States its strength are working here, and from the fusion of cultures which is still in progress a new civilization will one day emerge.

The English or American visitor to Australia is blissfully ignorant of the fact, as he sails under the harbor bridge or touches down at Mascot Airport, that he will soon have to start learning a new language. This is a problem which scarcely arises when one crosses the Atlantic, despite any statements that may have been made to the contrary. The Englishman has seen, and heard, so many American movies that he understands the meaning of most of the words he will encounter in the United States, though he may sometimes be baffled by their delivery if, for example, he gets caught in the cross fire between two Brooklyn cab drivers. And conversely, the American in England will have already read a good deal of the written language and will have been carefully warned about pavement, lorry, lift, and similar stumbling blocks.

Not so the new arrival in Australia. He will have seen no Australian movies (though there have been some good ones) and will probably have read no Australian books. He may be astonished to discover that the Australians have a vernacular whose richness, picturesqueness, and—ahem—virility put that of any other English-speaking nation in the shade. It is also highly infectious, and anyone leaving the country after a prolonged stay should allow himself at least two weeks to delouse his vocabulary.

This precaution is rendered necessary by what has been called the Great Australian Adjective, which creeps up on the visitor until he is quite unaware that he has started to use it. This sanguinary word, however, can hardly claim to be of Australian origin or exclusive usage; indeed, it embellishes the most famous line of dialogue that Bernard Shaw ever wrote. Suffice to say that only the most effete Aussie would use the expression "Not likely!" without inserting the inseparably linked adjective.

What baffles the visitor, however, are not familiar words used with unfamiliar freedom, but words he has never met before, or words that have acquired new meanings. It was some time before I realized that "crook" meant ill or, as applied to machinery, out of action; that a "bomb" was a beaten-up old car; that "grog" and "plonk" were beer or cheap wine; that "fair dinkum" meant genuine, O.K., on the level—and about a dozen other shades of rectitude. When the New Australians add their quota to the language, anyone entering the country will have to take an Anglo-Australian dictionary with him.

As Mike had already been in the country for almost a year, I was able to use him as an interpreter when things got difficult, but after two weeks I was talking good Australian in a mid-Atlantic accent.

The first problem which we had to face before our expedition could make any progress was that of ensuring that all our underwater equipment was suitable for the job ahead. This equipment fell into two classes—the cameras and the breathing gear.

The cameras I had brought with me from London comprised three Leicas, a Robot Star, and a Bell and Howell Automaster 16 millimeter movie camera. There were three waterproofed cases of various designs for the still cameras, and one for the movie camera. Though the lack of standardization was unfortunate, these were the only underwater cases readily available at the time—at least, the only ones at a reasonable price. Even so, this little collection represented an investment of about two thousand dollars.

Contrary to popular belief, most underwater photographs are taken by divers *not* using breathing gear, but relying solely on their ability to remain submerged long enough to get into position and to snap the shutter. When free diving in shallow water, indeed, it is often possible to take half a dozen photographs before having to return to the surface for another breath. However, there are occasions when some kind of diving equipment is essential; only a superman could use a camera fifty feet down if he had to depend upon his own lung power alone.

As everybody now knows, largely thanks to Captain Cousteau, there are two main types of diving equipment The conventional, old-fashioned kind uses a long, flexible pipe to connect the diver below the water with an air pump on the surface. The "classical" diver with his brass helme rubber suit, and lead weights is still doing most of the world's underwater work, but the more modern and—as result of the war—more glamorous self-contained equipment has now stolen all the limelight. The frogmen are their civilian successors are quite independent of any equipment on the surface. They take their air supply with ther compressed to a very great pressure in cylinders strapped on their backs.

The world-famous "Aqualung," evolved by Cousteau and Gagnan in the early 1940's, is the prototype of all modern compressed-air diving equipment. With the growing popularity of underwater exploration, however, there have been almost as many variations on the original design as there have been types of automobile since the first Model T emerged from Henry Ford's workshop.

We had both taken Aqualungs to Australia, but during the year he had spent in the country preparing for our expedition, Mike had tested the Australian-designed "Porpoise" diving equipment, and had decided that this surpassed any other equipment he had used. Instead of the two large corrugated tubes from air bottle to mouthpiece, familiar to everyone who has ever seen a photograph of the Aqualung in use, the Porpoise had a single, much smaller tube on the left side only, so that the chances of getting entangled underwater were greatly diminished. The very high pressure of over 2,000 pounds per square inch in the air cylinder was dropped to a manageable 150 pounds per square inch by a reducing valve, and air was fed at this pressure to a demand valve actually on the mouthpiece. The function of this valve was to feed air to the lungs whenever they asked for it, at exactly the right pressure required, by balancing the pressure in the lungs against that of the surrounding water. Breathing was completely effortless and the equipment was very little handicap to movement underwater—which was more than could be said of some type of gear I have used. (I can remember one that had its reducing valve strategically placed so that I banged my head against it every time I tried to look up. . . .)

In addition—though this was a feature we hoped we should never have to employ—the equipment had a built-in buoyancy pack which provided the underwater explorer's equivalent of a parachute. Pulling a string would jettison the heavy cylinder and leave the diver a poorer man, but at least able to float effortlessly on the surface.

The Great Barrier Reef was more than a thousand miles away, and it would be months yet before we could go there. But we were already semi-operational, and had no intention of remaining on dry land while the sea was so close at hand. Besides, there was one little question that we wanted to answer right away. Again and again we had been asked, "What will you do about sharks?" Usually we had laughed, shrugged our shoulders, and replied, "Oh, they won't bother us." We had found that to be true enough in Florida and the Red Sea, but from all accounts the sharks we had met there had been timid and inoffensive beasts compared to those that patrolled Australian waters.

There was only one way to find out.

III

White Water

There can be few cities in the world where it is possible to indulge in spear fishing in the suburbs, but Sydney is built around so many bays and beaches that the sea seems to lie at the end of every other streetcar route. Mike and I attracted no particular attention when, laden with flippers, face masks, and underwater cameras, we pushed our way (with a little help from the points of our spear guns) into the crowds of rush-hour passengers.

Our boarding house was not far from Balmoral Beach, a crescent of smooth sand flanked at its northern end by rocks which the waves had sculptured into fantastic shapes. I had had my first swim in Australian waters off these rocks—on a sun-scorched Christmas Day. It is a place much frequented by learner divers, as the water is shallow and deepens only slowly toward a sandy bottom twenty feet down. Near the shore there is a fringing band of kelp through which you must swim to reach the open water; until you get used to it, the continual backward tug of the long, perpetually moving tentacles of weed is distinctly unsettling. The bare flesh shrinks involuntarily from the clammy touch, and the eye peers nervously through the waving ribbons, wondering what may be concealed beneath them. It requires two or three dives to become accustomed to the kelp, but after a while you control your reflexes and no longer react with an automatic shudder to the intimate touch of an underwater tentacle.

During my first dive in Balmoral, I met nothing more dangerous than a small sting ray, which flapped slowly out of sight when I prodded it with my spear. My second dive was considerably more memorable—though just *how* much more I was not to know until two weeks later.

The sun was blazing, the sea calm, but the water was rather murky. Visibility was less than twenty feet, which is poor by Australian standards. I was using no breathing gear, merely mask and snorkle, and had been cruising around for half an hour on a general sight-seeing tour. Though I was carrying a seven-foot hand spear, I had no aggressive intentions. A spear is a very useful companion to have with you underwater, where you frequently meet mysterious objects which you may want to prod but feel disinclined to touch. I was also using the spear, which had been marked off in foot lengths, as a measuring rod to enable me to judge distances for photography.

My only memory of the early part of this dive is the striking temperature difference between the water on the surface and that on the bottom. It was pleasantly warm just under the waves, but twenty feet down I felt almost frozen as I coasted over the smooth sand. Temperature has a very great effect on a free diver's ability to stay submerged, and the longest time I remained under was a mere minute, which was not a very good performance. However, it enabled me to explore a tiny cave festooned with colorful marine growths. This cave was supposed to be the occasional residence of a small and (almost) harmless shark known as a wobbegong, but he was out when I called.

One does unaccountable things underwater, through irresponsibility, oxygen starvation, or sheer *joie de vivre*. I had grown tired of swimming, and decided to relax. My relaxation took the form of winding myself round my spear, like a ball of wool on a knitting needle, and sinking slowly into the depths. Actually there was a tenuous justification for this peculiar behavior: I wanted to see if my buoyancy altered as I changed from the outstretched to the curled-up position. I never finished the experiment (which for that matter, is still uncompleted) for at that moment I realized I had company.

A large shark was circling me at the very limit of vision its outlines completely unmistakable even through the underwater haze. Though all its details were lost, no one could have failed to identify that pointed nose and torpedo sleekness. It was a swiftly moving shadow, giving an overwhelming impression of effortless power. I watched it make half a circuit of me—which took only seconds though it must have covered fifty feet in that time—before I made any move myself.

I was much too excited and interested to feel any sense of danger; my only fear, indeed, was that the shark would go away before I could get a good look at it. When it showed no sign of coming closer, I took a deep breath, dived, and swam toward it as quickly as I could. But it is as useless to try and catch a shark as it is to try and swim away from one; all that happened was that the creature broke away from its circuit and disappeared at once into the haze.

The whole incident lasted less than a minute, and took place about thirty feet from the shore. Mike had been sunning himself on the rocks while this was going on, and when I lost sight of the shark I popped my head above the surface to shout to him: "Mike! Bring the camera! There's a shark here—a big one!" Then I dived under again, having a prejudice against floating with my head blindly out of water, particularly in circumstances such as these.

Mike joined me at once, and we swam around for ten minutes in the hope that the shark would reappear. When we finally gave up the search, we emerged to find a young spearman squiring his girl friend into the water. We told them of my encounter, but that did not stop them from going ahead—though they took their time over it. Perhaps they did not believe us and thought we were crying "Wolf." If they disbelieved us then, I am certain that they remembered our warning later, in view of what happened at this precise spot sixteen days afterward.

I am fairly sure that this shark was larger than I was; it is impossible to estimate accurately the size of an object seen by outline only, at the limit of visibility. Judging by the angle of vision it subtended, it must have been about ten feet long, I felt sorry, afterward, that I had not been a little more patient and remained motionless rather longer, instead of swimming toward the shark and so scaring it.

If my first introduction to Australian sharks was of the kind that breeds familiarity, the second was of the kind that breeds contempt—and it occurred on the very next day. We had now made contact with most of the leading skin divers in Sydney, who were hospitably determined to put on the best show which their waters could provide.

It was a pleasant, sunny morning when our good friend Reg Keegan, who looks as if he spends all his time lifesaving on Bondi Beach instead of running a Sydney pub, drove us to Bilgola Bay, about thirty miles north of the city. This bay has a fine sandy beach, across which the waves were breaking in endless lines of surf. But we were not interested in the great crescent of sand and the old-fashioned people who were merely bathing off the beach. Our objective was the rocky headland at the north of the bay, against which waves were crashing with a violence which did not seem to worry our companions in the least. By this time we had been joined by several other massive Australians, among them Keith Whitehead, who has swum for his country in the Olympic games and who would therefore, I felt, be a useful fellow to have around if I lost my flippers. (I am quite happy in the water without flippers, but don't actually *get* anywhere, however much effort I put into it. This information may encourage other nonswimmers to take up skin diving.)

It looked dangerous enough going in off these rocks, with the waves thundering against them and the spray breaking over us as we sorted out our equipment. But that was not good enough for Keith; he had a better idea. He wanted us to climb right round the headland, making our way (complete with weight belts and the rest of our diving equipment) for a couple of hundred yards over enormous broken boulders until we had rounded the tip of the promontory and had got into the next bay. I cannot remember the purpose of this maneuver, or why we let ourselves get talked into it, but will merely remark that since taking up underwater exploring I have done more mountaineering than in the whole of the rest of my life.

Four of us made the climb round the headland, and presently stood in a small rocky cove with the waves dashing against our feet. It was not too hard to get into the water, if you dived in at the top of a wave, but the problem of getting out again at the other end looked as if it might be a little more difficult. Any doubts that I had were considerably increased when the fourth member of our party, after one look at the heaving seascape beneath us, announced *his* intention of staying on land. He said he felt cold, and was afraid of getting cramp on the long swim back. This perfectly reasonable excuse, which I felt very much inclined to borrow, was greeted with jeers by Keith, but his countryman stuck to his guns and began the tedious scramble back over the rocks around the headland.

Feeling wistfully that I would have liked to see a little more of Australia before consigning myself to the deep, I followed Keith out into the sea. The technique was straightforward, but required careful timing. You had to hurl yourself off the rocks at the moment when an extra high wave came in, then swim like mad to get out of the white water and into the relative safety beyond the breakers. If you missed your cue and leaped into an already retreating wave, you were likely to be dumped on the barnacle-covered rocks.

Mike had already gone in, and a little later I too made the transition without mishap, joining him and Keith about fifty yards out. We could still see (whenever we happened to be on the crest of a wave) our colleague making his slow but undoubtedly sure way back along the rocky foot of the cliff. Half the time, however, we could see nothing of the shore, being entirely surrounded by small mountains of water which somewhat restricted the view in the horizontal direction.

Straight down, on the other hand, the view was fine. The water was very clear, and we could see an interestingly rugged vista over which countless small fish, and not a few large ones, were weaving to and fro. Sometimes the sea bed would be thirty feet below us—sometimes, when we were in the trough of a wave, it would be ten feet closer. Even when we dived down to the bottom, we could feel the pressure changing as the weight of water above us continually varied. It was an exhilarating experience, and perfectly safe as long as we kept away from the angry seas pounding against the shore.

We made our slow way around the headland and back into Bilgola Bay, where we were glad to see that the fury of the waves had somewhat abated. Mike, who was used to swimming in white water, had gone on ahead, leaving me in Keith's charge. I was getting rather cold, and a little tired, but there was so much to see that I was in no great hurry to reach land again. The sea bed above which I was switchbacking at the whim of the waves was dotted, with huge boulders and crevassed with innumerable small valleys. Sometimes I would take a deep breath and dive down into one of these, as often as not disturbing some great fish of a species as strange to me as I was probably strange to it.

Suddenly there was the unmistakable "spang" of a spear gun—a sound which can be heard through water for a distance of a hundred feet or more by human ears, and doubtless for much farther by the sensitive vibration detectors with which all fish are equipped. Looking up, I saw that

Keith's gun was floating on the surface, while Keith himself was down below wrestling with a fine thirty-pound parrot fish that had been impaled on his spear. Feeling tired and cold as I was, I felt no great enthusiasm to act as Keith's caddy and carry his gun back to land for him while he dealt with his still-struggling victim. This, however, was a somewhat shortsighted view, for later that day I was one of the twenty people who had a good meal out of this savory titbit—and still left quite a few helpings over.

We could now no longer avoid the problem of getting back to shore, for it is not advisable to swim in the neighborhood of struggling fish if there are sharks about. (And in Australian waters there are always sharks about, whether you can see them or not.) It is not as easy to get out of rough water, onto a rocky shore, as it is to get into it, but the same principles apply. You have to choose a likely looking spot where you can scramble up without being shredded by too many barnacles, then watch the pattern of the waves and seize the right moment to make landfall. This is not a simple thing to do while you are bobbing up and down in a maelstrom of broken water. If you have calculated correctly, you arrive at your chosen rock on the crest of a wave, and cling to it like a limpet when the water recedes. You then have a full five seconds to scramble ashore before the next wave arrives and tries to sweep you away.

Somewhat to my surprise, I managed to do this without any broken bones or major contusions, and now felt very proud of myself for being a fully qualified "white water man." I rather wished my Florida friends, accustomed to diving off a coast which is one enormous sandbank, could have seen this combination of mountaineering and aquabatics. At the sometime, I decided that I had had quite enough of this kind of thing for one day.

I had reckoned without my Australian friends. They clearly imagined that I was disappointed at so uneventful a trip to the seaside, and were determined to do something about it. No sooner had I warmed myself up on the rocks, well back from the spray still being flung up by the breakers, than there was a commotion fifty feet out. Reg Keegan and his colleagues, who had been off spear fishing on their own, popped up out of the waves and yelled at me, "Hey, Art! We've got a wobby for you—a six-footer!"

The wobbegong shark (*Oreotolobus maculates*) has already been mentioned. It is a normally inoffensive beast, which spends most of its time on the bottom, where it is quite hard to see owing to its excellent camouflage. But all six-foot sharks should be treated with caution—particularly when spears have been poked into them. I remembered a recent incident in which a diver got embroiled with a wobby and ended up, as he put it ruefully, looking as if he had a fight with a sewing machine. Until then, spearmen had tended to regard this shark as a joke, but now they took it more seriously. Though wobbegongs' teeth are not very big, they are extremely sharp, and there are an awful lot of them.

I looked out across the still-seething water, thought, "Save me from my friends!" and climbed reluctantly back into my flippers. When I had fought my way out through the boiling surf, I found Reg and his pals swimming around the punctured wobbegong, which looked much more than six feet. It was a broad, ugly beast, with a peculiarly repulsive fringe of tendrils dangling from its mouth, and it was weaving to and fro over the bottom apparently not much inconvenienced by the spear stuck in its left side. The spear, however, gave its hunters some control over its movements, for as long as the line held it was tethered to the gun which had shot it. The owner of the gun could "play" the shark just as an angler plays a fish, though with considerably less safety. Perhaps the shark could not get away from its captor, but it looked as if the reverse was also true.

I had just arrived on the scene, and was watching the tableau from a respectful distance, when another spear was planted in the shark—this time from the right. It at once turned over on its back, and for a moment seemed completely stunned. Then it recovered itself, but was obviously in no position to put up any further resistance. With lines now securely attached to it on either side, it could be steered in any direction, as effectively as if it had been fitted with bridle and reins.

When the shark was finally landed on the beach, it created a considerable sensation, for it was still very much alive and wriggled violently from time to time. Just to be on the safe side, we wedged a block of wood between its needlelike teeth, but some halfhearted attempts to finish it off with a knife came to nothing. It was impossible to get the point through the beast's skin, which was like very flexible chain mail. The knife merely formed a dimple in it, and skittered harmlessly around.

We eventually gave the shark—all six feet of him—to a small boy who seemed to think it might make a good pet. By this time it was in a somewhat moribund condition, so I doubt if this project ever got very much further.

As an introduction to Australian sharks, the wobbegong was hardly awe-inspiring. Perhaps it was not a fair example, but it certainly supported the general opinion that, to the underwater hunter or explorer, sharks were not a serious menace. This view was to be dramatically and tragically challenged, almost on our doorstep, just over two weeks later.

IV

Death of a Spearman

On the afternoon of January 17, 1955, a thirteen-year-old
boy named John Willis was spear fishing off Balmoral
Beach, at the exact spot described in the previous chapter.
The water was not very clear, and he was swimming alone,
but he was so close to a familiar shore that it probably
never occurred to him that he might be in any danger. A
few minutes earlier, another spearman had told him that a
large shark had been seen in the neighborhood, but John
had ignored the warning.

He was about twenty-five yards from the shore when
the spectators heard him scream for help and saw him
throw up his arms. He swam desperately toward the rocks,
while his blood incarnadined the water around him. Slash-
ing through the reddening waves was the dorsal fin of a
large shark, which attacked three times while the boy was
trying to reach safety.

He managed to get into the shallow water, then collapsed a few feet from shore. Some bystanders waded out

and carried him to the rocks, but it was too late. He was still breathing, but had ceased to bleed, because he had no blood left. There were gaping wounds on both legs, and it must have taken great determination and endurance for him to reach the shore at all. He died within seconds from shock and loss of blood, while the shark was still circling in the shallows only a few yards out. Soon afterward it was joined by two others, no doubt attracted by the blood staining the water. Local fishermen set out in boats to shoot the intruders, but by the time they arrived the sharks had left. All that could be done then was to set out baited hooks and hope that the murderer would return to the scene of the crime.

The death of John Willis provided the main headlines in next morning's Sydney papers. For a few days, there was a hurried check of the shark nets which guard many of the bathing pools, following complaints that some of these protective barriers were pierced with underwater holes several feet across. Balmoral Beach was deserted, except by morbid-minded spectators wandering over the rocks and looking at the two buoys from which the baited hooks were hanging.

Yet, within a week, Balmoral Beach was back in business. A few cautious mothers, amid much wailing and lamentation, had disposed of their offsprings' spear guns, but the setback to the rapidly expanding sport of underwater hunting was only temporary. Nevertheless, this tragic incident made many underwater explorers—including Mike and myself—have second thoughts about the dangers of the realm they were invading.

The Australians have a curiously ambiguous attitude toward their sharks. They are quite proud of them, and fiercely resent any suggestion that they are not the most dangerous in the world. Many of the splendid beaches have shark-proof enclosures, but far more people will be found outside the nets than within them. The swimmers know perfectly well that there are sharks around, but do not regard them as a hazard which affects them, personally. This is perhaps a reasonable point of view, since around the entire Australian continent only two people are killed by sharks every year. The same number of road fatalities occur each day in the state of New South Wales alone.

Two days after the attack on John Willis, Mike and I went down to Balmoral Beach again, carrying our underwater cameras and Aqualungs. The reason why we used breathing gear in such shallow water was simple. If the killer was still around, we wanted to be able to stay on the bottom, so that he would not mistake us for swimmers or snorkling spearmen.

Mike was carrying the Robot camera in its large metal case; I had the Leica, with flash attachment, in an almost equally massive container. A punch on the nose with a camera case is one of the approved methods of dealing with inquisitive sharks; the larger and stronger the case, the happier you feel behind it. I was also carrying my spear, and had a string bag full of spare flash bulbs tethered to any waist like a captive balloon. With all this equipment, it was some time before I was satisfactorily submerged, and as I wound my way through the clammy tentacles of the help I felt much more like the White Knight from *Through The Looking Glass* than a daring underwater adventurer.

Visibility was poor, and I was hard pressed to keep up with Mike—a better and less encumbered swimmer. Needless to say, I kept looking in all directions, wondering if at any moment I would see that gray, superbly streamlined shape slide out of the gloom. My general mood could be defined as alertness rather than apprehension; if the hark did appear, I was chiefly anxious to get him in the game picture as Mike, so that I could obtain a good photographic composition.

I was quite startled when, fifty feet ahead, I saw a weird white object hanging in mid-water. For a moment I could not identify it; it was something so out of its normal context that it was meaningless. Then I realized that I was looking at a joint of meat, impaled on a hook just as it night have been in a butcher's shop. It was a horrible, pallid white as it turned slowly in the haze; a few tiny fish were nibbling around it, but it had obviously been untouched by anything of real size.

With some reluctance, I grasped this rather repulsive object while Mike took some shots of me; then I photographed him doing the same thing. The water was so dirty that we had little hope of getting worth-while pictures, but it seemed a pity to have come thus far without using the cameras.

There was a second buoy about a hundred yards away, in rather clearer water. The hook here had been baited with two lumps of liver, but with equal lack of success. Either the sharks had left the area, or the tangle of wires and ropes around the bait made it too obvious a trap.

Mike and I spent some twenty minutes swimming through the gloomy waters in which John Willis had died two days before. We did not feel particularly brave, nor did we consider that our action was foolhardy. From the shark's point of view, we were a pair of unusually large fish, quite at home in the water and obviously well able to look after ourselves. Perhaps it was there all the time, keeping just out of range and waiting until we had gone away. Even without the vibrations of the Aqualung exhaust valves, its sensing apparatus would have told it of our presence. Sharks, like all fish, have extremely poor eyesight, and rely on vision only when they are very close to their target. It seems more than probable that many of the attacks made on human beings may have been due to mistaken identity, though that is poor consolation to the victim.

This may have been the case with John Willis, since otherwise it is difficult to account for this attack in an area where hundreds of other spear fishers had operated for years. Another plausible theory was that John had speared a fish or lobster, and it was that which had attracted the shark. There have been many cases of sharks stealing the catch from a spearman—sometimes when he had already tied it to his waist!—without doing more than nudge the hunter. In such circumstances a shark might well attack if the spearman lost his head and tried to swim away.

By the time Mike and I left the water, a small crowd had collected to watch our activities, and a press photographer was waiting for us when we emerged. It was at this point that I made an unfortunate mistake that I have never ceased to regret—I handed over our exposed films to the press. I had not realized that the subtleties of fine grain 35 millimeter processing are unknown in newspaper darkrooms, where films are apparently boiled in concentrated quicklime in order to produce results in two minutes. When the negatives came back from the darkroom, they were completely ruined—the images had been burned out, and only a couple of shots were even recognizable. It was a bitter lesson; thereafter we let no one else process our films.

John Willis has the sad distinction of being the first spearman definitely known to have been killed by a shark. Two weeks later, a twenty-six-year-old German immigrant was taken at a spot about two miles from Balmoral Beach. The injuries in both cases were almost identical—severe lacerations of the lower limbs, causing death in a few seconds through shock and loss of blood. The second victim, however, was not diving, but was merely swimming on the surface. The distinction may seem trivial, but is actually quite fundamental. A swimmer without face mask is blind, and does not know what is happening—or approaching—below him. A shark probably classifies surface swimmers, drowning men, and injured fish in the same category—but will be much more cautious in tackling an underwater explorer making his calm and confident way through an element no longer alien to him.

These two deaths, coming so close together, were hardly calculated to encourage us as we prepared to leave for the Reef. I have often wondered if the shark I met in Balmoral was the one responsible for the later killing. There is no evidence, of course, that John Willis and the young German were killed by the same animal, but statistics indicate strongly that shark fatalities occur in pairs in a given area, as if one particular shark acquires the taste for human flesh.

A single brief encounter was hardly enough to qualify me as an expert on sharks, but it was reasonably certain that I would meet a good many more on the Reef. Meanwhile, I no longer regretted scaring away the one that had circled me in Balmoral Bay. If I had not, this book might have ended abruptly at Chapter I.

Australian spear fishing received a distinct setback from this second tragedy, and it was not helped by the release, a week or so later, of a sensational film showing huge sharks being hooked off Bondi, the most famous of Sydney's beaches. Mike and I had already had some memorable experiences here, thanks to Don Linklater, the hospitable and energetic secretary of the Underwater Explorers' Club.

Don and his wife Lois form an underwater team which will doubtless be joined in due course by their daughter Margaret. They live on the cliff overlooking Bondi, and their back garden is usually full of the diving equipment which Don develops and sells through his company, Undersee Products. Our first trip out into the well-populated waters of Bondi Bay took place in one of Don's inventions, a large catamaran constructed from three flying-boat floats bolted to a framework of aluminum girders.

It was a boisterous day, but the catamaran was assembled and launched without much trouble from a sheltered cove near the headland which looks across the mile-wide bay. No less than six fully equipped hunters then climbed aboard and pushed out to sea, sitting uncomfortably on piles of air cylinders, underwater cameras, and spear guns. I was not among them; I had stayed ashore to film the launching. According to theory, the catamaran would come back and collect me when I had shot my movie sequence.

Unfortunately, as soon as the Linklater family yacht set out to sea the waves became so rough that it was impossible for it to turn back and pick me up. Those aboard waved to me to come and join them, but Mahomet was not only reluctant to go to the mountain—he was by no means sure that he could get there. My face mask and flippers were out in the catamaran, separated from me by the boiling surf. It never occurred to my Australian friends, who had been amphibious since childhood, that I couldn't swim. So I stood uncertainly with the spray breaking around me, while the catamaran circled a hundred yards out, its occupants wanting to know what the blankety blank I was waiting for. It was impossible to turn and slink away, pretending an urgent prior engagement, for I was now hemmed in by the large crowd which always gathers when any diving is in progress.

There was nothing for it but to hurl myself into the foam and to battle out from shore as best I could, using alternatively a spasmodic breast stroke and a kind of despairing, going-down-for-the-last-time overarm. After what seemed a very long time, the catamaran loomed up beside me and I was dragged aboard. The first thing I did was to put on my flippers so that whatever else happened, I would no longer be left to my own feeble resources if I had to enter the water again.

The catamaran then turned to sea, its outboard motor laboring heavily every time we climbed the towering waves crashing in toward Bondi. Once out of the shelter of the bay, it was perfectly obvious that we had no hope of diving; we would have our hands full getting back to shore in one piece. The sturdy but overladen little craft was swung round into the waves, and at this point I reluctantly consigned to the deep the excellent lunch that Lois Linklater had just given me.

When at last we got back into the relative shelter of the bay, it was still too rough for the catamaran to get ashore. Don brought it in as close as he could, then one by one its crew swam ashore with their equipment, using the typical Australian white-water technique I had already seen in action during the wobbegong hunt. I followed a little later; despite my still enfeebled condition, I was able to reach the rocks without much difficulty, as Mike had already taken my Aqualung and camera ashore. A few minutes later, Don followed in the now-lightened catamaran, and it was seized by willing hands before it had a chance of overturning in the surf.

That was the end of our first attempt to dive off Bondi. Two days later we had rather better luck, when we got the catamaran out in calmer weather and Don led me down to the bottom of the bay on a personally conducted tour.

He was using a two-cylinder unit, while my single cylinder was only half full and also had a slight leak. It took me some time to get below thirty feet, for at first my ears bothered me, but presently I pushed my way through the pressure barrier and joined Don on the bottom, sixty feet down. The water was quite clear, which surprised me since it had appeared dirty from the surface, and I felt rather sorry that I had not brought the camera with me. I had felt it best to avoid such complications on my first deep dive for a year, and in strange waters at that.

We swam to and fro over the rocky bottom, Don holding fast to a thin line which was our only connection with the distant, bobbling speck of the catamaran. Up there on the surface, Mike was holding the end of the cord and trying, in vain, to interpret Don's occasional signals. We disturbed several large fish—including one, a banjo skate, whose name describes it perfectly.

I was right on the bottom when I realized that my air supply was practically exhausted, and that only a couple of mouthfuls were left. My Aqualung was a shallow-water unit, with no reserve supply, and it was admittedly bad practice to stay down until the last gasp. I grabbed hold of Don, indicated that my cylinder was empty, and started to swim to the surface. As long as I didn't dawdle on the way up, I was in no danger. When ascending, an Aqualunger has to breathe *out*, not in, as the compressed air in his lungs expands. Moreover, during the climb to the surface the relaxing pressure enables one to suck a few more gulps of air from the cylinders; I timed it rather nicely, and broke water just after swallowing the last cubic inch of air.

During the rather long swim back to the catamaran, I breathed through the snorkle tube which no Aqualunger should ever dive without. All the way back, Don held my hand—a touching gesture which he hastened to explain as soon as we climbed aboard.

"They catch all the big sharks just where we were diving," he told me. "I wanted us to stick together so that my air bubbles would frighten them away." I was so deeply moved by this charming and considerate act that I felt quite unable to frame any suitable reply.

Mike was also somewhat speechless when we got back to the catamaran. He had calculated that I had not more than fourteen minutes of air for the depth at which we were working, and I had actually been down about twenty minutes. When I did reappear, he was just about on the point of going down to see what had happened.

As a suitable finale to this dive, Don then took us to view the impressive collection of sharks' jaws kept on display at the Dorsal Club, a small boathouse overlooking the bay. Here were jaws up to two feet across, filled with scores of razor-sharp teeth. Most of them had been removed from sharks ten or fifteen feet long, all of them taken off Bondi.

I looked at the grinning white jaws and their serrated

ivory fangs—and then I glanced across the bay to the crowded beach, thinking how many of these imposing sets of dentures must be hungrily patrolling these now placid waters. And I shook my head wonderingly as I considered the fantastic risks people took in search of amusement. . . .

It is impossible to leave the subject of sharks without mentioning one of the most fantastic murders ever recorded in the bulging annals of crime—the so-called "Shark Murder Case" which caused a great stir in Australia some years ago. A large shark had been captured alive and placed in a tank in the Sydney Zoo, where it swam round disconsolately looking rather sorry for itself. It was obviously sick, and after it had been in captivity a few hours it regurgitated its last meal. The zoo attendants were startled, to say the least, when they noticed a human arm floating around in the pool.

The Criminal Investigation Branch got to work on this gruesome Exhibit A, and were able to identify the arm's owner from the fingerprints. In due course his suspected murderers were arrested and tried, but because this is true life and not fiction, no one was ever convicted.

One can draw several conclusions from this extraordinary event. The first is that sharks take a long time to digest their food and probably don't really enjoy human flesh. And the second, which is hardly original, is that no writer of fiction ever dare attempt to match the improbability of truth.

V

Enter the Cops

"We've got the cameras, we've got the Aqualungs, and we've got Sydney harbor," said Mike one evening. "There's just one thing we need to make a good underwater picture."

"And what's that?" I asked.

"A pretty girl. Look at Lotte Hass—"

"Willingly."

"—she's the star of half the pictures Hans sells to the magazines. Why shouldn't we try and get into the act?"

"Doubtless you have someone in mind," I said resignedly.

"Her name's Margaret, and she lives just across the bridge. I've fixed everything up. After breakfast tomorrow, I'll drive over and collect her while you get the cameras and lungs ready."

It seemed quite a good idea; at the worst, it would give us some practice in underwater photography. The sun was shining, and everything seemed all set for an interesting morning beneath the waters of the harbor. Whistling cheerfully, Mike went out to the car and promised, "I'll be back in an hour."

"O.K." I answered, "I'll have everything ready by then."

It took me less than half that time to assemble the necessary equipment in the hall of the small private hotel where we were staying. Then I sat down inside the door to read a book and to await the return of Mike—and Margaret.

I had barely made myself comfortable when there was a knock, and I looked up to see a rather large gentleman standing in the entrance.

"Does a Mr. Mike Wilson live here?" he asked me.

"That's correct," I said. "But he's out at the moment."

"When will he be back?"

I explained the situation, said that I was Mike's partner, and was there anything I could do to help?

The large gentleman looked me over with a coldly professional gaze.

"No," he said. "It's Mr. Wilson we want to see."

Not until then did I notice, parked on the other side of the road, a black Holden sedan sporting a whip antenna and containing two other characters who, though not built on quite the scale of the one confronting me, were obviously cast from the same mold.

"Uh-huh!" I said to myself. "What the heck has Mike been up to now?"

"We'll just wait outside," said the uncommunicative visitor, and joined his companions, leaving me in a somewhat agitated frame of mind. There was nothing I could do about the situation; I didn't know Margaret's phone number, and in any case Mike was probably on the way back by now. I tried, without much success, to get interested in my book again. And then, by one of those improbable coincidences which would never happen in a well-constructed novel, another crisis blew up in the house behind me.

Our landlady, whom I shall call Mrs. Morgan, was a rather overpowering person with a quiet and inoffensive little husband. We got on well enough with both of them, but this morning it was obvious that they were not getting on very well with each other. For some time I had been aware that Mrs. Morgan's voice had been growing shriller and more agitated, while Mr. M.'s had been becoming more and more subdued. I had tried to ignore this evidence of domestic disharmony, but could hardly continue to do so when Mrs. Morgan grabbed the phone in the hall just behind me and began to call for the police.

Despite Mr. M.'s efforts to stop her, she must have managed to get through to the local station, for this sort of conversation ensued:

"Hello—is that the police? I want protection—my husband is trying to murder me."

(Slight interval, while Mr. M. manages to get hold of the phone.)

"Don't worry, officer. I'm afraid my wife's a little hysterical."

"Hysterical! *I'm* hysterical?" (Quantities of high-pitched laughter.) "I want the police! Give me Detective-Inspector Smith!"

(Another scuffle over the phone. Several guests pass through the hall, looking rather embarrassed. The Battling Morgans take no notice of them at all.)

"It's quite all right, Inspector. My wife's just imagining things."

(More laughter, but no further phone conversation. At this point, I rather fancy, the police lost interest and hung up on the prospective murderer. Five minutes later, all was peace and quiet again.)

And ten minutes later, Mike arrived, with Margaret beside him. She was certainly decorative, but I was a little too worried to notice that. As soon as Mike had come bounding up the garden path, waiting to introduce us, I broke the news to him.

"Don't look now," I said, "but there's a carful of cops over there waiting to have a word with you."

With more unconcern than I could have mustered in the same circumstances, Mike strolled over to the waiting patrol car, leaving me to entertain Margaret as best I could. She, poor girl, obviously did not know what to think. Perhaps she wondered if we were part of an international gang that had been planning to ship her to Buenos Aires. . . .

To our vast relief, Mike's conversation with the cops was short and moderately friendly. It turned out that they were rather anxious to know exactly why he had just paid a visit to his ex-colleague Billy Black, now in jail awaiting trial for stealing a car, borrowing a yacht without the owner's permission, shooting three policemen, and similar minor infractions of the law.

The case of Billy Black (this is not, of course, his real name) was a sad one. He had been a good friend and partner of Mike's for six months out on the Reef as a diver, and as a frogman in an act they had done together. But he had got himself involved with too many girls and, judging by his behavior, had suffered some kind of breakdown during which he had literally run amok. He had been caught only after a state-wide hunt culminating in a running gun fight, and Mike had been to visit him purely out of sympathy for a friend in trouble. The police, who were busily preparing their case—knowing that Billy had the cleverest criminal lawyer in the country defending him—were naturally curious and suspected some ulterior motive.

The whole affair gave us some anxious moments, for we were afraid that one side or the other might call on Mike to give evidence regarding Billy's character and actions—which could have been highly inconvenient just when we were planning to leave for the less accessible regions of the Reef. But we never heard any more about the matter, and in due course Billy was given five years to consider the folly of his actions. I thought he was rather lucky, but in Australia shooting at policemen (even when you hit them, as Billy did) is not regarded too seriously when it is only a first offense.

A few weeks after the trial, one of the national magazines came out with a lavishly illustrated life story of Billy under the tear-jerking title, "A Mother's Boy in Search of Death." In an attempt to analyze his psychology, the writer decided that Billy's love of diving was a proof of a hidden death wish. This produced a great splutter of indignation from his ex-partner. "If wanting to dive proves that you've got a death wish," snorted Mike, obviously thinking of his parachute activities, "what does that make *me?*"

Though I felt sorry for Billy, I also felt sorry for the policemen he had punctured. However, it was certainly bad luck that their colleagues had chosen that particular moment to visit us. We tried to explain the situation to Margaret, but I don't know if she really believed our story. For that was the last we ever saw of her, and the end of our attempt to provide some competition to Lotte Hass. At least, the end of *that* particular attempt, for from time to time Mike still goes down to the sea with a pretty girl and an underwater camera. I am still, however, waiting to see any photographic results.

VI

How to Call on an Octopus

The road to the Reef was a long one, both in terms of distance and of time. It was more than four months from the moment when I met Mike at the end of 1954 to our first landing on an island of the Great Barrier Reef. Most of that time was fully occupied with obtaining and testing equipment, making contacts with everyone who could conceivably help our expedition, and waiting—not long enough, as it turned out—for weather conditions in the north to improve.

During this period, we made two trips south from Sydney. The first was to Canberra, Australia's unique capital, where we met the Secretary of the Prime Minister's Department and other government officials, all of whom did their best to assist our plans. Canberra is like no other city we had ever seen. Fifty years ago, the site was one vast sheep farm, stretching as far as the eye could see in every direction. Now it is a city of some twenty thousand people, most of them civil servants. But it is a city so completely integrated into parks and wooded areas that except in the shopping and residential quarters it is seldom possible to see more than one building at a time. Calling Canberra a garden city does scant justice to it; on several occasions we thought we were miles out of town in some well-kept forest—only to find that we were in the very heart of Canberra all the time. The extreme devotion of the capital's planners to the unspoiled countryside, and their refusal to build more than two or three stories high, has naturally caused much controversy. Nothing is sacred to the Australians (except possibly cricket) and one of their descriptions of Canberra is "six suburbs in search of a city."

For both of us, our most vivid recollection of Canberra is concerned with the Mount Stromlo Observatory, magnificently sited on a mountain a few miles from the capital. When the instruments now being installed there are operating, this will be one of the finest observatories in the world—certainly the finest in the southern hemisphere.

A few years before, a forest fire had swept over the mountain, destroying some of the observatory buildings but luckily not affecting the main installations. It was a little depressing to see the seventy-four-inch reflector—which I had admired four years before when it was on display at the Festival of Britain—concealed beneath a maze of scaffolding, with its great mirror still in the case that had brought it halfway round the world. It must have been still more depressing for the astronomers who were anxious to start using the great instrument.

Mike and I were wandering over the mountaintop when we encountered a ruggedly handsome stockman wearing a vivid checked shirt and mounted on a fine chestnut pony. He explained that he was on his way to doctor a sick cow, and I engaged him in conversation for some time while Mike photographed us from various angles. One day, I shall have great pleasure in exhibiting these colorful mementos of Mount Stromlo Observatory at a meeting of the British Astronomical Association—for the bronzed and burly cow doctor we met patrolling his mountain range is now Her Majesty's Astronomer Royal. We very much wished that these cartoonists who always depict astronomers as spindly, bulbous-domed creatures peering through thick-lensed spectacles could have seen Dr. Woolley galloping over the landscape.

It was on the Canberra road, also, that we met our first motorized gypsies. They waved us to a halt, told us some cock-and-bull story about running out of gas, and then insisted on reading our hands and "blessing" the contents of our wallets. We think we got away without loss, but other motorists—judging from subsequent court proceedings—were not so lucky. When we returned from Canberra the gypsies were still putting on their act of waving from the roadside like stranded travelers, but this time we roared past them with rude gestures. We waited anxiously for a couple of miles to see if anything would happen to the car, but we must have been going too quickly for any of their curses to catch up with us.

Our second journey to the south was to a picturesque speck of land, Bowen Island, a hundred miles down the coast from Sydney. At this point lies the important naval base of Jervis Bay, the entrance to which is guarded by Bowen Island, although all the gun emplacements and military installations have now been removed. The island's only permanent human inhabitants are an elderly Scots couple who act as caretakers and look after the anglers and spear fishers visiting the place. Bowen Island also supports a colony of minute but extremely bad-tempered penguins, standing about nine inches high. These are so pretty and so easily caught (especially when they emerge from their burrows at night) that it is hard to resist picking them up. They then belie their attractive appearance by cursing madly and removing all accessible pieces of hand with their needle-sharp beaks.

We made the trip to Bowen Island in the hope of giving all our equipment a thorough test, under operational conditions, before we set off on the much longer journey to the Great Barrier Reef. My most vivid memory of the island, however, has nothing to do with underwater exploration. We lived in small, isolated wooden huts which had once formed part of a military base guarding Jervis Bay, and one dark and dismal night I was alone on our little hilltop, a quarter of a mile away from any other human being, as Mike had driven up to Sydney for the weekend. The wind was howling, but I had settled down comfortably enough in my sleeping bag on the lower level of a two-tiered bunk, so that I was supported about a foot from the floor.

I was just dozing off when all thought of slumber was banished by a sound which shot me straight out of my sleeping bag. Something large and very determined was digging its way *up* through the floor immediately beneath me. It was putting so much energy into the excavation that the entire wooden bunk in which I had been resting quivered as if with a fit of ague. I sat there in the darkness, while the wind moaned around the hut, the rain fell in torrents, and the Thing underneath the floor came steadily nearer. Cheerful little tales like H. P. Lovecraft's *The Rats in the Walls* flashed through my mind, and I remembered the wicked bishop who had been eaten alive by the army of rats that gnawed their way relentlessly through the walls of his castle.

I am not ashamed to admit that without wasting any more time I climbed out of the lower bunk and scrambled upstairs. The cause of the disturbance still baffled me; I could not believe that a rat could make so much noise. As the tin roof was now only a couple of feet above my face, and the rain had worked itself up to a crescendo, I felt as if I were inside a kettledrum during the finale of Ravel's *Bolero*. However, I decided that it was better to be deafened than to be eaten by whatever it was that still shook the wooden framework beneath me.

I don't know how long it took me to identify my tormentor—if there was only one, which seems hard to believe. Those infernal penguins were on the move, enlarging their burrows. I climbed out of the bunk and banged vigorously on the floor until the mining operations ceased. Then I went back to bed—still upstairs, just in case. . . .

It was on Bowen Island that, quite unexpectedly, I met an opportunity for which I had been waiting for several years. I was able to make my first social call on an octopus.

By this time, the octopus is somewhat thoroughly deflated as a menace to divers, so no one will expect this encounter to be a notable addition to the epic literature of Man against Beast (Marine Biology Section). I have no intention of entering for the Hemingway Stakes, but octopi (or octopodes, if one wishes to be pedantic) are interesting creatures, well worth the trouble of getting to know. Blasé octopus-fanciers can profitably ignore the next few pages.

I was skin diving around a small reef off Bowen Island,

in about ten feet of water, when I noticed a small rock beneath which something had obviously been burrowing. There was a little cave under the rock—a cave which appeared to be occupied by old bicycle tires. More detailed examination showed that these bicycle tires were covered with suckers, and as I dived closer and peered into the cave I could see a slitted yellow eye staring back at me. The octopus was so nearly the color of the surrounding rocks that it was quite hard to see; only the regular rows of suckers, and the birdlike eye, betrayed its presence.

It was impossible to judge its size from the little I could see of it; what was more, I had no idea how large an octopus had to be before it became advisable to keep out of its way. I swam around for a while, analyzing the situation, and wondering whether to be valiant or discreet. The reef was almost a hundred feet from land, I was by myself, and there was no one on the shore to give me any help. The octopus remained in its hole, providing me with no vital statistics of size and strength on which to base my plans.

After a while, I decided that Trojan Horse tactics offered the most promising approach to the problem. My seven-foot-long spear, though its only use so far had been as a focusing-aid, was still a useful weapon, and I had no difficulty in impaling a nice two-pound fish that came up incautiously to have a look at me. I could have hit something considerably larger, but that would have been a waste.

With my victim wriggling on the end of the spear, I swam back to the octopus and dropped the fish on its doorstep. I hardly expected that such an obvious ruse would work—for octopi were supposed to be shy beasts—and was both surprised and delighted when tentacles started to creep coyly out of the cave and wrap themselves round the bait. I could now see that the octopus was about three feet across, and that its body was as large as a coconut. This appeared a reasonable size for a beginner to tackle, but before I got too close it seemed a good idea to test the beast's strength. It requires very little effort to hold a diver on the bottom, and being drowned by an octopus of this size was a fate too ignominious to bear contemplation.

When the animal had emerged completely from its hole and enveloped the bait, I began a tug of war. The fish was firmly fixed on the end of the spear, and the barbs prevented the octopus from getting it off. I fully expected that when it encountered opposition, the mollusc would retreat into its lair; to my surprise, it remained outside and prepared to give battle. From time to time I dropped the spear on the sea bed and took a few photographs, then continued to inch the octopus farther and farther away from the safety of its cave.

When I had succeeded in getting it into the open, I made an interesting discovery. The cave—or rather burrow—had two entrances, and the right-hand mouth was still occupied by a tangle of tentacles. The octopus had a companion, presumably its mate. I wondered if it would come out and give a hand—or perhaps several—if the conflict got too one-sided, but it showed no interest in the proceedings at all.

That was perhaps just as well, for though the octopus I was teasing was small, it was surprisingly strong. When I was tugging at the end of my spear, my breathing tube barely reached the surface of the water when I held the spear at arm's length, and as there was a fairly rough sea running I could get air only when the trough of a wave happened to pass overhead. I could not exert enough force to pull the octopus away from the rocks to which it was clinging, and neither of us would let go our respective ends of the spear. For a while it seemed an impasse, but the octopus got fed up first and finally relinquished the fish.

It did not, as might be expected, then retreat to its lair, but remained clinging to the rocks outside, giving me ample opportunity to photograph it. As a camouflage expert, it would have taken high honors, for it was very hard to distinguish the creature from the lichen-covered boulders on which it was sitting. From time to time it changed the mottled pattern on its body in order to match its surroundings, being quite dark when it was in shadow and lighter when it came out into the sun.

It seemed to have no particular fear of me as I swam round and round waving my camera in its face. Indeed, it began to show signs of annoyance, and started to vibrate to and fro as if working itself up into a lather. This annoyance communicated itself to me, and my intentions, which had been fairly honorable, began to change. I remembered that the anglers on the island had told me that octopus made the best bait, and I decided to do my bit to cement relations between those fishermen who go underwater and their more effete brethren who stay on top. (Those relations sometimes need improving; I have known charter boats to "bomb" spearmen with their anchors, and not to desist until the aggrieved parties threatened to shoot their guns through the hulls below the water line.)

"Very well," I told the angrily undulating mollusc, "if that's the way you feel about me, you can end up as fish bait." Thereupon I speared it neatly, and the water promptly filled with a cloud of ink. The ink did not make a very effective smoke screen, for it disappeared almost at once.

According to all the authorities I had read on the subject, it is a foolish thing to shoot an octopus, since it is likely to climb up your spear and enmesh you in tentacles. I don't think that my victim had much fight left in him, but in case he felt like coming at me I swam rapidly toward the shore, towing the spear behind me. The water resistance kept him safely at arm's length, and a few minutes later I handed him over to the anglers who, with cries of glee, cut him up as bait for their hooks.

After lunch I went back to look for the creature's mate, which was still skulking in its hole. I had no intention of harming the bereaved survivor, but wanted to catch it and bring it back to land so that I could examine it at close quarters. This time, my attempts to spear a fish as bait failed completely; all the fish had now left the area, now that they knew that I could no longer be trusted. After swimming around vainly for thirty minutes, I came across the corpse of my earlier victim, and carried this back to the octopus' apartment. The animal came out quickly enough, but refused to engage in a tug of war with me and shot back into its cave—taking the fish with it. Eventually I had to prod my spear in the back door until the octopus emerged from the front one, and after some gentle persuasion I managed to prize it off its rock and start it swimming around. It was a very feeble swimmer, its jet propulsion equipment apparently operating at low efficiency. This was partly due to the fact that it was still carrying the dead— now *very* dead—fish, which it stubbornly refused to drop until it realized that its position was now serious. Once I had got it into open water, away from any rocks to which it could cling, it was relatively helpless and I was able to shepherd it toward the shore. As soon as we were in shallow water, I picked it up and carried it onto the beach. It is by no means easy to pick up an octopus, unless it is co-operating. This one was not, and slithered out of my grasp so promptly that it required a positive juggling act to keep it under control.

I knew that an octopus has a small, parrotlike beak, but was not exactly sure where it kept it. While the animal was sitting on my arm, I felt a sudden sharp prick and hastily prized it loose to find that blood was welling from a small bite. It was no more painful than the stab of a hypodermic needle, but I was very careful to clean the wound thoroughly. Not long before, a man at Darwin, in the Northern Territory, had died after a bite from a very small octopus. There seems to be some kind of poison associated with the parrot-beak, since crabs attacked by an octopus are quickly paralyzed. When I turned the octopus over, I was just in time to see the beak being retracted into the animal's mouth, which is situated on the underside of the body at the meeting point of all the tentacles.

As soon as I had got the beast to shore, I placed it in a bucket of salt water, where it lay panting for breath. This is a perfectly accurate description of its behavior, for it kept squirting water in rhythmic jets from the tube or siphon on the side of its body. At no time, however, did it emit any sepia, as captured octopi sometimes do, nor did it make any serious attempt to climb out of its bucket. It just sat and looked at me with its yellow, strangely intelligent eyes, and made no particular fuss when I picked it up and played with it.

I kept it for a couple of hours, changing the water

frequently, before tipping it back into the sea. It would have been a novel pet to have taken back to the mainland, but hardly a practical one. Could I have trained it to act as a retriever when I went spear fishing, thus solving the major problem of what to do about injured fish that creep under rocks? I commend the idea to someone with unlimited time and patience. . . .

These two octopi were the only ones of any size that we net during our entire stay in Australia. There must be plenty on the Great Barrier Reef, but we saw no sign of them. And only once did we come across their cousins, the squids, though the porous white cuttlefish "bones" were common enough on the beaches of many of the Reef islands. These animals are in some ways even more interesting than the octopus—and they come in considerably larger sizes. A few years ago, Mike was walking along the shore of the Red Sea, near the outpost of Abu Zenima, when he came across a single rotting tentacle lying on the beach with the sea gulls pecking at it. It was devoid of suckers, so it must have been one of the twin arms, terminating in grasping palps, which the giant squid whips out to grasp its prey. Holding his nose, Mike paced the tentacle as accurately as he could—and he swears that it was a hundred feet long. If I ever meet this sort of character, I hope it will be at the remote end of a TV circuit.

It was at Bowen Island that I almost achieved another ambition—that of going for a swim among porpoises. Every evening, just before dusk, a small school of these delightful mammals would go gamboling across the little bay above which our hut was sited. They would be punctual to the minute, and when I had got to know their habits, I made ready one evening to go out and meet them, carrying the camera and a spear just in case they got *too* playful.

The sun was almost setting when a couple of curved fins came slicing around the headland, and as quietly as I could I slipped into the water. It was rather gloomy in the failing light, but I could see twenty feet or so. I saw no sign of the animals while I was underwater, but once when I came up for air a sleek, shiny back was breaking the surface fifty feet away. I took a bearing on it, and swam toward it as quickly as I could. At the same moment I heard a curious, high-pitched squeaking noise—a loud squeak followed a fraction of a second later by a fainter one, then the pair repeated after a pause: SQUEAK, squeak. . . . SQUEAK, squeak. . . . It seemed an oddly feeble and ineffectual sort of noise for such a large animal, and I had no doubt that the beasts were "ranging" me by their sonar equipment in exactly the same way as a bat detects obstacles in the air. That regularly repeated pulse with its fainter, answering echo awakened a haunting memory in my mind, but it was not until a long time later that I identified it. I had once heard a recording of a radar transmitter beaming its power out across space and receiving, two and a half seconds later, the returning echo from the Moon. There had been that same insistently repeated double pause; the principle was just the same—only the scale was slightly different.

Unfortunately, I was not equipped to send back the correct identification signal, and once they had discovered the presence of an unknown body in the neighborhood the porpoises shot off out to sea. When I saw them again they were half a mile away, pirouetting in the last rays of the sun, and there was nothing to do but to creep shivering ashore.

I have often thought what a pity it was that I arrived

in Australia about a hundred years too late to see porpoises and men co-operating in a fashion that would have made a wonderful film sequence. And lest anyone suppose that the following is all a figment of the imagination, they can look it up (if they have access to an unusually good library) in the *Proceedings of the Zoological Society* for 1856, pages 353–4. I quote verbatim from an article concerning the natives of the Moreton Bay area (on the Queensland coast not far from Brisbane).

> Some of the natives may constantly be found during the warmer months of the year fishing for mullet . . . in this pursuit they are assisted in a most wonderful manner by the porpoises. It seems that from time immemorial a sort of understanding has existed between the blacks and the porpoises for their mutual advantage, and the former pretend to know all the porpoises about the spot, and even have names for them.
>
> The beach here consists of shelving sand, and near the shore are small hillocks of sand, on which the blacks sit, watching for the appearance of a shoal of mullet. Their nets . . . lie ready on the beach. On seeing a shoal, several of the men run down, and with their spears make a peculiar splashing in the water. Whether the porpoises really understand this as a signal, or think it is the fish, it is difficult to determine, but the result is always the same; they at once come in towards the shore, driving the mullet before them. As they near the edge, a number of the blacks with spears and hand-nets quickly divide to the right and left, and dash into the water. The

porpoises being outside the shoal, numbers of the fish are secured before they can break away. In the scene of apparent confusion that takes place, the blacks and porpoises are seen splashing about close to each other. So fearless are the latter that strangers, who have expressed doubts as to their tameness, have often been shown that they will take a fish from the end of a spear, when held to them.

Several other independent observers have described this same unique method of fishing, and one adds: "The cooperative principle was so well understood between these fellow adventurers that an unsuccessful porpoise would swim backward and forward on the beach, until a friend from the shore waded out with a fish for him on the end of a spear."

Fantastic though these accounts may have appeared to many who read them at the time, they would not surprise anyone who has seen the playful and intelligent porpoises showing off their tricks at such places as Florida's Marineland, or at the Theater of the Sea on the highway to Key West. Porpoises are at least as clever as dogs, and have a much superior sense of humor. As I clambered back over the rocks on Bowen Island, I think those distant dorsal fins gave me a mocking farewell salute as they disappeared into the sunset.

VII

In the Wet

From Sydney to the southernmost of the islands in the Great Barrier Reef is a little matter of eight hundred miles— and the Reef itself stretches northward for twelve hundred miles more. The problem of transporting our heavy equipment over such distances was a formidable one, and after much argument we decided that the most practical thing to do was to buy a car and to drive up to Queensland. Not only would we then always have our gear in our own possession, but the car would be invaluable at any stopping points on the coast where we might decide to go diving. We planned to go by road to Cairns, about fifteen hundred miles north of Sydney, and the last town of any size along the coast. From there, we calculated, it would be a simple matter to take a boat to Thursday Island, in the Torres Straits, just off the extreme northern tip of the continent. This, as it turned out, was an interesting theory but overlooked a few stubborn facts.

Neither of us had ever possessed a driving license;

indeed, I had never driven a car. After a concentrated course of lessons a sympathetic inspector from the Police Traffic Branch certified us as safe to be on the roads, a verdict with which I privately disagreed. Indeed, as soon as my license had been filed away I decided to have nothing further to do with so obviously impracticable a method of transportation, at least until completely automatic steering and obstacle avoidance had been perfected. Keeping my license in reserve in case of emergency (and if I drove it *would* be an emergency) I then handed the car over to Mike, together with full responsibility for the parking tickets that thereafter were to roll in with monotonous regularity. In Sydney, we soon discovered, it is illegal to leave a car anywhere—but anywhere—in the central area. As the public transport system is almost as bad as that of New York, this creates a situation in which the unhappy traveler spends much of his time trying to escape the notice of a diligent but very unpopular corps of men—known as Brown Bombers—who prowl the streets with notebooks jotting down number plates. They jotted down AEK942 at least six times, and it was a great relief when we were able to post their final warning back to them from the safety of a New York address.

Despite these hazards, and others which we were yet to meet, our beige-colored Chevy sedan was an invaluable asset for moving heavy air cylinders and underwater cameras, and for getting us to otherwise inaccessible beaches. We (i.e., Mike) drove it several thousand miles around Sydney before we finally set out for the north during the last week in March.

Even had we been ready, we could not have left earlier. From January to March is the rainy season, referred to throughout the north as "the Wet." This year abnormally heavy rains had brought the worst floods since the country was discovered. Several low-lying towns had been almost wiped off the map, and millions of dollars worth of damage had been done. The roads to the north had not merely been blocked; they had frequently been eliminated. We had to wait until this havoc had been rectified, and we were gloomily aware that the countless tons of mud and debris swept out to sea by the flooded rivers would ruin underwater visibility at the southern end of the Reef.

It was a fine sunny morning, giving no hint of the recent rains, when we squeezed the last box of flash bulbs into the car and headed north toward Brisbane. After some discussion, we had chosen the coastal route—the Pacific Highway—rather than the inland road. We had been warned that this was in poor condition, but at that time we did not realize what a road had to be like before the Australians considered it "poor," and we were anxious to keep as close to the sea as possible. It was a gamble, and we lost.

The road was fine for the first two hundred miles or so; then it literally went to pieces. First the macadam surface began to disintegrate, so that every few yards Mike had to take violent evasive action to avoid potholes which might be anything up to a foot in depth. After a few more miles, there was no sign that there had ever been any macadam; we were driving over a plain dirt road, creased with innumerable corrugations where the rivulets of rain had dug their tiny channels. The aftermath of the floods was everywhere: bridges had been damaged and their parapets half torn away by rivers twenty or thirty feet above their normal level; creeks were still littered with debris and their slopes caked with mud. We very soon ceased to complain to each other about the state of the road, but accepted thankfully the fact that there was a road at all. The expedition might have turned back there and then had we guessed that much worse was yet to come.

Our first goal was not Brisbane, the capital of Queensland, but the little coast resort of Coolangatta, about sixty miles to the south, on the border of New South Wales. One crosses the state border under a large notice which warns the traveler that the importation of live rabbits into Queensland is illegal—a reminder of the days when this unwisely introduced rodent menaced the state's agriculture, and it was necessary to erect thousands of miles of rabbit-proof fencing to protect the great sheep farms from being overrun.

Coolangatta is an attractive little town set on one of the magnificent beaches of the south Queensland coast, and we had been invited to stay there by the first of the many hospitable friends we were to meet in Queensland—Charlie Mustchin, possessor of one of the most comprehensive science fiction collections in Australia. It is sometimes a surprise to those who judge science fiction by the crude and often hideous magazines displayed on the sleazier newsstands (forgetting the contributions to the genre of Stevenson, Doyle, Kipling, Wells, Foster, Huxley, Orwell . . .) to discover that its readers can be staid and sober citizens, respected by the rest of the community and showing no other sign of mental aberration. Charlie was a prominent building contractor with a quiet sense of humor and a charming family, and seemed only too glad to let Mike and me take the shine off a brand-new apartment he had completed on the very morning of our arrival.

The fact that I had a foot so firmly in two camps—that of the underwater explorers and that of the science fiction enthusiasts—sometimes made life rather complicated, and was particularly confusing to newspaper reporters who often couldn't decide what line to take in their interviews. It also resulted in not a few underwater explorers starting to read science fiction, and in quite a few science fiction "fans" (a horrid but convenient word) descending cautiously into the depths with mask and goggles. It was at Coolangatta, indeed, that we used one of them as a guinea pig in an experiment which I rather hope no one else will try to repeat.

The victim was Frank Bryning, a professional editor and a leading member of the Brisbane science fiction group. Frank, who is in his forties, will not take it amiss when I say that no one would imagine him to be an athletic or adventurous type, but it seems that he is one of those perpetually young in heart who are always willing to try anything new.

Coolangatta is near the mouth of the River Tweed, which flows out to sea under a breakwater pierced with short tunnels through which the rushing waters surge to and fro with such impetus that the unwary diver can easily find himself caught in their suction. It is not particularly difficult to swim through these tunnels, if you catch the current when it is heading in the right direction. If you mistimed your entry, however, and were caught in the middle when the current reversed its flow, it could be very unpleasant even if you did not run out of breath before you could extricate yourself. The walls of the tunnels are completely covered with razor-sharp barnacles and oyster shells which can slash the unprotected skin to ribbons. I made just one dive through the breakwater, to see if I could do it, and then left it severely alone.

Inside the breakwater is a deep submerged valley through which the river flows out to sea. It was on the slopes of this valley, about fifteen feet below the surface, that Mike decided to give Frank Bryning his first diving lesson.

Frank had never been underwater before, but it was not hard to get him in. He was fitted with face mask, flippers, and a borrowed Porpoise unit and then, to quote his own words, "assisted by three strong men, picked a laborious way over the rocks like an aged Martian in Earth gravity for the first time." Mike, wearing one of the three Porpoises that the manufacturers had loaned us, accompanied him into the water and they both disappeared in a cloud of bubbles.

The remaining members of the party remained on the breakwater; we could not see what was happening down there on the bottom, but the steady stream of bubbles—*two* streams—assured us that all was well. After about ten minutes, however, no one had reappeared and it seemed to me that far too much air was bubbling up to the surface to be accounted for by a pair of divers who were doing nothing but sitting on the bed of the river. I dropped back into the water to see if anything had gone wrong.

Frank and Mike were sitting on the bottom, each with a large rock in his lap. They had unharnessed their breathing equipment, and were now in the process of swapping mouthpieces, like a couple of Red Indians exchanging pipes of peace. Mike was giving all the instructions in sign language which he made up as he went along, and Frank—who had received no warning at all of this underwater transposition—seemed to have no difficulty in understanding. Once he got a little flustered, and showed some anxiety to get back to the surface, but Mike just piled another rock into his lap and prevented his escape.

It requires a good deal of confidence, when you are underwater, to remove the mouthpiece through which you are being supplied with air. When you try to replace it, you are up against the problem of getting it back between your teeth without filling your mouth with water. Most novices trying the experiment for the first time end up spluttering ignominiously on the surface—and this even after they have had plenty of practice with the equipment before-hand.

Yet Frank seemed to be managing without any difficulty, and went trustingly through the unrehearsed routine of taking out his mouthpiece, holding his breath until he had exchanged it with Mike's, and then completing the operation by swapping air cylinders and harness. Even this last stage is not as easy as it sounds; unattached cylinders try to escape from your clutches while you are underwater, and buckles put up a stiff fight against opening or closing. In due course, to the astonishment of his waiting friends, Frank came back to the surface wearing Mike's unit, and vice versa. To this day we have not decided whether the whole episode was a greater tribute to Mike's ability as a sign-language instructor, Frank's aptitude as a pupil, or the foolproof design of the Porpoise units.

Our stay in Coolangatta was also enlivened by Charlie Mustchin's discovery of some youthful indiscretions of mine in deservedly defunct magazines, and by a visit to one of the few platypuses (platypi?) in captivity. This ex-traordinary little beast, which is an egg-laying mammal with a beak like a duck, was apparently designed for the express purpose of confusing naturalists. The specimen we saw, like all its kind, was extremely shy, but took much delight in wrestling with a mop that its keeper lowered into its pool. At the click of a camera shutter, however, it would dive out of sight and take a couple of minutes to reappear.

If the platypus was designed to madden naturalists, the koala bear, which we met for the first time at the same animal sanctuary, must have been designed to delight the hearts of children. No one can see one of the animated Teddy bears without wanting to cuddle it, and indeed they are completely docile and good natured. They spend much of their time crawling slowly through the eucalyptus trees which provide their sole source of food, or curled up in motionless furry balls which are quite difficult to see among the leaves. When frightened they will cry like babies; like kangaroos, they are marsupials, the mothers carrying their tiny infants in pouches. It is hard to believe that these enchanting little beasts were once slaughtered in thousands for their fur.

We were preparing to leave Coolangatta on our way to Brisbane when the rains came once more. The second cyclone of the season, Bertha (Anne had already done a good job a few weeks before), came roaring in from the Pacific and the skies began to fall. The storm did not last for long, but as usual the rivers promptly flooded, and we got barely halfway to Brisbane before we found that the road was six feet underwater. There was nothing to do but to turn back and try again the next day.

This time we succeeded, though we had to get out and push on one occasion when the car stalled in water that was luckily only a couple of feet deep. And so under cloudy, lowering skies we drove into the capital of the Sunshine State.

Brisbane is a pleasant subtropical city, well laid out and not, like Sydney, so crowded that even the pedestrians have to battle their way along the streets. Even in the center of the city, there seems plenty of room for everyone.

We had been booked into a hotel which, as it turned out, was a temperance one. Now both Mike and I have a total alcoholic intake of perhaps a quart a year, and regard ourselves virtually as secret teetotalers. But we disapprove of compulsory prohibition, and regard the right to buy a drink for our pals as one of the essential freedoms. However, what lost this hotel (which in other respects was quite a good one) our future patronage was a clever little gimmick which I have never met before or since.

There were two lights in our bedroom—a main overhead light and a table lamp between the beds. When the table lamp was switched on, *the main light automatically went out.* I recommend this niggling economy—which probably cost more in extra wiring than it saved in electricity—to any hotel keeper desirous of antagonizing his guests. It inspired us to invent yet more penny-pinching brain waves which we thought of suggesting to the management—such as slot-machine metered bath water and rationed toilet paper.

The same hotel, we were later told, had once been the scene of a piquant episode from which it is very difficult to draw any moral. It seems that, rather surprisingly, a theatrical touring party was once staying there, and that during her toilet the leading lady suddenly became aware that she was being observed by a Peeping Tom. Hearing her screams, the male star promptly rushed to her rescue and, using the first weapon that came to hand, knocked out the offender in the best tradition of knight-errant and lady-in-distress. Right, however, could hardly be said to have triumphed, for the hero was promptly ordered to leave the hotel.

The weapon he had used was an empty beer bottle...

We spent two weeks in Brisbane, following up the contacts we had already made in Sydney and Canberra. The Underwater Spearfishermen's Association of Queensland was kind enough to make us honorary members, after we had given it a screening of our color slides and movies, and its president, Lyle Davis, saw to it that our expedition was properly equipped with the exceptionally powerful guns which bear his name.

Underwater guns are of many types, but fundamentally they all depend on the use of stored energy to shoot a harpoon (usually attached to the gun by a line) into the target. Compressed air, explosives, powerful springs, rubber bands—they have all been used. For simplicity and ease of maintenance, however, it is hard to beat the rubber-powered gun; Lyle's design incorporated two thick rubber cables, and had the unique advantage that if either of them broke it could be readily replaced while the hunter was still in the water. The gun could also be easily loaded while one was swimming, as the two rubber cables could be tensioned one at a time. (To have stretched them both at once would have been a feat comparable to Ulysses' stringing of his bow.) Mike, who had used many spear guns in various parts of the world, went into raptures over Lyle's piece of underwater artillery and could hardly wait to try it out on the biggest fish the Reef could offer.

It was in Brisbane, in the quite literally fish-lined office of Tom Marshall, the Government Ichthyologist, that the shadow of Hans Hass first fell across our path. "Have you heard," said Tom, "that Hass is due out here at the end of the year?"

Mike and I looked at each other with very thoughtful expressions. We both had a great admiration for Hans (and for Lotte) and were extremely anxious to meet him. But we also knew of the resources and experience he had acquired in fifteen years of underwater exploration, and the news that he was heading for the Reef filled us with considerable alarm. This was the sort of competition we did not care to face, and we could only hope that *our* book was safely out before Hans could catch up with us.

We had arrived in Brisbane without any definite plan of action, confident that when we had spoken to the people on the spot, we would soon discover which were the right places to visit and which the right ones to avoid. So it turned out; after a conference with Mr. Ferguson, the Director of the State Tourist Bureau, we had mapped our itinerary along the Reef and had decided that we would make our first contact with it at Heron Island, in the Capricorn group. We had to wait a week before the boat could take us across, but there were plenty of things that had to be done in that time.

One of the most important of these was contacting the Great Barrier Reef Committee through its secretary, Dr. Dorothy Hill, at the University of Queensland. The G.B.R.C. is a scientific body concerned with the investigation of every aspect of the Reef; when we arrived on the scene it was in the process of setting up a Marine Biology Research Station on Heron Island. The laboratory was still under construction, but we were offered what facilities were available and gladly accepted them.

So, in the middle of April, over roads still bearing the marks of yet another storm, we set out for Heron Island and the southern boundary of the Great Barrier Reef.

VIII

Out to the Reef

From Brisbane the Bruce Highway runs north along the coast of tropical Queensland. The word "highway," however, no longer conjured up in our minds the picture of long miles of smooth cement. We were not in the least surprised when, a couple of hours after leaving the city, we were once more bouncing on corrugated dirt. The trailer we were towing, which was packed with the heavy compressed-air cylinders, gave us some anxious moments, and after one particularly bad bump there was a violent crash as the rear light came adrift. We didn't bother to pick up the fragments.

As some compensation, the country through which the road wound its way was attractive and interesting. From the crests of hills we caught occasional glimpses of the sea, its waves marching against beautiful but lonely beaches which, a generation or so from now, may be as famous as Miami or Waikiki. Most of the time, however, we were ten or twenty miles inland, passing through plains covered with the gaunt skeletons of gum trees that had been killed by bush fires years before, but which still stood in countless thousands. Farther north, the land was very fertile, and we entered the sugar belt, the gum trees giving way to vistas of red earth and green canes. Apart from the exotic crops, I might have been back among the rolling hills of my native Somerset.

Dusk had fallen when the Bruce Highway—which had at least been recognizable as a road until now—played a dirty trick on us. I had been navigating, trying to reassure Mike that we were still on the main road and not lost in some country lane. On the whole it was easier to drive by night than by day, for when the sun was up the shadows of the gum trees lay in bands across the road and concealed many of the potholes, which were revealed much more clearly by the slanting beams of the headlights.

We had seen no other traffic—or indeed any other signs of life—for many miles, and we were driving under a star-filled sky through a land that was completely wrapped in darkness. There were not even the occasional lights of isolated farmhouses, and civilization seemed a very long way off indeed. In actual fact, the nearest town was barely twenty miles away, and anyone from the real Australian "outback" would probably have felt oppressively hemmed in. But after the bright lights of the cities, this was as lonely as I cared to be.

Suddenly there *was* a light ahead of us. Standing in the roadway was a man waving a torch, and he had disturbing news. A large trailer had swung across the highway, and it might be hours before any traffic could get through. "But they're building a by-pass through those fields on the right," he told us. "If you go carefully, you can get the car through there."

We dutifully turned off into what appeared to be a roughly plowed field. After a few yards, it was quite possible to decide which was the best—or rather the least impossible—route to take. Bulldozers had been at work and we were surrounded by embankments of piled-up earth. The only thing to do was to get out of the car, take a flashlight, climb up one of the mounds, and survey the landscape.

I did this and reported back to Mike that if he could surmount one hillock and then make an S-curve there seemed a good chance of getting through. So we made a run for it, the mounds of earth looking enormous as our headlights picked them out against the utter darkness of the night. For one anxious moment car and trailer seesawed on top of a crumbling embankment; then the tires got a grip and we were over. After a little more cross-country work, we managed to find our way back to the main road, which to our relieved eyes now had all the attractions of a superhighway.

The first night on the road out of Brisbane we spent at the little town of Maryborough, which was still in the process of recovering from the disastrous floods of a few weeks before. All the obvious damage had been cleared away, and a casual visitor might never have known that not so long ago all the streets had been canals. Almost the only visible reminder of the floods was an occasional notice in a shop window: BACK IN BUSINESS ON BARE FLOORS.

The next day, as far as the roads were concerned, was a repetition of the first. From time to time our spirits would be raised by a stretch of smooth concrete, and we would

get up to sixty just in time to hit the next section of corrugated dirt. Once we passed—with considerable difficulty—
a convoy of enormous circus trucks, laden with all the
gaudy props and accessories of the Big Top and the Mid-
way. It was hard to see how these huge vehicles could get
through some of the places we had negotiated, but presently we found that they had one advantage denied to ordinary motorists. In the middle of the convoy we came
across a truck loaded with elephants, which stood patiently
side by side waving their trunks back and forth in hypnotic
rhythm. When the trailers were bogged, the elephants could
always get out and push. . . .

Toward evening, over a soggy stretch of freshly laid
gravel, we drove into the little port of Gladstone. It had
taken us a day and a half to travel four hundred miles, but
in the circumstances we were only too glad to have arrived
with the car undamaged (as far as we could tell beneath
its coat of mud and dust) and all our property intact.

Gladstone is a landlocked port surrounded by mountains and protected from the sea by an island barrier. When
we arrived it was very warm and humid, and it was easy
to believe that we were now in the tropics. If I had had
any doubts on that score, they were dispelled when a weird
flying Thing, which I was completely unable to identify as
long as it remained airborne, came blundering into our
bedroom out of the night. When it finally touched-down
on the dressing table it turned out to be a giant praying
mantis, a good three inches long. It took quite a fancy to
us and didn't leave until next morning.

The link between Heron Island and the mainland is the
sixty-foot motor vessel *Capre*, which makes the crossing
twice a week. She was due to leave at eight in the morning,

so we had taken the precaution of loading all our heavy gear the night before. There was no need for us to have swallowed our breakfasts so hastily, for it was not until ten-thirty that the last stores and tourists had been loaded aboard and we got under way.

It was a bright, sunny day, with a slight breeze and a gentle swell on the water. The *Capre* negotiated the channels leading out of the harbor, the mainland fell astern, and we were heading out toward the Reef. An hour after leaving Gladstone, we noticed something that warmed our hearts, and raised our expectations. The brown and turbid coastal waters, stained by the sediment from the still-brimming rivers, were giving way to the deep blue of the open sea.

An hour later, the first island of the Reef appeared on the horizon. It was not more than a dozen feet clear of the water line, and was thickly wooded so that from the sea it appeared as a tightly packed forest bounded by a narrow fringe of dazzling white sand.

I stood on the wind-swept deck of the *Capre* and stared across at my first coral island. It was lovely, with its gleaming beach dividing the blue sea from the verdant forest. Yet there was a loneliness about it, even a desolation, for it was a place that had nothing to do with man. A castaway would soon perish amid all this beauty, the tides and the winds would efface his footprints from the virgin sand, and the legions of ants and crabs would make short work of him.

An hour and several islands later, our goal appeared as a dark cloud on the horizon, but it seemed a long time before it humped itself out of the sea and we could distinguish the buildings set among the trees, the rust-stained wreck lying on the edge of the reef, and the little fleet of dinghies and cabin cruisers moored offshore. Almost five hours after leaving the mainland the *Capre*—which is an unusually fast boat—came to rest at her anchorage a couple of hundred yards from the beach. That was as close as she—or any vessel drawing more than a few feet of water—could get, even when the tide was at its highest. The reef that completely surrounds Heron Island like a vast, barely submerged plateau prevented any closer approach, and the last stage of our journey had to be made in dinghies. We were welcomed on the beach by a large tribe of painted cannibals from the tourist settlement, who danced round us uttering wild cries and were not appeased until we handed over our prettiest lady passenger as a sacrifice. The remainder of us walked up the beach into the cool, green shelter of the pisonia trees, trying to realize that what for most men could never be more than a romantic dream had now come true for us.

Heron Island is typical of its class, being a perfect example of one of the "low islands" which comprise most of the outer regions of the Reef. The phrase "coral island" probably conjures up in most people's minds a picture of a palm-crowned ring surrounding a still, blue lagoon. This is merely one type of coral island—the atoll—and it so happens that though they are common in the Pacific, atolls are virtually nonexistent in the Barrier Reef. Even the few ring islands that do occur fail to merit the name, for the true atoll rises out of the great ocean depths—a thousand fathoms or more—while the waters inside the Barrier Reef average little over a hundred feet in depth.

The Reef islands fall into two main classes—the hilly or even mountainous "high islands," and the "low islands," which are often little more than glorified sand dunes and may rear themselves less than a dozen feet above the sea. Only these latter are the true coral islands—that is, islands which are literally made out of coral. The high islands are formed of ordinary rock and were once part of the mainland, a change of sea level having cut them off from it. Though they often have extensive coral reefs around them, the coral grows upon them as barnacles encrust a ship—the islands themselves would have existed whether there was such a thing as coral or not.

Heron and the other low islands have quite a different origin. Without getting ourselves involved in the argument that has raged among geologists for more than a century, we can regard them as reefs that have managed to stay permanently above the water line, and have acquired a coating of sandy soil in which vegetation has taken root. The process is a continuing one, and the time may come when all those reefs which are now submerged at high tide will become islands.

It is easy to see how this can happen. Coral cannot live permanently out of the water, yet it needs sunlight so it is continually growing up toward the surface. Eventually it establishes a kind of equilibrium, the tougher corals, which can stand exposure to the air for several hours at a time, forming the upper layer of the reef. When these corals finally die, their chalky skeletons—which often form massive boulders—may be piled up by storm-driven waves so that they form a pin point of land, just beyond the reach of the highest tides. Such an islet, at first only a few feet across, may become a nucleus for future growth. Birds may rest upon it, leaving as a memento the seeds of plants and trees which they have eaten. Drifting debris—sometimes carrying lizards and other small animals—may make further contributions to its flora and fauna.

And so the island will grow from a barren speck in the ocean to an entire self-contained world of life and beauty—unless the storms which gave it birth destroy it before it can consolidate itself. The war between sea and land is never-ending, and each side has its victories.

Coral islands can, of course, be formed in other ways. Sometimes the immense forces which lie slumbering in the darkness beneath the earth bestir themselves, and the land rises or the sea falls. This can happen in a few minutes—there is one record of a ship in the Reef area which was lifted out of the water by a rising rock as if on an elevator—but normally it takes millenniums.

Heron Island is a tiny oval of land only about half a mile long; it can be circumnavigated in a brisk thirty-minute walk along the beach. However, I think it unlikely that anyone has ever performed the feat, because there are so many interesting distractions—flotsam to be picked up, pools to be investigated—that no time limit can ever be set for a stroll. The island is completely covered with a dense forest of pisonia and pandanus trees, the home of thousands of sea birds, and all the buildings that have been erected on the island are set in clearings that have been cut in this small jungle.

Four times every day, as the tides rise and fall in their eternal rhythm, Heron Island undergoes a complete transformation. At high tide, all that is visible above the water line is the tree-covered sand key, no point of which is more than twenty feet above the sea. But when the tide turns, the water drains away to reveal a vast, flat tableland, and the island multiplies its size a hundredfold as the reef around it is exposed. In some directions, the water's edge is miles away; at an unusually low tide, the distant sea is no more than a strain of deeper blue on the horizon. Endless acres of coral are exposed, if only for a few hours, to the sightseer who cares to wander among them and explore the contents of their countless pools. (The verb "to fossick" describes this sort of activity; "fossicking" is an old English word imported during the Australian gold rush and now extinct in its country of origin.)

Although the normal tide range is only about six feet, the coral slopes so gently to the sea that immense areas of reef are exposed in a very short time. And, conversely, as many incautious tourists have discovered, the tide can come in with equally surprising speed. It is all too easy to find oneself half a mile from the shore, wading waist-deep in water and keeping an anxious lookout for triangular fins.

The reef on which Heron Island stands is a long oval lying approximately in the east-west direction, and the island itself is at the western end of the reef, at the nearest point to the Australian mainland. At low tide, therefore, it is relatively easy to walk right out over the exposed coral until you come to the western edge of the reef, for it is only a few hundred yards from the sandy beach. But on the other side of the island, the reef edge is unattainably remote, except by sea. No one could ever scramble across those miles of slippery and often treacherous coral before the tide turned and they were forced to head back to land.

This, then, is a thumbnail sketch of Heron Island, and indeed of a hundred other islands in the Great Barrier Reef. It was to be our home for the next six weeks and was to provide us with some of the most exciting, most frustrating, and most dangerous moments of our lives.

IX

Heron Island

Heron Island, like ancient Gaul, is divided into three parts. One is leased to the owners of the tourist center, who have built small, two-berthed cabins which form a compact little settlement complete with its own power plant, refrigeration system, water storage tanks, and most of the necessities of civilized life for an isolated—apart from the twice-weekly trips of the *Capre*—colony of a hundred people. Another is leased to the Great Barrier Reef Committee; the only buildings on this portion are the research station (half completed at the time of our visit), the Superintendent's house, and a small hut which we used as home, photographic laboratory, office, and storehouse for our equipment.

The remaining portion is the exclusive property of some thousands of noddy terns and muttonbirds (wedge-tailed shearwaters) who form two distinct communities—one nesting in the branches of the pisonia trees, the other digging burrows underground.

We were met on the beach by Eric Hasting, the

Superintendent of the Research Station, who was quite surprised to see us as the letter announcing our arrival was still in the mailbag upon the *Capre*. All our equipment was also out there off the edge of the reef, and when it was finally brought in it monopolized the services of one dinghy. Visitors to the island are asked to bring not more than two suitcases; we had four or five each, plus half a ton of diving and photographic equipment. It made a most imposing pile when laid on the beach, and we did not look forward to the task of transporting it a hundred yards or so through the jungle.

Fortunately the tourist center came to the rescue by lending us its ancient truck; we had hardly expected to meet any motor vehicles on an almost completely wooded island with no roads. When the *Capre* anchors at low tide, however, the truck is a very useful asset as it can trundle along a ribbon of sand that, in one area, extends almost out to the edge of the reef. Stores can then be loaded and brought back without waiting for the tide to rise high enough to float the dinghies. I am quite sure that, sooner or later, the truck is going to get bogged down somewhere out on the reef, and Heron Island will be deprived of its solitary motor vehicle.

We piled our equipment aboard the truck, and it set off into the apparently trackless jungle, squeezing dexterously through the thickly set trees and scraping under overhanging branches. Several times the driver had to duck to avoid decapitation, but at least he had no worry about oncoming traffic. We ground through the forest for little more than a hundred yards, but there were so many twists and turns that I got lost a dozen times the first week before I could guarantee to retrace the path.

The Research Station was so enclosed with trees that it might have been in the middle of Africa; it was hard to believe that the sea was only fifty yards away, and that there was a flourishing holiday resort at about twice that distance. In next to no time, the virgin concrete floors of the lab were covered with air cylinders, cameras, flippers, snorkles, spear guns, weight belts, film processing equipment, and all the other impedimenta of our expedition. The landing area around the first lunar rocket would have presented a very similar appearance an hour or so after touch-down. . . .

Although the jungle on Heron Island is dense enough to provide all the solitude anyone could desire, it is not so thick that one cannot force a way through it in almost any direction. The island, presumably because of the absence of animals, is completely free from plants that scratch or sting. Nor are there any poisonous reptiles or insects; it is safe to walk barefooted even through the densest undergrowth. Safe, yes—but occasionally rather nerve-wracking, owing to the ubiquitous muttonbirds.

These quite attractive birds, about the size of pigeons, spend all day out at sea foraging for food and return to the island when darkness falls. The sandy soil is literally honeycombed with their burrows, which can make even a short walk quite a hazardous adventure. Without the slightest warning, the (comparatively) solid earth will open up beneath you and you may sink up to your knees in the sand. You may get one foot free, rest your weight upon it in an attempt to extricate yourself—and promptly go through the roof of the muttonbird residence next door. Every year, during their seasonal stay on the islands, hundreds of these birds and their broods must, one would imagine, be killed by the collapse of their flimsy homes.

It seems odd to find birds burrowing underground like rabbits, but on treeless sand keys there is no other way of finding shelter, and the muttonbird has so adapted itself to this subterranean existence that even when it lives in a spot where there are more trees than open ground, it still digs its nest in the soil. At night, if you walk through the forest with a torch, you continually come across these birds squatting outside their burrows and blinking in the sudden light. They make only halfhearted attempts at protest when picked up.

The muttonbird really makes its presence felt in the hours before the dawn. When, during our first night on Heron Island, we had finally dozed off and had ceased worrying about what absolutely essential items we had left on the mainland, we were awakened in the small hours of the morning by a din which we would never have believed birds were capable of making. A chorus of shrieks, groans, screeches, and twitterings came from the pisonia trees all around us, and no two birds seemed to be making the same kind of noise. Indeed, when that next morning I looked up the section headed ULULATION in Roget's *Thesaurus*, I decided with reluctant admiration that of the forty-six basic animal noises the muttonbirds could provide good examples of all except "buzz" and "hiss."

Oddly enough, the dawn chorus did not bother us after the first night. Since it seems unlikely that the muttonbirds had changed their habits just because we had arrived, this must be yet another proof of the way in which the human ears can adapt themselves even to the noisiest company.

There are two ways, which really complement each other, of growing to know a coral reef. One is by walking over the exposed reef when the tide is out; the other is by diving, preferably around high tide. Only by diving, of course, can one explore the permanently submerged areas of the reef, which in many ways are much the most interesting. And only by diving can one hope to meet, literally face to face, the largest and most fascinating of the reef's inhabitants.

We soon found that any program we drew up for the systematic exploration of the reef was so much wasted effort. A coral island is not, as most of the world imagines, a place of perpetual sunlight and crystal seas. It has weather—plenty of it. For days, even weeks, at a time it may be lashed by winds of hurricane strength, and drenched with torrential rains falling at the rate of an inch an hour. Even when there is no wind, and the sky is clear, the island may still feel the powerful influence of far-distant storms. It is a strange experience, on a lovely night when the sky is packed with steadily shining stars and there is not a breath of wind stirring among the trees, to hear a continuous roaring thunder as great waves that have been on the march for a thousand miles come smashing in against the reef. One almost expects, when the dawn breaks, to discover that the very foundations of the island have been swept away; but in the morning there will be no sign that energy equal to that of many atom bombs has spent itself in vain against the living ramparts of the reef.

The underwater explorer is completely at the mercy of the weather; when it is rough, he cannot dive in safety, and even when the storm is past, two or three days may have to elapse before the disturbed water becomes really clear again. As often as not, the water will not have returned to normal before the next storm comes along to stir it up once more. Then there is nothing to do but to sit and wait, in the hope that tomorrow—or the day after—or the day after—will be better. . . .

We had planned to stay on Heron Island for no more than three weeks before moving further north along the Queensland coast. In that time, we optimistically calculated, we should be able to obtain most of the photographs we needed. Three weeks, surely, was long enough to guarantee a certain amount of favorable weather. We remembered Professor T. C. Roughley telling us that, when he was collecting material for his *Wonders of the Great Barrier Reef*, his island sojourn had coincided with a month of absolutely perfect weather. If we were a quarter as lucky as this, we would be reasonably content.

As it turned out, we stayed on Heron Island not three weeks but six. And in that time we had perhaps four perfect days and about as many more which, from the underwater explorer's point of view, were usable. The rest of the time it was overcast, there was a gale blowing, the water was dirty, or all three. It was the old story; by the end of the six weeks, which was the longest we could risk staying if we wanted to see the remaining twelve hundred or so miles of the Reef, we got more than a little tired of being told "You should have been here *last* season." Toward the end of our visit we had ten continuous days when there was little point in stirring from our hut, and I shall never forget one night when the fusillade of the rain on the tin roof reached such a noise level that sleep was out of the question. In the morning some empty buckets that had been left outside were brimming with water, which was hardly surprising as according to the radio seventeen inches of rain had fallen in twenty-four hours. All this when the Wet had officially ended weeks before! As we rubbed the mold off our camera cases, we began to suspect the existence of a hitherto unrecorded phenomenon, which we christened the Damp.

What increased, if possible, our frustration was the fact that from every other point of view the island was ideal. The reef was superb; we had the Research Station dinghy at our disposal; Mrs. Hasting looked after our meals and laundry, and, being a trained nurse, doctored our cuts and toothaches; and when any of our equipment went wrong, Eric Hasting would promptly fix it in his workshop. He had built an elaborate lathe-cum-drilling machine out of an astonishing collection of parts, including the undercarriage of a Kamikaze plane that had dive-bombed the ship in which he had served as a Chief Petty Officer in the Royal Australian Navy. There was nothing that Eric could not fix—except the weather.

Despite this, our extended stay on the island produced worthwhile results, and when we finally left for the mainland we were not too disappointed. One day, we promised ourselves, we would return; and return we did, three thousand miles and two months later. The following chapters, however, are the record of our adventures on that first visit, when for me at least everything I met was fresh and strange. I was to see many other islands—some more beautiful and more romantic—but for the rest of my life the words "Great Barrier Reef" will always conjure up a certain submerged coral garden forty feet down and half a mile out from Heron Island.

X

The Stone Jungle

Fossicking over the exposed coral, when the tide is out, is the most comfortable though least adventurous way of getting to know a reef. Even this is not without some hazards; it is necessary to wear boots, or at least thick sand shoes, since coral is dangerous stuff to walk on and inflicts cuts which may take a long time to heal. (As I type these words, I have a four-month-old scar which has failed to close completely despite penicillin, aureomycin, and several other "ins.") And there is always a risk—remote, but nevertheless present—of accidentally stepping on one of the reef's poisonous inhabitants, such as the dreaded stonefish, whose venom-tipped spines can cause an agonizing death.

From a distance, when the sea has drained away, the exposed reef presents a somewhat drab and unimpressive appearance. Only a few boulders of dead coral, thrown up by the last cyclone, break the uniform flatness that stretches—perhaps for miles—toward the distant sea. It is not until you actually walk out among the rock pools and begin to explore this living tableland that you realize how much variety it holds. Tiny crabs scuttle away beneath your feet; fish trapped by the receding tide dart for shelter— but you hardly notice these dwellers on every seashore as you examine the fascinating shapes which only a coral reef can produce.

Here is a giant mushroom, sunk in the sand. There lies the wrinkled replica of a human brain—there a forest of bifurcated branches resembling the patterns etched upon window panes by the frost that never visits these islands. Half buried in the rock is a partly opened clam, more than a foot across—a close relative, you realize, of the giant which is rumored to trap divers in its jaws. A gorgeous blue mantle fringes the gap between the shells, and as you approach, this exquisite welcome mat is hastily withdrawn. The clam must have sensed the vibration of your footsteps, for it jerks closed as you bend over it. You reach down and try to pry it loose from its rocky bed—and get a surprise as the agitated bivalve squirts a small geyser of water into your face. As you wipe your eyes, you decide that it is most improbable that any diver could get near enough to one of these nervous molluscs to be trapped by its jaws.

If the reef has not been picked over by too many earlier visitors, you will find countless shells of all types and sizes. Many of them will have been vacated by their original inhabitants, but that does not mean that they are neces- sarily empty. You will often see one scuttling across the sand and, if you turn it over, will catch a glimpse of a hermit crab's spidery legs as it retreats into the inner sanc- tum of its spiral home. Some of these crabs are very large— perhaps twelve inches long if stretched out straight, which they never are. The biggest specimens are colored a beautiful red, and have one outsized claw which they use as a door to seal their home against intruders. Sometimes it seems impossible that so much crab could squeeze itself into a relatively small shell.

One of the commonest and most unmistakable creatures of the reef is the *bêche-de-mer* or sea cucumber, specimens of which may be seen lying in almost any pool. These repulsive objects, which often look like slimy black sausages, are sometimes two or three feet long. They can be seen feeding through the feathery tentacles which fringe their mouths, and if you annoy them they will sluggishly contract to half their original length, perhaps ejecting a mass of sticky, silken threads at the same time. In a real emergency the *bêche-de-mer* will abandon all its internal organs, hoping thereby to entangle or confuse its adversary. The fact that this animal lies around in the open, with no attempt at concealment, suggests that it had few natural enemies until some hardy Chinese decided that it made a delicious soup. Before the Second World War, a thriving industry exported dried *bêche-de-mer* to China at prices ranging up to a thousand dollars a ton.

Some of the shells which may be found on the reef are of astonishing size. The giant clams have already been mentioned; Mike has seen one six feet across. One authority (Saville-Kent) quotes rumors of specimens fourteen feet long. Though it is tempting to dismiss such stories as typical fishermen's (or divers') tales, some real monsters must exist in the unexplored regions of the Great Barrier Reef.

There were none of the giant clams on Heron Island, but myriads of the smaller (only one or two feet across!) Tridacnidae. One of the most remarkable accomplishments of these bivalves is their ability to bore into the coral, so that it is often quite impossible to dislodge them without a crowbar. At first sight one might get the impression that the coral has grown around the clam, so snugly does it fit into its cavity. In actual fact, the clam bores into the coral by rocking to and fro—a method of excavation probably unique in the animal kingdom.

The bailer shell must come next in point of size. It is the home of a mollusc not unlike a giant snail; one that I discovered weighed about ten pounds (with the animal inside it) and was over a foot long. It gets its name from the fact that it can be easily gripped by the hand and used as a ready-made—though rather fragile—scoop for liquids.

Dwindling down the scale of size are hundreds of other varieties of shell, many wonderfully colored and of exquisite design. One—a small, truncated cone about two inches long—possesses a tiny, poisoned sickle with which it will try to stab you if you pick it up. The weapon has little range of movement, so it is quite safe to handle the shell if you know which is the end that bites. If not, it is best to leave it alone, for the stab is quite painful and has been known to cause death.

Starfish of a vivid blue color, and sea urchins pricked out with curious beaded designs, are also very common on the reef. If you are lucky, you may find in a rock pool one of the most fantastically beautiful of all the creatures of the sea—a nudibranch, five or six inches long, looking like a gorgeously colored Persian carpet and undulating through the water with all the grace of a ballet dancer. No one can really believe in the nudibranch the first time he sees it in action. It is too beautiful, and too obviously impracticable, to be true.

Even at low tide, there are plenty of fish on the reef,

though you may not see them. They will be lying hidden among the coral, and sometimes you may startle a fairly large one from under your very feet, both of you probably jumping out of the water in your mutual fright.

If you know where to hunt for them, you can also find many crayfish lurking beneath the coral, their presence betrayed by their long antennae. These armored and often marvelously colorful creatures, looking like lobsters without claws, provide excellent eating and were the main course in many nocturnal feasts while we were on Heron Island. Mike would sometimes bring back six or more—the largest almost two feet long—after a trip to the shallow pools in which they lived.

To go fossicking successfully, you need bright sunlight to reveal the delicate colors of the coral, and a dead calm so that there are no disturbing ripples on the surface of the water. One of the frustrations which the reef can produce from its extensive repertory is a brilliant, sunny day with a ten-knot wind corrugating the water so thoroughly that nothing is visible through it, and you might as well be standing on the wrong side of a sheet of frosted glass.

If you wish to walk out to the very edge of the reef, you have to choose your time carefully, setting out an hour or so before extreme low tide. A mile an hour is a good average speed over a reef; there are so many obstacles to overcome, and so many things to stop and examine. At first there will be extensive patches of open sand, littered with dead coral—an uninteresting desert whose only inhabitants will be the ugly *bêche-de-mer*. You will hurry through this without wasting any time, and soon you will find that the coral is encroaching upon the sand and is becoming more colorful and varied. You are entering the region of living coral, and very soon will have to scramble over its spiky palisades if you want to make any further progress.

This requires a great deal of care, for much of the coral is brittle and will give way beneath your weight without any warning. The more massive, boulder-like corals are quite safe to walk on, but the fragile staghorns are treacherous, and you can crash painfully through their branches with the greatest of ease. Though you will not fall more than a foot, you can easily cut your legs so badly that you will be out of action for several days. About halfway between the island and the reef edge the territory through which you are passing will be equally divided between shallow pools and flat-topped plateaus of living coral, projecting a few inches above the water. I once had an odd experience in one of these pools, when a very decorative little shark swam right up to my feet and lay there motionless for at least two minutes, exactly like a dog waiting to be patted. There was time to set up the camera tripod and take a couple of carefully composed photos before the shark got tired of my company and wandered off again.

Near the very edge of the reef, the character of the coral begins to change. It becomes much more solid and close set, and accordingly much safer to walk upon. You have reached the massive rampart protecting the reef from the fury of the sea, which on all but the calmest days will be smashing its breakers against these living battlements.

It is an unforgettable experience to walk along the very edge of the reef at low tide. Although you may be a mile from the nearest land, you will feel as secure as if you are walking on a concrete road. In many areas, indeed, the pounding of the seas will have welded the coral into a completely solid and almost smooth surface, which would require little treatment to convert it into a first-class highway.

If the tide is still ebbing, a surprising volume of water will be draining off the reef flat and falling in cascades into the sea. These waterfalls at the edge of the reef are an unexpected and beautiful sight; in many places they will have cut what are virtually river mouths in the solid coral, which may be seen glowing in all its lovely pastel shades through the moving, crystal water. It seems quite surprising that such a large difference in level—often amounting to a couple of feet—can exist between the extensive pools on the reef and the sea with which they are connected through countless channels.

On most days, even when the sea appears to be calm, there will be waves breaking in spray over the edge of the reef and you will not be able to look into the deep water beyond it. On rare occasions, however, the sea may be as flat as the proverbial millpond, or will have no more than a slow, oily swell upon its surface. Then, and only then, you can stand on the wetly glistening outer slopes of the coral rampart, and look right down into the blue waters that forever wash around it. The great flat shelf whose very limit you have now reached plunges abruptly into the sea. Behind you, stretching back to the island, will be the region that can be thoroughly explored with no more equipment than thick-soled sand shoes, but ahead lie mysteries that are never uncovered by the tide, and which only the diver can ever reach.

Under ideal conditions, when the sea is flat, the water clear, and the sun high enough for its rays to pierce like blue-tinted searchlights far down into the depths, it is possible to see fifty or sixty feet down the coral-covered hillside. You will see legions of colored fish, most of them quite small, wandering to and fro along the edge of the reef, and darting for shelter when danger threatens. And further down, where the light fades and the thickening layers of water veil everything with a penumbral mistiness, you may glimpse huge and shadowy shapes moving among the great boulders and through the aisles of the stone jungle.

This aspect of the reef—the wide, massive rampart suddenly shelving down into deep water—is typical of the parts which face the prevailing winds and which have, therefore, to withstand the violent storms which hurl themselves against the Queensland coast every summer. The sheltered, or lee, side is less rugged, and the transition zone which divides the reef proper from the deep water beyond it is considerably wider.

On a clear, warm day one is reluctant to tear oneself away from the life and color at the edge of the reef, and to start the long walk back to the island. But if you delay your departure too long, you will suddenly realize that the countless clumps of exposed coral which lay between you and land are no longer visible. The tide has turned and slowly, stealthily, the water behind you has been rising as it seeps back through the myriad interstices of the reef. The little pools through which you waded an hour ago are now linking themselves together into wide lakes, and deepening minute by minute. Unless you want to swim—and share the water with the sharks which come in on the rising tide—it is time to head for home.

XI

Rendezvous with Sharks

It was on a partly overcast day, with the sun breaking through at intervals, that Mike and I made our first dive off Heron Island. We piled our equipment into the Research Station's dinghy, and rowed out across the reef flat until we had got clear of the dead, sandy bottom and were over live coral in about fifteen feet of water. The spot we had chosen was on the lee side of the island, well sheltered from the prevailing wind, and as far as we could judge through our waterscopes—glass-bottomed cans which gave a clear though narrow view through the surface—visibility was quite good.

We put on our face masks and flippers, adjusted our weight belts, blew the sand out of our snorkles, and dropped quietly over the side. Below us was a bewildering profusion of weird shapes; it almost seemed as if we were hanging above a forest of fantastic trees or giant fungi. By comparison, the corals we had seen while fossicking along the exposed reef were no more than withered, stunted shrubs.

The commonest variety was the branching staghorns, whose spikes formed an impenetrable thicket within which countless tiny fish would retreat for safety if we came too close. The larger staghorns resembled the giant cacti of the Arizona and New Mexico deserts, and it was hard to realize that they were animals, not plants. Or, to be accurate, the skeletons of animals, for a piece of coral is all dead lime-stone, covered with a thin and still-growing film of living polyps.

Less common, but equally unmistakable, were the con-voluted domes of brain coral, forming massive boulders sometimes a yard or more across the base. The labyrinth of ridges and furrows covering them forms such an un-canny resemblance to the human brain that no other name is possible. Often, as I was swimming among them, I was irresistibly reminded of the "giant brains" imagined by Wells, Stapledon, and other science-fiction writers.

At rarer intervals there were wide, flat plates of coral, often growing one upon the other, and providing shelter for large fish which we could see lurking in their shade. Some of these corals were quite delicate, veined with in-tricate traceries like those which spring from the tops of the columns supporting the roof of an ancient cathedral. There were, however, none of the frail vertical fans com-mon in the Caribbean and off the Florida coast. Probably the movement of the water was too violent here for such fragile structures to survive.

As a garden on land has its butterflies, so these coral groves had their legions of gorgeously colored fish. They were cautious, but not shy. We could get so close to them that it sometimes seemed easy to reach out and catch a handful. If we tried this, however, they would effortlessly elude our grasp.

The larger the fish, the more nervous they were—and with good reason. Neither Mike nor I approved of the indiscriminate piscicide which has wiped out the underwater populations in some areas of the world, but, when we were in Brisbane, Lyle Davis had given us the most powerful spear gun he manufactured and we were very anxious to try it out. Apart from indulging in what is one of the few sports where hunter and hunted meet on equal terms, we had good moral justification for what we were doing. Our unannounced arrival on the island had caused a slight food crisis in the Hasting household, and a few fish for dinner would be very welcome.

With his first three shots, Mike speared three fish totaling just over fifty pounds. We decided that was quite enough for one day, and heaved fish and gun into the dinghy while we started on the serious business of photography.

For the next few days, when tide and weather conditions allowed, we returned to the same spot so that we could test our cameras in familiar territory. We met no very large fish—above all, no sharks—but we did not expect to do so, for we were inside the boundary of the reef and in comparatively shallow water. When we were quite sure that we had a reasonably good chance of photographing anything that came along, we prepared to make our first dive over the edge of the reef. Mike had made one preliminary reconnaissance, under bad conditions, some days before. The water was still dirty after a recent storm; he had dived off the dinghy, just to have a look around, and had climbed hastily back into the boat with a very thoughtful expression.

"It's weird down there," he admitted, "and there's some big stuff moving around. It won't be safe until the water's clearer—you can't see what's coming at you now."

I was content to take his word for it; there was no point in running unnecessary risks by diving in water which was too dirty for photography—and photographs were, after all, the main object of our expedition.

It was about an hour after noon, and on a falling tide, that we rowed out to the reef and tried our luck for the second time. I slipped quietly overboard, with the Leica strapped round my neck, and found myself drifting twenty feet above a dense thicket of staghorn coral. The anchor of our boat lay supported in the topmost branches of the petrified forest, with a few small fish playing around its stock.

Visibility was excellent; when, a few seconds later, Mike followed me into the water we could see each other clearly when we were sixty feet apart. The sun, though it had passed its noonday peak, was still powerful enough to throw patches of dappled light on the coral beneath us.

There were some very large fish moving sedately over the sea bottom, but never venturing far from the shelter of some cave or cranny into which they could retreat if danger threatened. Keeping one eye on Mike, who was prowling around with his spear gun at the ready, I made several dives to the bottom to take close-ups of interesting coral formations. After a while I decided that there was a better way of reaching my goal than swimming, which used up a lot of energy and air. The anchor line provided a convenient stairway into the depths, so I flushed out my lungs, then filled them to bursting, and pulled myself hand over hand down to the sea bed.

When I arrived at the bottom most of my reserve of air was still intact; I twined my legs around the anchor and relaxed in the water to survey the situation in comfort. I hoped that if I remained motionless for long enough, some of the larger fish would let their curiosity overcome their natural caution.

Nothing whatsoever happened for almost a minute, and I was just about to head back to the surface when the utterly unmistakable shape I had been hoping to see slipped into my field of vision. Thirty feet away a small shark, with a startlingly white tip on his forward dorsal fin, was sailing smoothly above the coral undergrowth. It was no more than five feet long—just about the right size for an introduction to the species. As soon as I had refilled my lungs, I began to stalk it with the camera, and had no difficulty in securing a couple of shots as it passed over sandy bottom and was silhouetted against the dazzling white of pulverized coral.

Then I surfaced and yelled to Mike, who was in the water some distance away. I tried to indicate with my arms the direction the shark was taking, and Mike set off towards it as if jet-propelled. When I ducked my head under the surface, I had lost sight of the beast, and regretted my missed photographic opportunities. Almost at once, however, there was a flurry fifty feet away, and Mike emerged momentarily to yell, "I've got him!"

Ignoring the excellent rule that one should swim quietly on the surface, without making too much of a splash, I stern-wheeled across to Mike at maximum acceleration. When I arrived on the spot, I found him using his gun to fend off a very angry shark, which was turning and snapping on the spear that had passed right through its body below the rear fins. Though its crescent-shaped mouth was only about six inches wide, I did not at all like the way in which its teeth kept grinding together in rage and frustration.

I took two hasty photos, then moved in close (or as close as I cared) with my own hand spear, to help push the beast away from Mike if it showed signs of coming to grips with him. He had swum slowly backward toward the boat, towing the spear with one hand and using the discharged gun to keep the still violently wriggling shark at bay.

We had an acquaintance in the dinghy, who had come along for the ride and seemed slightly taken aback when we drew alongside and yelled at him to help haul our captive aboard. He reached down and tried to grab the tail, which was about the only thing he could do—though even this is not recommended in the best circles, since sharks can curl round to snap at their own tails with no trouble at all. They also have skins like sandpaper, which further discourages contact with the bare hand.

We had managed to get the shark halfway out of the water when, in a sudden paroxysm of fury, it succeeded in tearing itself loose from the spear. I caught a final brief glimpse of it shooting away across the coral, apparently none the worse for its encounter. When I surfaced again I found that Mike had climbed into the boat and was doing a dance of rage, accompanied by suitable sound effects, which were being greatly admired by another boatload of spear fishers who had now arrived on the scene. He stated, in no uncertain terms, what would happen to this particular shark if he ever met it again, with or without spear gun.

He added several footnotes, containing information which would have surprised ichthyologists, about the ancestry and domestic behavior of sharks in general. In fact, he managed to convey the distinct impression that he did not, at the moment, feel very kindly disposed toward sharks.

When we had succeeded in calming him down a little, we went back into the water and did a search for the weight belt he had lost during the battle. After five minutes' hunting, he was lucky enough to find it on a patch of sand, and this did something to restore his good humor. The loss of these weights would have been quite a serious matter, as without them it would have been difficult or even impossible for him to remain in effortless equilibrium at any depth. Though we had brought spares of all our other equipment, we had drawn the line at an extra ten or twenty pounds of lead, which somehow always seems to be even heavier than it actually is.

While engaged in the search for Mike's belt, I had swum a considerable distance against the prevailing current, and had noticed that the water "upstream" was much clearer than in the region where we had been operating. So we pulled up the anchor, and rowed a hundred yards against the current to try our luck further round the edge of the reef.

The character of the bottom had changed greatly, even in this short distance. Huge coral boulders, ten feet high, were spaced at irregular intervals through the blue-lit twilight. The water was also considerably deeper, and much richer in fish life. Horned rhinoceros fish, coral trout, and grouper swarmed beneath us, playing hide-and-seek around the submerged hillocks when we tried to get close to them. I noticed a fine grouper, well over a hundred pounds in weight, moving along a valley below me, and surfaced to draw Mike's attention to it. As I did so, a large turtle, moving with surprising speed for so ungainly a beast, shot past me and disappeared into the depths. I had no opportunity of giving any of this information to Mike, however, for no sooner had I broken surface than he shouted "Shark!" and pointed back into the water.

For a moment I wondered if our earlier victim had been rash enough to return. It took only a second's glimpse to dispose of *that* theory.

This was a real shark—a good ten feet of ultimately streamlined power, moving lazily through the waters beneath us. His body was a uniform metallic gray, with no trace of markings. He seemed aware of our presence, for he was cruising in a wide arc as if wondering what to do about us. I swam slowly above and behind him, trying to get a picture every time he was in a good position. If I kept moving steadily toward him, I felt quite sure that he would not come to me; indeed, my only concern was that I might make too violent a move and frighten him away. I was far too lost in admiration of this beautiful creature—the first large shark I had ever met in clear water—to feel the slightest sense of alarm.

But then I saw something that made my blood run cold. Mike, apparently thirsting for revenge, had reloaded his spear gun. He was getting into position to attack this monster who was bigger than both of us put together.

I shot up to the surface like a rocket, and as soon as Mike came up for air yelled at him, "For God's sake—don't shoot!" The spear fishers in the boat fifty feet away heard every word; mike, a yard from me, appeared to be stone-deaf. I followed him all the way down, making all the sign gestures I could think of to try and dissuade him, but it was no use.

Things sometimes happen so quickly underwater that often one can never clearly recall a sequence of events. I cannot remember the actual moment when the gun was fired; I can only remember my vast relief when the spear missed, and the shark veered away from its course. It did not, however, show any sign of fright as the steel arrow whizzed past its nose; indeed, it swept round in a great circle and swam toward Mike, who had now reeled in his spear but—luckily—had not had time to reload the gun. As the shark came slowly up to him, Mike suddenly realized that it was about time he did something, and began to shout into the water in the approved textbook fashion. The shark took no notice at all, but continued its leisurely approach. Mike jabbed his empty gun in its direction; still it came on. Not until it was about five feet away, and Mike could see its myopic eyes staring straight into his face mask, did it apparently decide that this was just another of those annoying and indigestible human beings, and swing contemptuously aside. I caught a last glimpse of it, a blurred torpedo lit by the slanting sunlight, as it vanished along the reef.

We climbed back into the boat, and recriminations continued as we rowed homeward. Mike swore, not very convincingly, that he thought *I* wanted him to shoot the shark. I produced all the witnesses within earshot to prove the contrary, and loudly lamented the masterpieces my camera had lost. "If you *must* shoot a shark," I wailed, "at least wait until I've finished photographing it."

Looking back on these events from the comparative calm of the present, I am inclined to believe that Mike never actually intended to hit the beast, but merely wanted to express his feelings. He is a dead shot at fish anything more than nine inches long, and it makes no sense at all for him to have missed something that occupied most of his angle of vision when he fired at it. At the crucial moment, his subconscious mind must have decided that this nonsense had gone far enough, and made him deflect his aim.

That evening, as soon as we could borrow the necessary ice from the tourist center, we set to work to develop the color film I had shot during the day. After two hours' work, pouring liquids from one bottle to another and running round with lumps of ice to maintain all the solutions at the right temperature, we knew that our photographic efforts had not been in vain. There was our gun-metal friend cruising over the coral, the undisputed master of the reef.

Undisputed? Well, one day, Mike may decide to put that to the test again. I hope he does it when I am not around.

XII

Devil on the Reef

No two days under the reef are exactly the same. Tide, wind, water clarity, cloud cover, elevation of the sun—all these factors are constantly changing, and with them the whole aspect of the underwater world. It is a strange and wonderful sensation to go twenty or thirty feet down, when the sun manages at last to break through a heavy blanket of clouds. At one moment you are floating in a somber blue mist, able to see only a few feet even if the water is at its clearest. You will feel depressed and a little apprehensive, for out of that closely encompassing blueness anything may appear without a moment's warning. The slopes of broken coral beneath you will be drab and colorless, the whole submarine landscape drenched in a twilight and autumnal gloom.

Then the clouds part, and the sun bursts forth. Though you can see neither sun nor cloud, at once everything around you is transformed. The coral hills and pinnacles become radiant with life; the constellations of tiny fish glitter as they turn in the sunlight whose slanting rays you can now see driving into the depths. Your horizon expands as if a fog had suddenly lifted; the dreary, monochrome gloom that had hemmed you in and oppressed you with its hidden menace now becomes a wide, enchanted vista glowing with soft colors, so lovely that any thoughts of lurking danger vanish at once.

This transformation is the most dramatic that the reef can know, for it can happen literally in a matter of seconds. But there is also something else that can alter the whole mood and aspect of the underwater scene. The reef, after all, is primarily a background, a living yet immobile stage against which the multitudes of fish act out their little lives. After a few visits one gets to know them all, not only as types but even as individuals. There is that mournful and aptly named pipefish, the perfect underwater equivalent of the dachshund. Circling that rock is the dignified angelfish, who never strays far from his home and who flaunts his brilliant colors as if certain that nothing in the sea will molest him. Down there in the shadows is a splendid fifty-pound grouper who suspects that you have designs on him and watches you with a wary eye; the white scar below his jaw shows that he has encountered Man before. . . .

These are the permanent residents, the actors who are always on stage. But ever and again there will come in from out of the ocean depths an intruder who does not belong here, an actor who dominates the scene so completely that all the other characters are forgotten. You may dive at the same spot a dozen times and meet exactly the same fish, haunting the same places in the coral garden. And then, one day—

The tide was falling that morning when Mike and I

rowed out over the flat fringe of dead coral and came to the living edge of the reef, where the bottom shelves abruptly away into deeper water. Though there was some cloud, most of the time the sun was shining and the water was wonderfully clear. There was hardly a trace of wind, and the surface of the sea was so still that for long intervals we could observe every detail of the coral-encrusted slopes forty feet down.

We had chosen a favorite spot—a fantastic grotto on the edge of really deep water—at which to dive, our main object being to test the new Ektachrome color film we had just obtained from New York, at vast trouble and expense. I had already mapped out a series of carefully planned shots, with and without flash, to discover just what this new film could do. Nothing—but nothing—would be allowed to distract us from taking these test shots; on three earlier occasions we had been diverted or conditions had conspired against us, but this time....

When we reached our selected site, there was such a powerful current flowing that we decided to move on to quieter waters, by rowing further around the reef. Mike took the oars, not trusting me with them, though I had expressed my willingness to try and experiment—like the man who wanted to find out if he could play the violin. While Mike provided the motive power, and bemoaned for the $(n + 1)$th time the fact that we had no outboard motor, I kept a careful watch on the undersea landscape that flowed slowly past beneath us. We were moving above new and unexplored territory, and at any moment we might see some attractive coral vista that would demand to be photographed with all the different combinations of flash and filter we could muster.

The glass-bottomed box through which I was surveying the sea bed gave a rather restricted view, so I kept swinging it from side to side, scanning the zone over which we were passing. Although we had traveled not more than a hundred yards from familiar territory, I had already seen several new types of fish, including one with a long, pointed nose that had obviously been designed for cruising at supersonic speeds. The scenery below us was not spectacular—an almost continuous thicket of staghorn coral, with occasional patches of clear sand.

Through the surface of the water, distorted by a momentary ripple, I caught a glimpse of something large and white. I swung the viewing box toward it—and gave an involuntary yelp of astonishment. There beneath us, and looking quite as large as our dinghy, was a magnificent manta ray. The gleam that had attracted my attention was the pallid white flesh on the inner sides of the two horns or palps extending ahead of the creature's mouth. It was cruising very slowly around in wide circles, its great triangular wings—more than ten feet from tip to tip—flipping with lazy grace. A couple of pilot fish were keeping accurate station beneath its belly, mimicking every movement it made, while above it swam several smaller satellites. Indeed, it seemed to have almost as big an entourage as a prize fighter.

I had seen many photographs of mantas, but it was quite a different matter to find one of these weird beasts swimming immediately below me, looking like nothing that had any right to exist in this world. To have come across it under conditions of such perfect visibility seemed too good to be true; very gently, without making a sound, we lowered the oars into the boat and gingerly let down the anchor. Gone were all thoughts of my carefully worked-out test exposures; we were desperately anxious to get some pictures—*any* pictures—of this splendid apparition before it took fright and vanished out to sea.

Moving with catlike caution, we put on our flippers and face masks, glancing over the side every few seconds to see if we still had company. There was no need to use the viewing box, for the manta's startlingly white palps revealed its presence immediately. It continued its slow orbiting, each circuit taking it a little further along the edge of the reef. Apparently it was feeding on the stream of minute organisms being swept along by the current.

With the camera round his neck, Mike slipped overboard and I followed a moment later, easing myself into the water so gently that I made scarcely a ripple. Now we could see the manta clearly; now, indeed, we were two more parasites trying to join its retinue. Mike swam down to within five feet of it and shot off a couple of pictures; it did not seem to mind in the least, even when a flash bulb exploded right in its face. We could not have hoped for a more tractable subject. It knew that we were there, for it kept a watchful eye on us, and once when Mike swam straight toward it, it deviated from its orbit just enough to avoid him. I have known human subjects who were much less co-operative.

When we had used half the roll of color film, I decided to switch to black-and-white as an insurance policy, and Mike climbed back into the boat to change the film while I remained in the water. I was reluctant to miss any chance of observing this strange creature, which bore such an uncanny resemblance to a modern delta-winged bomber. The upper half of its body was a dark blue-black, but its underside was a ghostly white, broken by the parallel slits of its gill openings. Its back had been scarred by numerous scratches or lash marks, perhaps caused by the whiplike tails of its companions.

Mike handed the now reloaded camera over the side and I went into action again. We had brought one of our Porpoise compressed-air breathing units with us, and when Mike rejoined me in the water he had put this on in the hope that he would be able to take his time getting into position for a real studio portrait. If you are free diving down to twenty feet, you do not have a great deal of surplus breath and there is time for no more than a couple of shots before you have to start climbing back for air.

It was now that we had our first momentary qualms about sharing the water with this large and powerful beast. Manta rays have a fondness for rubbing their horns against anchor lines or divers' air hoses, just as a dog may scratch itself against a chair—and for much the same reason. The ocean has its fleas, or their equivalents. Unfortunately, this habit sometimes has disastrous consequences; mantas get entangled in moorings, become frightened, and may tow a small boat for miles. The results can be even more serious when a diver is involved, and there have been several deaths from this cause. This has not helped the manta's reputation, already somewhat damaged by its popular name of "devil ray."

I became distinctly anxious when I noticed the manta showing a great curiosity in our anchor line. It would be a long swim back if we lost the dinghy, though we had no objection to the ray rubbing itself on our property as long as it did not overdo matters. When it had got to within a yard or so of the line, however, the arrival of Mike made it abruptly change its mind.

Until now it had taken little notice of us—we were just a couple more hangers-on following it around. By now Mike was emitting clouds of bubbles as the air gushed out of his Porpoise exhaust valve. The manta gave one look at him, and reared up in the water exactly like a startled horse. It banked round in a great circle, its pilot fish scattering in confusion. Then it drove off downstream with powerful beats of its great black wings, and we knew that we would have no chance of catching it again.

It did not matter; we had been luckier than we had any right to expect, and the final flurry of action had given us some dramatic pictures. We had been literally face to face with one of the most hideous and, to the ancients, most feared of all the creatures of the sea. At one time it was believed that manta rays would wrap their great wings around a man and crush him to death; today we know that for all their ugliness and unfortunate nickname, they are perfectly inoffensive beasts. They do not even possess the barbed spikes which make the sting rays, their smaller relatives, much more dangerous creatures to approach.

And is it really true to call the manta hideous? At first sight, perhaps, its appearance is diabolical, even terrifying. Yet it is doubtful if anything in Nature is really ugly. Ugliness, like beauty, exists only in the mind of the beholder; it is a purely human conception. At no time did I feel, as I was swimming around the manta, that there was anything in the least repellent about its form. It seemed rather to me that it possessed the whimsical grotesqueness of an amusing gargoyle. . . . Indeed, as I grew to appreciate the grace of its movements and the fitness for purpose of its design, it began to acquire a starkly functional beauty.

Fishermen sometimes amuse themselves by spearing mantas and letting the terrified great beasts tow their boats—often for miles—before they are exhausted. Why quite decent men will perpetrate on sea creatures atrocities which they would instantly condemn if inflicted upon land animals (has anyone ever harpooned a horse to make it tow his car?) is a question which is not hard to answer. Fish live in an alien element, and many of them have outlandish shapes; therefore we feel none of the sympathy, none of the kinship, for them which often links us to the creatures of the land. Few of us overcome the reaction that classes anything strange as automatically dangerous.

Let us hope that we will not always retain this primitive behavior, and will ultimately learn to base our judgments on something more than mere appearance. For one day, when the frontiers of space are down, we may meet creatures who are much more hideous than the manta—and much more intelligent than Man.

XIII

The Wolf Pack

The scene of our encounters with the manta ray and the two sharks became our favorite area of the reef, and whenever conditions allowed it we would row out and drop anchor here, very quickly following the anchor overboard ourselves. We never knew what we would meet and we hoped that if we came back here often enough, we would eventually run into everything that was worth meeting . . . even up to and including whales.

The water here was about thirty feet deep, but the bottom very rapidly sloped down to depths of sixty feet or more as one swam away from the reef. Great pinnacles of coral, some of them as large as houses, soared toward the surface, reaching within five or ten feet of it. One supported a huge overhanging bulge on a massive vertical column, so that it seemed a copy in stone of the A-bomb's mushroom cloud.

Though on the whole Mike and I preferred to go diving by ourselves, believing that too many people in the water at one time would scare away the fish, our most crowded—and most hair-raising—day off the reef occurred when we had company. Two high-school boys—typical young Australians already pushing the six-foot mark—had come along with us to give us a hand with the equipment and to see how we operated. The sea was very calm, but there was a good deal of cloud and the sun broke through only at rare intervals.

Our private underwater sanctuary was about half a mile from the island, and we usually located it by lining up a couple of trees and then rowing out until we recognized the coral beneath us. Today, for some reason, we could not hit our target, and after rowing round in circles for ten minutes in the general area, decided not to waste any more time searching but to anchor where we were and start diving. We could not be more than a hundred feet from our favorite pinnacles and grottoes, and would be bound to run into them as soon as we started exploring.

Mike went in first, with the spear gun. We wanted fish for dinner, and it took Mike only a minute to find and spear a large cod. Unfortunately it was a bad shot—and an expensive one—for the cod broke the nylon line and promptly disappeared into the distance with the spear and the detachable warhead which Mike had spent a great deal of effort perfecting.

However, it was soon clear that the shot had produced an unexpected bonus. The struggles of the injured fish had attracted company, and almost at once a fleet of several dozen barracuda appeared. Splendid, five-foot beasts with long, needle-toothed jaws, they came cruising in out of deep water, staring at Mike and his companion Irvin with coldly appraising eyes. While this was happening, I was in the dinghy with the other neophyte diver, pressurizing the camera cases with a bicycle pump—a routine we always carried out conscientiously, to reduce the danger of leaks. From time to time Mike or Irvin would pop up to the surface and give us a running commentary.

The magic word "Shark!" shouted by Mike during one of his appearances made us redouble our efforts to get the cameras ready. The barracuda, it seemed, were not hunting alone; a rather plump six-foot shark was swimming in the middle of the pack. A few seconds later two more materialized; that is the only word for it—you may see a shark leaving, but never arriving.

Mike treaded water while I handed him the Robot camera, which had just been returned to us after a major repair. Irvin also bobbed up, yelling to his mate to join him. "Come and see these sharks!" he enthused. "They're real beauts!" In a few seconds the dinghy was quite deserted.

Mike swam round the sharks, photographing them from all angles—even from below—until they decided that they were wasting their time and disappeared into the distant blue haze along the reef. The barracuda also departed; we were rather sorry to see them go, though in a few minutes we were to be much sorrier to see them come back.

Throughout all this, the two boys were having the time of their lives, though, I could not help wondering what their parents would have thought had they known what their offspring were doing. It was the first time they had ever dived in deep water, and the reef had certainly put on its best display for them. Like most skin divers being introduced to sharks, they were much too excited and interested to be at all frightened. There is something about the sheer beauty and grace of large sharks which, when you are watching them in action, suppresses thoughts of personal danger.

We continued swimming around for another ten minutes, always keeping in sight of each other but quartering a large area of the reef. In one of my circuits over deep water I came across a flotilla of sting rays, slowly cruising round and round a huge coral boulder. Their backs were covered with a beautiful and intricate pattern of white spots, and they trailed long, thin whips on which the dangling barbs could be clearly seen. One of the rays had a broken tail; there was a sharp kink halfway along it, so that the slender whip drooped away disconsolately.

Rays are fascinating creatures to watch, as they flap through the water like enormous butterflies, and it is hard to resist photographing them. I took a deep breath, and dived as swiftly as I could toward the dimly seen creatures circling down there in the gloom. Keeping well clear of those dangerous whips, I took one shot—but the flash bulb failed to operate and I knew that the picture would be a failure.

On my second dive, the flash operated correctly. I was already well on my way back to the surface when I glanced at the depth gauge strapped to my wrist and saw that I was just passing the 30-foot mark. This was probably the deepest dive I had ever made without breathing gear, though the 40-foot level I had just managed to attain was barely a third of the way toward Raimondo Bucher's astonishing record of 128 feet in the Mediterranean.

Only a few minutes later, as I was cruising high above an isolated patch of coral, I noticed a perfectly good anchor lying beneath me. This was an immediate challenge, for no diver can resist the opportunity of making the sea give up some of the wealth it has stolen from mankind. A lost anchor is not quite as glamorous, or as valuable, as a brass-bound chest full of pirates' treasure, but one has to make a beginning somewhere.

The boys had now climbed back into the dinghy, but Mike was still in the water and I called him over to have a look at my discovery. At first he was not particularly interested, but presently he made a quick reconnaissance dive to see if the anchor was worth recovering. He dwindled swiftly toward the bottom until he seemed no more than a small doll far below me; the modest forty feet which was the best I had done immediately shrank to insignificance in my mind. When Mike had climbed back and recovered his breath, he informed me that the anchor was in good condition, had a long chain attached to it which had become embedded in the coral—and was, according to his depth gauge, sixty feet down. There was no question of being able to raise it by free diving, but there was a Porpoise unit in the dinghy which would make the job a simple one. I remained in the water, marking the position of the anchor, while Mike swam to the dinghy and collected his breathing gear. The cylinder was dropped over the side while he trod water and adjusted the harness—a much easier and simpler procedure than climbing back into the boat and then staggering out again with the heavy equipment on your shoulders.

Mike submerged in a long slanting dive, after telling the boys to follow his bubbles with the dinghy and then to lower a line to him when he gave the signal. He reached the isolated clump of coral and, without much difficulty, unraveled the chain that had become wrapped around it. Then I saw him shoulder the anchor and trudge across the sea bed, stirring up a great cloud of sand as he did so.

Meanwhile, from the dinghy above, our own anchor on

the end of its line was being slowly lowered. The whole operation was beautifully timed; when Mike looked up, the big metal hook was just descending toward him and he merely had to loop the chain over it. Unfortunately for his peace of mind—and for mine, for I was a good fifty feet further away from the dinghy—he was now being intently watched by a very large crowd of spectators.

The barracuda had come back. What was more, they had brought reinforcement. Although the sharks had gone, there were now at least a hundred 'cuda in the pack, some of them up to six feet in length. They formed such a compact ceiling above Mike that he could no longer see the boat, sixty feet above his head. He waved his arms and blew bubbles out of his exhaust valve in the recommended fashion, but the fish took not the slightest notice.

"This is it," he thought, as the anchor began to move upward through the almost solid mass of sleek, ferociously fanged beasts. He had grabbed the anchor line, so that the boys in the boat would save him the trouble of swimming up to the surface. Now he began to wonder if they would find anything on the end of the line apart from two anchors and a rather chewed-up Porpoise unit.

The barracuda followed him all the way up, eying him as if trying to make up their minds. They were, luckily, still undecided by the time he had reached the dinghy. To give himself time to climb aboard, Mike gave a final blast of bubbles and made a short dart at the circling 'cuda. They retreated for a few feet, and before they could come back Mike—air cylinder, lead weights, and all—was out of the water like a flying fish and into the dinghy.

I saw all this from fifty feet away as I swam around just under the surface, but took little notice because I "knew" that barracuda were quite harmless. I had met dozens—though never ones so large—while swimming in the Gulf of Mexico and the Straits of Florida, and had photographed speared ones at close quarters while they were still struggling on the harpoon. They had been inquisitive and fearless, but had never shown any signs of aggressiveness. When a friend of mine had cut his hand open within sight of twenty or thirty of them, and had stained a cubic yard of water with blood, they had shot toward him—and then turned away, apparently uninterested.

Accordingly, when the pack that had been surrounding Mike swam toward me, my first reaction was one of extreme pleasure. "Now," I said to myself, "you'll be able to get some *really* good close-ups." I waited until I was completely encircled—not that there was much else that I could do—and fired off my first shot. The silent but dazzling explosion of the flash bulb lit up the lean silver bodies that surrounded me like a living wall. It did not disturb them in the least; they continued to spiral inward, until they were no more than six feet away. It was then that I began to suspect, for the first time, that these barracuda might be very different from their innocuous Florida relatives. I felt like a tempting morsel surrounded by a pack of hungry wolves; it would only need one of these great fish to be a little bolder than the rest and it would all be over in a couple of seconds. Rather irrationally, I felt quite aggrieved at the prospect of being eaten by what were, after all, only overgrown pike. A shark—preferably not less than twenty feet long—would have been much more acceptable.

I surfaced long enough to yell for the dinghy, then dived under again so that I could keep an eye on the steadily encroaching fish. A second flash bulb produced as little reaction as the first—though it left me with an unanswered enigma. Between the two photographs, which were taken only seconds apart, the entire huge pack had reversed its direction of movement. In the first, it was moving clockwise—in the second, counter-clockwise. It is only now, months later, as I examine the still uncut strip of film, that I have realized that. I would have been prepared to swear on oath that the 'cuda had spiraled in towards me in one continuous sweep.

The photographs also correct another impression. I would have guessed that there were about a hundred barracuda in the pack—but no less than thirty are visible in the relatively small area covered by each photograph, so the total number surrounding me must have been at least two hundred. I could scarcely have provided an entree for so many ravening appetites.

Before I could take another photograph, the close-packed bodies began to disperse; the 'cuda were drifting slowly, reluctantly away. The dinghy was overhead; perhaps that had finally scared them off, or perhaps they had decided that I was inedible. This is a question to which I shall never know the answer, but I am quite certain of one thing—that from now on both Mike and I will take barracuda very seriously indeed. We may fool around with sharks, but not the giant sea pike—at least when they come in swarms of two hundred at a time.

We rowed the dinghy in a rather thoughtful silence for a hundred yards along the reef, then suddenly noticed the area that we had been looking for earlier but had failed to find. There was no sign of the barracuda, so I dived again and finished off the film in the camera. But I was careful to keep very, very close to the boat.

XIV

"Spike"

After devil rays, sharks, and barracuda, this chapter may seem something of an anticlimax. But the creature which is widely regarded as the most dangerous animal on the Great Barrier Reef is a lazy and completely inoffensive little fish which spends most of its life lying motionless on the bottom of coral pools, and seldom grows to a greater length than ten inches. The adjective "inoffensive" may seem surprising, but is perfectly accurate; the trouble with *Synanceja horrida* is not that it is offensive, but that it is highly *defensive*.

The stonefish—to give it what would be its popular name, if there were anything at all popular about it—also has the additional distinction of being one of the most hideous creatures which Nature has ever designed. Indeed, into its mere nine or ten inches of length have probably been packed more concentrated ugliness and venom than could be found anywhere else on Earth.

It is common all along the Great Barrier Reef—though

just how common, nobody knows since it is so extremely difficult to see. Men have spent years on the Reef without ever encountering one, despite the fact that in that time they must have walked within a few feet of dozens. The stonefish is a supreme master of the art of camouflage, tucking itself in beside rocks and bending its squat body to conform to their shape with such skill that it looks exactly like a piece of rotten coral. To add to the resemblance, its warty skin is usually covered with a green scum of algae, and its body is humped and indented in such a manner that the usual smooth lines characteristic of most fishes are completely lost.

Having worried its way into the sandy bottom of a pool by wriggling the wing-shaped fins that run along the lower side of its body, the stonefish sits and waits. Two tiny eyes, looking like warts on the top of its head, survey the surrounding scene. Sooner or later, along comes some unsuspecting little fish, completely deceived by the camouflage expert. Then a semicircular mouth, hinged at the bottom, drops like a swiftly falling drawbridge, and dinner is served. As the mouth opens, it reveals for a moment a tongue and throat of a corpselike pallor, in quite surprising contrast to the creature's dingy exterior.

If this summed up the appearance and habits of the stonefish, it would not be of much importance or interest. However, along its back the creature has a series of thirteen spines, which normally lie flat and are linked together with a band of skin. If stepped on or otherwise molested, the stonefish erects these spines, each of which can inject a poison of appalling virulence. The spines are sharp enough to go through thin shoe soles, such as those of light tennis shoes, and the venom is so potent that death may follow in a matter of seconds. The pain is so agonizing that even if the victim recovers he may have to be given sedatives for prolonged periods, and since it is usually impossible to get really swift medical attention to anyone injured out on the jagged assault course of the average exposed reef, the chances of survival after an encounter with a stonefish are rather small. Or so, at any rate, most authorities maintain with a certain macabre relish.

Although they are so dangerous, and not at all rare, these unprepossessing little beasts actually cause remarkably few casualties. This is because it is physically impossible to walk over a coral reef without wearing good shoes, which give almost complete protection even if one steps directly on a stonefish. Moreover, the fish do not lie around in the middle of pools, where one would be likely to step on them, but nestle against rocks which the careful wader would tend to avoid in any event.

The stonefish, then, is one of those dangers which everyone on the Reef talks about but which few people have actually met. During my first few days on Heron Island, I could hardly walk a dozen yards through the coral pools without coming across something that looked like a stonefish to my ultra-cautious eye, but which on prodding with a spear turned out to be a perfectly ordinary lump of rock. After a while I ceased to see stonefish everywhere, and realized that my chances of coming across any were minute. Professor Younge, leader of the Great Barrier Reef Expedition in 1928, never found a stonefish during the entire year he spent on Low Isles—though the sharp-eyed native helpers did so. Professor Dakin, of Sydney University, author of one of the best books on the Reef, failed to find one in a lifetime of study.

I was lucky. One afternoon, during our last week on Heron Island, I was wading out from the beach toward the distant line of foam where the now almost exposed coral shelf dropped away into the sea. I had gone little more than a hundred yards, and was not paying much attention to the pools through which I was passing. The coral here was almost all dead, having been choked by sand swept out from the beach in a cyclone a few years before. I was in a hurry to get through this drab coral graveyard so that I could set up my cameras along the colorful living growths that the receding tide had just uncovered.

However, you cannot walk on the face of a reef, with its treacherous crumbling coral, its sudden, unexpectedly deep pools, and its possibilities of discovering interesting shells, without keeping a fairly watchful eye on the ground beneath you. I was just passing through one very dull and lifeless pool when I half-consciously noticed a dirty, oval object lying beside a larger rock. Automatically, I gave it a gentle jab with my spear. It didn't move—but it seemed to be slightly less than solid. I gave it a harder poke—and my first stonefish jerked itself spasmodically about six inches through the water, and once again tried to pretend that it wasn't there.

In a surprisingly short time, a small crowd of tourists, photographers, and vacationing schoolboys had gathered around the pool. It says much for the stonefish's powers of camouflage that, even though it had been disturbed from its chosen resting place and now lay out in the open, several of the spectators were quite unable to find it until it was pointed out to them.

After a brief photographic orgy, the problem now arose of carrying the creature back to land. Luckily, one of the schoolboys had with him a glass-bottomed viewing box, and we tipped the fish into that by prizing it cautiously off the bottom with a large knife. Throughout the proceedings it made no effort to escape, or even to move. It still seemed unable to believe that anyone could actually see it.

The ten-year-old who had contributed the viewing box then gallantly carried box and contents back to shore, while I followed with the cameras. This performance was criticized in some quarters, and I had to point out that two Leicas were more valuable than all stonefish and most small boys. The fish was then installed in a large tank, surrounded by blocks of broken coral, so that the way in which it merged into its background could be studied at leisure. It seemed incapable of swimming, but when disturbed merely flopped along the bottom for a few inches and tried to dig itself in with its fins. After a while, also, it no longer erected its frill of poisoned spines, having apparently realized that its standard operational procedure had ceased to be effective.

Because it seemed so improbable that the stonefish should have *exactly* thirteen spines, I made a special point of counting them carefully. (And no nuclear physicist manipulating two subcritical lumps of plutonium could have been more careful.) Rather to my surprise, thirteen was quite correct. The spines were normally retracted in a sheath of skin, so that the only sign of their presence was a series of warts. When extended, however, some of them were fully half an inch in length, and looked like needles of translucent glass.

"Spike," as I christened him, lived for several days in one of the laboratory tanks and was visited by so many of the island's tourists that I felt tempted to charge an admission fee. When lifted out of the water, Spike put up no resistance but lay morosely inactive until he returned to the tank, when he would start scuffling his way back into the sand. Stonefish can live completely out of water for several hours. They would hardly have survived otherwise, since so much of their time is spent in shallow pools which must often be drained as the tide recedes.

When I got back to the mainland, feeling that I now had a personal interest in stonefish, I started to make further inquiries about these creatures. Everything I read increased my respect, though hardly my affection, for them. In Professor Younge's *A Year on the Great Barrier Reef* I found these cheerful words: "There have been many cases of human beings stepping on these creatures with their bare feet or in sand shoes—and suffering terrible agonies. Days of blinding pain and three or four months of illness have been the usual result, and death has been by no means infrequent. . . . Little can be done for the patient except to keep him unconscious by injections of opium until the pain becomes bearable."

I also read that the aborigines have an extreme horror of this fish, and in their initiation ceremonies a man pretends to step on a wax model of one and falls to the ground uttering shrieks of agony—a very direct and effective object lesson. Now the aborigines are intelligent and practical people, only slightly more superstitious than the average white. (Anyone inclined to doubt this can look at the horoscope page of his Sunday newspaper.) The fact that they are afraid of the stonefish is proof enough that it should be taken seriously.

And yet—I cannot help wondering if here is another case of a creature whose appearance has given it a worse reputation than it deserves. Some months later, in Cairns, I was discussing the stonefish with Dr. Hugo Flecker, a well-known Queensland naturalist. He stated categorically that in twenty years he had never heard of a single death caused by these creatures.

Since then, I have come across several cases of people who have heard of people who were killed by stonefish— but firsthand evidence, never.

So the case against the stonefish must still be regarded as "not proven." Most people, after taking one look at the beast, will probably decide that no further proof is necessary.

XV

North to the Sun

We had twelve hundred miles of reef to look at and six months to do it in; we could not remain on Heron Island forever. Besides, disquieting rumors of Hans Hass's imminent arrival continued to reach us, though no one was ever able to substantiate them. There was also another rumor, equally persistent—that Hans had been eaten by a shark. Everywhere we went we kept hearing this report, which we did our best to ridicule. We did not deny that sharks might exist sufficiently ill-mannered to eat Hans; what we did deny was the possibility of it happening without our hearing all about it through our excellent information channels. In one case I was able to point out that, after the date of his reported demise, I had seen Hans with my own eyes, as he sat listening to Captain Cousteau address an enormous audience at the Royal Festival Hall, London. He looked a little envious, I thought, but if he was a ghost he was a very substantial one.

The long string of islands and sand keys which

constitutes the Great Barrier Reef has a general uniformity which makes it possible to judge the Reef as a whole by a few representative samples. We had agreed on a general policy of spending all the time we could on one island, in the hope of getting to know it thoroughly, and making quick "spot checks" of any others we were able to fit into our program. Ideally, we would have liked to sail the length of the Reef, stopping at any place that looked interesting. (One day, perhaps, we may be able to do just that.) Since we were short of time and of millionaire yacht owners, this plan had to be abandoned. Instead, we decided to see what we could by flying the length of the Reef and spending a few weeks exploring its extreme northern end among the maze of islands in the Torres Straits. We were encouraged to do this because Thursday Island—the administrative center of the islands off the north tip of Queensland—is also the center of the pearling trade; and much of the Reef's history is bound up with the quest for pearl.

The plane from Brisbane skirts the coast for most of its journey into the north. Less than two hours after take-off we were crossing the Tropic of Capricorn, which it had taken us almost two days to reach by road. The first islands of the Reef began to appear as dark smudges on the eastern horizon, and everywhere beneath us were the telltale shadows of barely submerged shoals and reefs. Each island had the same characteristic pattern; there would be the vast fringe of coral around the tiny pin point of exposed land, and on the weather side a crescent of white water, often many miles in length, would show where the waves were breaking against the Reef.

Further north, the high or mainland islands began to make their appearance. Between the little towns of Mackay and Bowen lies the picturesque Whitsunday Passage, considered by many to be one of the most beautiful spots on the Queensland coast. Here the land has subsided—or the sea has risen—so that a chain of mountain peaks has been cut off from the mainland. Many of these islands are covered with rain forests and tower more than a thousand feet above the sea, and it is not surprising that an area of such great beauty has the largest concentration of holiday resorts of the entire Reef. Brampton, Lindeman, Long, South Molle and Hayman Islands all have tourist centers on them; as we flew above the heavily wooded peaks we could see below us the little huts and clearings and beaches basking in the sun. But for all their loveliness, these islands were of less interest to us than the sandy flats of the Capricorn group. They were so near the mainland that the chance of finding really clear water there was much less than on the outer islands of the Reef.

As we flew steadily into the north, the land below became more and more empty. It was not desolate or barren—indeed, far from it, for much of it was heavily wooded and obviously very fertile. In places the trees were so dense that they had almost obliterated the rivers winding through the landscape; the watercourses were visible merely as ribbons of lusher green. Here were endless acres of rich land with never a road—not even a solitary footpath—hinting at the presence of man. One day, no doubt, all this wilderness will be tamed and cultivated, parceled out into sugar farms or sheep and cattle holdings. Yet though Queensland is primarily an agricultural state, with two million acres under crops, most of it must still look as it did when Captain Cook first set eyes on it in 1770.

Late in the evening we touched down at Cairns, the last

town of any size along the coast. We were a thousand miles from Brisbane, but five hundred miles of almost completely uninhabited coast still lay between us and our destination. Cairns is the gateway to the far north of Queensland, and is important both as a harbor and as a center of agriculture. Though it is a place where winter never comes, we saw little of the tropical sun during the ten days we stayed there. Indeed, for almost the whole of that time the town was blanketed by clouds which occasionally disgorged their contents on the sodden land beneath. One cannot have it both ways, I suppose; much of the area's prosperity depends on its rainfall, which sometimes exceeds a hundred inches a year. As usual, we were assured by the locals that this rain was all concentrated in the wet season, that never before had this sort of thing happened in June, that we should have been here last week, and so on and so forth.

From our point of view, the most interesting thing about Cairns was that here the Great Barrier Reef is scarcely ten miles away from the mainland. What is more, the visitor can meet its inhabitants under ideal conditions, at the Underwater Observatory on Green Island.

Green Island, a ninety-minute launch trip from Cairns, is a true coral island about thirty acres in extent. Most of it is a national park, and consists of thickly grown jungle with occasional paths winding through it. The tourist settlement is on the western or mainland side of the island, and a long jetty extending out to the edge of the surrounding reef makes it possible for goods and passengers to go ashore without having to be transshipped in small boats.

The observatory is at the very end of the jetty, and is a large steel chamber anchored to the bottom by chains and weights. Visitors enter the observatory by walking down a narrow flight of steps, as if descending into the bowels of a ship. They then find themselves in a porthole-studded metal room, large enough to contain twenty or thirty people. Around them is what must be one of the world's first—but certainly not last—examples of underwater rock gardening. Admittedly the term is not accurate, since corals are not plants, but it will serve until a better one comes along.

Living corals from various parts of the island's fringing reef have been gathered here, together with giant clams which lie with their serrated jaws gaping wide. Anyone who wants to go underwater without getting wet could have no better introduction to the creatures of the Reef, for countless small fish gather round the portholes to stare at the strange animals inside the tank. An underwater observatory of this sort must run a close second to a planetarium as a means of combining education and profit. As Mike and I left Green Island, we both wished that we had some shares in this submarine gold mine.

Flying up to Cairns we had traveled in DC-4 comfort; for the last five hundred miles of Australia we were in DC-3 territory, and as we climbed aboard the faithful old war horse, Mike, who has done much of his jumping from DC-3's, seemed a little unhappy without his parachute. We took off in the bleary hour before the dawn, and the light slowly strengthened around us until the hills above Cook-town began to climb into the first rays of the sun.

Cooktown, a hundred miles north of Cairns, is famous as the involuntary landing place of Captain Cook, the first European navigator to sail the length of the Great Barrier Reef. Keeping as close as possible to the mainland, Cook had sailed north for a thousand miles along the Queensland coast without ever suspecting the existence of the vast wall of reefs fifty or a hundred miles to the east—a wall which was closing in upon him, and becoming more continuous, as he proceeded into the north. Cook named many of the capes and islands, and his men made several landings in the quest for water and food. Though they encountered aborigines, they were lucky enough to have little trouble with them, being much more fortunate in this respect than many later voyagers.

Trouble enough, however, was to come. On June 11, 1770—a clear, moonlit night—the little *Endeavour* was proceeding northward about ten miles from the coast when she struck hard upon the reef which is now named after her. A great hole was breached in her side, but she was kept afloat by dint of continuous pumping and by throwing overboard all guns and ballast. A temporary repair was made by stretching a sail over the breach, and after six desperate days, during two of which the *Endeavour* was kept at anchor by a gale, Cook brought his damaged craft to shore. The ship was beached on the banks of a river (now named the Endeavour River) and repaired after six weeks' hard work by the carpenters.

Though Cook was to tangle with the Great Barrier Reef again before he escaped from these treacherous waters, he was never to know its full magnitude and complexity. Later navigators—including the much-maligned Bligh—were to fill in the details, often at the cost of their lives.

A hundred years after Cook had extricated himself from the dangers of the Reef, the town named after him became a thriving seaport through which the wealth of the Australian gold fields flowed out to the world. But with the collapse of the gold boom, Cooktown collapsed also, and the settlement we flew over during the first light of dawn was little more than a village.

A few miles north of Cooktown, we had a reminder that these waters, despite all the charts and navigational aids which modern science can provide, still take their toll of shipping. Our plane began weaving over the Reef and descending to within a few hundred feet of the surface to inspect a couple of luggers sailing toward the south. One of the local boats was overdue at Cairns by several days, and our pilot was trying to identify the craft beneath him, so that he could radio to land if either was the missing lugger. Very few of these small boats carry radio transmitters—though many of them have receivers—and the regular airliners perform a valuable service by keeping an eye on the scattered shipping of the Reef.

The whole region north of Cooktown—five hundred miles of peninsula stretching to Cape York—is almost completely empty of human life. Beneath us, thickly wooded hills stretched as far as the horizon, and the eye looked in vain for roads or clearings. We touched down twice at tiny airstrips linking remote mining settlements with the outer world, then flew on again over the endless wilderness. As we neared the ultimate tip of Australia, we came across proof that Cooktown was not the only spot in the north that had once been the scene of vast enterprises, now abandoned by Man. Suddenly there appeared below us the immense rectangle of a great airfield, with all its intricate network of perimeter tracks and dispersal sites. It must have cost millions to have carved this remote base out of the jungle, and to have kept its voracious machines supplied with everything they needed. Now the jungle was winning back the mile-long runways which such a little while ago had hurled their bombers into the Battle of the Coral Sea.

At last there appeared below us the maze of islands scattered across the Torres Straits. After traveling steadily for two thousand miles from Sydney, we had finally run out of Australia.

Thursday Island is too small, and too hilly, for aircraft to land on it. But it is surrounded by considerably larger islands, and on one of them—Horn Island—is another of the airstrips brought into existence by the war. This airfield is still serving a useful purpose, though the great radar antenna on the hill overlooking it ceased to search the sky a decade ago.

We landed on Horn Island, exchanged greetings with the southbound passengers who had been waiting for our plane to take them back to the mainland, and half an hour later (with our two hundred pounds of excess baggage) were in the launch heading across the narrow channel to T.I.—as Thursday Island is usually called by Queenslanders.

T.I. is so completely surrounded by other islands that only in a few directions is the open sea visible on the horizon. It thus provides an ideal harbor for the pearling fleet, which can ride safely at anchor even when cyclones are raging the Torres Straits. When we drew up to the battered jetty, about a dozen luggers were in port, preparing to set sail on the next favorable tide. Also at her moorings, and looking much smarter than her rather dingy companions, was the Fisheries Research Vessel *Gahleru*, which was to be our home for most of our visit to the Torres Straits.

F.R.V. *Gahleru* is the property of the Commonwealth Scientific and Industrial Research Organization, which maintains a laboratory on Thursday Island specializing in the study of the pearl oyster. We had made contact with the C.S.I.R.O. while in Sydney, and it had been agreed that we could go out on the *Gahleru* if we could fit our plans into her program. This appealed to us much more than the prospect of setting to sea in a commercial pearling lugger— an experience which Mike had already undergone and which he had described to me in all its horrid details. He had expressed grave doubts (which I fully shared) as to whether I would survive for a week at a time on a diet of rice and turtle eggs, with an occasional dugong steak to break the monotony. And he had made a special point of emphasizing the giant cockroaches, a good two inches in length, which emerge at night from their hiding places and nibble hungrily at your toes until they have succeeded in drawing blood. I was only too glad to discover that the *Gahleru* could take us out within the next couple of days, and that I should thus be able to forego these pleasures.

Meanwhile, we had T.I. to explore. Though it is no longer the great—and wealthy—pearling center that it was fifty years ago, the island still handles about $850,000 worth of shell a year. As to the value of the actual pearls, that, as we shall see later, is something that nobody knows.

The population of the island must be one of the most mixed and colorful for any place of its size in the world. On a speck of land a couple of miles across may be found some two thousand Europeans, Chinese, Torres Straits islanders, mainland aborigines, Polynesians, Malays, Indians, Japanese, and every conceivable intermediate gradation of race and color. Since no particular nationality predominates (the whites are outnumbered about five to one) there is no serious interracial friction, apart from occasional

fights between mainlanders and islanders, which are effectively dealt with by a minute corps of excessively large
policemen.

The built-up area of the island consists of a few score
bungalows (some of them, particularly those in "Pearlers'
Row," very large and well appointed), three or four hotels,
a dozen shops, a cinema, several churches, a power station,
the post office, a couple of banks, and a hospital. Facing
the harbor are the sheds where the pearl shell is sorted and
packed for dispatch to London or New York. There are no
properly surfaced roads, only the usual dirt tracks with
which the Queensland motorist is all too familiar. The taxi
and jeep population is fairly large, and the speed limit of
five miles an hour in the main street is frequently respected.

On the whole—and I hope my many friends there will
not take it amiss—T.I. often made me feel that I was in the
middle of a western movie. The hot sun, the dirt roads, the
wooden buildings—only the hotels boasting a second
floor—yes, it was all very familiar. At any moment I expected Shane to come riding around the corner, and even
the abrupt appearance of a battered truck driven by a
dusky islander failed to destroy the illusion completely.

All my memories of T.I. are pleasant, perhaps because
I was not there long enough for boredom to set in. But
there was one minor incident that I am not likely to forget,
and which might have had unhappy consequences.

The house in which we were staying, like many Australian homes, had an outside shed which was fitted up as
a laundry, complete with washtub and sinks. Needless to
say, we had annexed this for photographic purposes, and
one morning when I went out to check some of our

equipment I noticed a large spider clinging to the wall at waist level. It was about three inches across—nothing outstanding for the tropics, of course—and I took no notice of it, but walked back into the house without giving it a second thought.

At least five minutes later, I decided to have a belated shave and went into the bedroom. I picked up my shaver, walked over to the mirror—and swallowed hard. The spider was sitting on my shoulder, right beside my neck.

If it had been an English spider I would have carried it carefully back to its home, but I knew that this one was probably poisonous. I stood completely still and shouted for Mike, who came up behind me and then swept the creature away with his hand. It was, he told me cheerfully, one of the jumping spiders, and could have made me very sick if it had bitten me. As I had not passed closer than two feet from it, it must have been quite an athlete, and I would still like to know what its intentions were. Perhaps it merely wanted a free ride into the house, but I am afraid we could not afford to give it the benefit of the doubt.

The entire economy of T.I. is based on the pearl oyster, and it is not generally realized that the Australian pearling industry is concerned with the gathering of shell, not the collection of pearls. Despite heavy and increasing competition from plastics, pearl shell is still extensively used for the production of buttons, knife handles, and a whole range of similar goods. Yet the knowledge that any single shell may contain a fortune transforms what would otherwise be merely a tough, squalid, and dangerous occupation into one of the most romantic in the world.

Two types of pearl shell are found in the Great Barrier Reef, but only the large "gold lip" is of commercial importance. These shells may grow up to a foot in diameter and a pair may weigh as much as fifteen pounds, being worth about five dollars if of the best quality. Since a pearling lugger may collect several hundred shells on a single day's working, if it is lucky enough to strike a good patch, it will be understood why the pearling masters are more interested in shell production than in the occasional bonuses provided by the pearls themselves.

Moreover, there is absolutely no way of guaranteeing that any pearls discovered will ever reach the lugger owners. The boats are entirely manned by native crews, the shells are opened on deck—and any pearls found are promptly popped into little bags or bottles whose accumulated contents will be disposed of in some shady corner of a T.I. bar.

By far the majority of the pearls discovered are small and irregular, often attached to the shell itself. Sometimes several small pearls will be joined together to form odd shapes; in 1886 a group of nine pearls in the form of a cross was discovered, though it has never been decided how far the natural formation was assisted by a little dexterous "touching up."

The really perfect pearls are found loose in the actual body of the mollusc, and not attached to its shell. They may be spherical or drop-shaped, and the largest ever discovered was about the size of a sparrow's egg. The value of a large pearl varies rather widely according to whether one is talking to the owner or the potential purchaser; it may run to as high as ten or twenty thousand dollars, though such a monster will turn up only once in a decade. The average good pearl will change hands on T.I. for a few hundred dollars. What happens to it when it gets to Fifth

Avenue or New Bond Street is quite another matter.

As everybody knows, pearls are produced when the animal secretes some of its nacre to seal off a source of irritation, such as a grain of sand or, more usually, a parasite. Once formed, the pearl continues to grow in concentric layers as long as the animal lives, and only if this growth is regular and undisturbed will a perfect pearl be formed. Minor irregularities can sometimes be removed by "skinning"—i.e., filing off the outer layers of the pearl. This is something of a gamble, even in the hands of an expert. It may result in a smaller but flawless and therefore more valuable pearl—or it may reveal worse defects which the outer skins had partly concealed.

The pearl oysters seem peculiarly liable to infection by parasites, and almost every one houses a small crab which has found a safe home inside the shell. The only pearl oyster I have seen opened contained not only a crab but also a tiny, brilliantly colored crayfish. If these crabs die while still inside the oyster, their corpses may be found outlined perfectly in a mother-of-pearl tomb attached to the shell.

When the shell is brought back to land (after having been opened and cleaned on board the luggers) it is then sorted into the various grades, weighed, and packed into wooden crates to be dispatched to the manufacturers of mother-of-pearl articles. There is nothing in the least romantic about the land-based side of the pearling business, since the pearls themselves never go near the sheds where the shell is sorted and packed. All the danger, the drudgery, and the rare excitement takes place out at sea, or in the wide channels between the mangrove-covered islands of the Torres Straits. It was to these islands that the *Gahleru* was to carry us, so that we could see how the divers earned their living, and also how the scientists studied the life cycle of the pearl oyster.

On the afternoon before we sailed from T.I., I had a sudden vivid reminder that the most awe-inspiring of all natural phenomena was taking place a thousand miles to the north. I had walked out under the trees, which were tossing their branches incessantly in the perpetual wind which blew across the island all the time that we were there. Countless images of the sun, projected pinhole-camera fashion through the gaps between the moving leaves, were dancing restlessly to and fro across the sandy ground. And all these images were crescents, not the normal circles. The moon was moving across the face of the sun; in an hour there would be the longest total eclipse for more than a thousand years. We should miss it, being outside the zone of totality, but in a narrow band across the Pacific night would fall for as long as seven minutes in the middle of the day.

Almost a year ago I had seen the last total eclipse on the other side of the world, under conditions which could hardly have been more different from those in which I was living now. Then I had left a hotel on Broadway to catch an American Airlines DC-4 at LaGuardia, and had flown up to the southern tip of Hudson Bay with my friends from the Hayden Planetarium. Fifteen thousand feet above the barren Canadian wastes, with the cold, thin air roaring through the gaps in the cabin wall where the emergency hatches had been removed, we had watched the sun shrink to a glimmering thread of light, while darkness fell from the air upon the rolling cloudscape a mile below. At the moment of totality, a brilliant silver ring had flashed forth against the midnight blue of the now magically darkened sky, and I had seen the sun's corona for the first time in my life. That glowing ring had hung poised there for sixty seconds that raced past all too quickly. Then the moon's disc—the invisible shield that held back the sun's over-whelming glare and permitted us to see the millionfold fainter fires of the corona—slipped aside, and day returned in an explosion of light.

That had been a year ago and half a world away. Now I stood on Thursday Island—a place of whose existence I had never heard when I was flying through the moon's shadow above Hudson Bay—and looked at the shrinking images of the sun dancing at my feet. Here the eclipse was only partial, and even at its maximum a third of the sun would remain unobscured. The weakening of heat and light was no more than would have been caused by a passing cloud, and probably not more than a few people on the island even knew that an eclipse was in progress. I felt very envious of those astronomers—my erstwhile colleagues, I hoped, among them—who would soon be feasting their eyes upon the beauty of the corona for longer than any men had done in the last twelve hundred years.

And as I started to pack the diving gear and cameras for our early-morning departure on the *Gahleru*, I suddenly remembered an odd coincidence. Everyone who has ever seen the soft light of the corona reaching out around the sun has used the same adjective to describe it—and that adjective is "pearly."

XVI

Through the Torres Straits

The *Gahleru* pulled out of T.I. harbor at seven o'clock in the morning, into the teeth of a twenty-knot wind which soon brought the waves smashing into the scuppers. We sat on deck, talking to the crew and taking photographs whenever the spray allowed us to uncover the cameras. The ship's complement consisted of four whites and five colored: the skipper, Bill Parker; the research station's technical assistant, Dave Tranter; Mike and myself; Horace and Gordon, the divers; Johnnie and Korea, their tenders; and Stephen, deck hand and cook. The four whites became more and more dusky during the course of the voyage, through the positive effect of sunlight and the negative effect of washing in salt water; but the rest of the crew always managed to keep a few shades ahead of us.

After seven hours' cruising in a northeasterly direction from T.I., we anchored off the low, mangrove-fringed beach of Long Island. The dinghy was lowered, and a small expedition equipped with spears, rifles, and Leicas landed on the dead coral strand. It was a lonely place, but far from lifeless, as the cries of unknown birds, disturbed by our presence, came echoing out of the jungle.

The beach was about a hundred yards wide, and consisted entirely of fragments of dead coral which had been smoothed by the waves and bleached a nondescript gray by the sun. There was no sand whatsoever, at least on this side of the island. We walked for a mile along the flat carpet formed by this coral graveyard, coming occasionally across larger boulders which had not yet been broken down by the waves.

Gordon, who had brought a spear, waded through the shallows jabbing occasionally at a passing fish, though without any success at all. Johnnie had disappeared with a large sack and a metal spike, looking for a sandy beach beneath which turtle eggs might be buried. The technique for finding turtle eggs is quite simple; you walk along likely sections of the beach, jabbing your spike into the sand until it comes up sticky and with sand glued to it. Then you start digging, and a foot down you will come across a hundred or so white and leathery eggs, looking exactly like somewhat dented ping-pong balls.

Mike and I, on the lookout for crocodiles, crept along the edge of the mangrove swamp with gun and camera at the alert. A mangrove forest is a mysterious and rather depressing place, with its mixture of sunlight and shadow, its slow streams winding through the tangled maze of roots. Each mangrove tree, to anchor itself in the wet and shifting soil, is supported by a widespread system of roots which begins a yard or more from the ground, and resembles the flying buttresses of a medieval cathedral.

We met no crocodiles, which was disappointing but

may have been lucky, for in this part of the world they grow to twenty-five feet in length. But we did come across the largest and most magnificent crab I have ever seen, which crouched in a rock pool and waved its huge claws menacingly at us as we approached. Gordon, moving with extreme caution, crept up on it from the rear and grabbed it at the base of the claws, so that it could only snap at the empty air. To give it something to grasp, we rather foolishly let it grip the stock of Mike's brand-new rifle, and there was a crunching sound as the hard wood caved in beneath the great pincers. It was perfectly obvious that this crab could have performed a minor amputation with the greatest of ease.

On our way back to the *Gahleru*, we met Johnnie, who was briskly scooping turtle eggs out of a patch of sand he had found in the shade of the mangrove trees. Later I sampled one of these eggs, but as the ship was rolling badly at the time I lacked the enthusiasm needed to make such an experiment a success. It tasted powdery, but not unpleasant, and I have no doubt one could get quite used to it in time. It was an interesting object lesson to see how two men, in about half an hour's walk along an apparently barren beach, could collect enough food for a dozen meals. Certainly no one need starve to death on one of these islands, though his diet might eventually prove a little monotonous.

We had missed the tide and it was too late to do any diving that day. As soon as the sun went down, and we had tuned in to T.I. radio to see if it had any messages for us, we all climbed into our bunks. The gentle rocking of the ship as it lay at anchor off the reef was very restful, and by the fantastic hour of 7 P.M. we were all fast asleep.

I cannot truthfully pretend that the *Gahleru* was completely free from cockroaches, but at least they were not the large, carnivorous variety, and we were not awakened by any attacks on our toes.

We were up with first light and breakfasted on fried bread and jam, washed down with cups of sweet tea. The sky was cloudy, the wind slight, but the water was so turbid that it looked like blue milk. Though there was little chance of seeing much, we decided to test out the diving gear we had brought with us.

At this point, it is necessary to say something about the type of diving equipment used in the pearling industry—equipment which has remained virtually unchanged for half a century, but which is now definitely obsolete. Everyone is familiar with the standard diving suit, with its goggle-eyed helmet and air hose leading to a compressor on the surface. The Torres Straits divers use the helmet and corselet only, without any rubber suit. They wear canvas shoes and an old pair of trousers to protect themselves from coral scratches, and the helmet sits on their shoulders by its own weight. There are not even any straps to hold it in place; it is, essentially, nothing more than a little chamber full of air, a one-man diving bell, sitting over the diver's head. Unless he keeps upright, the helmet will fill with water; if the compressor fails, the same thing will happen. Nevertheless, a diver working under these conditions is probably better off than one inside a suit; if anything goes wrong, he can duck out of the helmet and swim unencumbered back to the surface. This helmet-and-corselet working (the corselet is simply the shoulder piece carrying the lead weights) is, of course, possible only in waters which are so warm that a man can stay submerged for hours without discomfort.

A life line is attached to the helmet (*not* to the diver) so that he can signal to his tender, and get pulled up whenever he wishes. On more than one occasion, a helmet has been pulled up with no diver in it. . . .

The discomfort and danger of working under such conditions, often more than a hundred feet down in water where visibility is less than ten feet, are not easy to imagine unless one has tried it. The boat is not at anchor, but drifts before the wind and the divers have to keep up with it. This means that they may have to walk briskly along the sea bed, grabbing any shell as they pass it—for they will not have another chance as their life line and air hose drag them along. Pearl shell is not easy to see as it lies on the bottom, for its drab exterior gives no hint of the iridescent beauty within, and it is often covered with weed and coral growths. As it is picked up, the shell is dropped in a net bag which the diver has hooked in front of his chest.

When the boat has drifted right across the patch of shell, the diver will signal to be pulled up and will dump his load on deck. The lugger will then retrace its track to the original starting point, when the diver will go down again and work another drift parallel to the first, so that eventually the whole patch will have been worked over. A pearling lugger will normally have at least three divers working on the bottom at once, and sometimes as many as four.

This procedure is all very well when the bottom is flat, but if it is rugged the diver's task is both difficult and dangerous. His lines may be "snagged," and the movement of the ship may drag him under overhanging rocks. He may step into an unexpected crevasse, and be crushed by the sudden change in pressure as he drops into deeper water—for the compressor supplying him with air cannot automatically compensate for a large variation in depth. All these hazards are quite apart from the intrinsic dangers of diving—the menace of sharks, manta, and giant grouper, the more serious and ever-present peril of the "bends" as nitrogen bubbles are absorbed into the blood. It is hardly surprising, therefore, that according to some estimates more than a thousand divers have lost their lives in the Torres Straits since pearl was discovered there. During a relatively short period as trainer-diver on one lugger, Mike had seen one of his colleagues killed (through being accidentally dropped nineteen fathoms) and another paralyzed by the "bends."

Pearl diving will never be a safe occupation, but there is no doubt that it can be made much safer. Modern, self-contained breathing gear like the Aqualung or the Porpoise sets we had been using is not practical when one has to stay underwater for many hours, and the air cylinders and the compressors to charge them are too expensive. But by a simple modification this type of equipment can be made ideal for all purposes where the diver is working from a boat on the surface.

Forget all about the massive copper helmet, its tiny little windows and its heavy lead weights. Use instead the simple modern face mask, covering eyes and nose and giving two or three times the area of visibility of the old-fashioned helmet. For breathing, use the Aqualung-type mouthpiece, with its completely automatic control of air flow to the lungs. Instead, however, of feeding it from a cylinder of air at a very high pressure, connect it through a long hose to

Pearling lugger under sail.

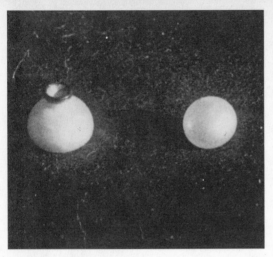

The "Chalice" double pearl—exactly as found.

A few hundred dollars' worth of imperfect ("baroque") pearls.

St. Michael. Michaelmas Day.

Blowing strong breeze S.E.
although not so hard as
yesterday.

No eggs.

An Heifer killed by the Blacks
over at the "Farm"
An Arm found less seal
which was the only proof.

30 FRIDAY [273-92]
Divs. due on India Bonds. ⅜ 48ᵃ P.M.

Natives down on the beach
about 7. P. M.
Fired off Riffle and revoler
they went away.

1 Oct SATURDAY [274-91]
Cambridge Michaelmas Term begins

Natives 4 Speared An Arm
4 Places in the right side
and Face on the Shoulder
Got three spears from Natives
Saw 10 Men Altogether

2 Sunday—16 aft Trin [275-90]

D 11

The last page of Mary Watson's diary.

Darnley Islanders celebrating.

Like a delta-wing bomber, a big manta swoops around Mike.

An anxious moment: a manta starts to inspect our anchor line.

Four-foot leopard ray.

Thursday Island.

Mike goes down for shell.

A massive brain coral.

Mike with oxygen rebreather, skirting the base of a coral reef.

Skyful of fish.

The marine dachshund, the pipefish.

A coral castle.

Housing problem: how does such a small shell hold so much crab?

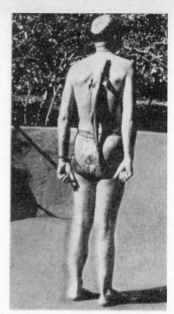

Left: Sixty feet down on pure oxygen, coming up with a salvaged anchor. Right: The remora's suction pad still works out of water.

The author heads for the Reef.

The Reef at low tide, Heron Island.

The stonefish, ugliest and most venomous of all the Reef's creatures.

Bêche-de-mer.

a small compressor on the surface; the type used to run paint sprayers will do very well.

The diver can now stay underwater as long as he pleases, without worrying about the limited air supply in his cylinder. He can work in any attitude—standing on his head if he feels like it. If he accidentally falls fifty feet, the demand regulator on his mouth will take up the pressure difference without his even noticing it. Moreover, since the functions of breathing and seeing are no longer the responsibility of a single piece of equipment—the helmet—the safety factor is much increased. Should the diver's hose get entangled, and he be compelled to abandon his equipment, he will still have full vision through his face mask as he swims back to the surface. The psychological importance of this can hardly be exaggerated, and a face mask contains a couple of breaths of air which may make all the difference in an emergency.

Since this type of equipment feeds air to the lungs only when the diver inhales, it is far more economical than the helmet, which is spilling out air in one continuous stream. We had some difficulty in persuading the divers that this was actually an advantage, since they felt that a constant stream of bubbles helped to scare away sharks. However, we were able to demonstrate that the diver could always produce a cloud of bubbles when he wanted to, by inhaling and exhaling rapidly.

We had flown up with us two sets of this aptly named "Hookah" equipment, together with sixty feet of hose. It had been Mike's idea; I had not been at all keen on encumbering ourselves with additional gear which we might never get round to using. The two pipe lines were plugged into a T-joint we had had fitted to the *Gahleru's* compressor, and watched with vast interest by the native crew, Mike prepared to descend. He took with him Dave Tranter, who had never used the gear before but was accustomed to the helmet and corselet.

They buckled on the harness, adjusted their face masks and lead weights, and disappeared over the side, their tenders playing out air pipe and safety lines. We saw their two streams of bubbles bursting intermittently on the surface as they exhaled, and the bubbles slowly wandered away from the *Gahleru* as the divers perambulated along the sea bed. They were not down for very long, as there was a strong current and, as Mike put it, they were on "grouper bottom," meaning that this was the sort of rugged territory in which the giant cod, one of the most dangerous of sea beasts, was likely to lurk. Big groupers have jaws three or four feet across, and have been known to bite off legs and arms—and occasionally to bisect divers completely.

As soon as Mike returned to the surface, bringing back Dave in good condition, he tried to get the native divers down with the equipment. Here he ran into a little consumer resistance: Horace, the head diver, was too accustomed to helmet and corselet and felt disinclined to try out these new-fangled inventions. Gordon, however, was quite willing to experiment, and let Mike take him down for a brief walk on the bottom.

The weather then became rapidly worse, and further diving was abandoned for the day. Not until the next morning, when the sun was barely above the horizon and the mangrove trees were transformed with the golden glow of the day's first light, were we able to watch the native divers go down with their conventional equipment.

The *Gahleru* had two sets of diving gear, the thick red

air hoses, more than an inch in diameter, being piled in great coils on a flat platform between the masts. The compressor was driven by the ship's motor and large air tanks provided a reserve which would allow the divers to return to the surface in the event of a power failure. The normal working pressure in these tanks was about 125 pounds to the square inch, which in theory would allow the divers to go down almost 300 feet. In actual practice, 200 feet is the limit for ordinary working, and it is quite unusual to descend as deeply as this.

Horace and Gordon pulled on their tattered long pants, and adjusted the felt shoulder-padding which takes the weight of the helmet.

Below decks, the compressor was thumping away, charging up the air tank. Johnnie and Korea, the tenders, were cleaning the helmet face-glasses with diluted vinegar, to prevent them from misting up with the diver's breath. A rope ladder had been hung over the side; Horace walked down it until his head was level with the deck and he was half immersed in the water. There was no other preparation; the helmet was placed on his shoulders, he let go of the ladder, and dropped swiftly out of sight, the life line and air hose being fed out continuously until he had reached the bottom. Gordon followed him a moment later, but both the divers were back on deck almost at once. The current was too strong, and the water too dirty, for them to do any useful work.

We decided to abandon Long Island and try our luck a few miles further on. After bucketing along in very rough seas for several hours, we came to anchor again just off the reef around Poll Island, another small, thickly wooded speck of land like a thousand others in the Great Barrier

Reef. Apart from the presence of coconut palms, we might have been back on Heron Island, a thousand miles to the south.

Unable to resist the opportunity to do some exploring, we rowed ashore and started to walk round the island. Mike and Johnnie were carrying fish spears, and waded out in water up to their knees looking for victims. Though they hurled the spears into the sea at least fifty times, they never hit anything. I was deeply disappointed, for I had hoped that Johnnie at any rate would do better, since I had heard so much about the natives' deadly accuracy when fishing by this means. Angling with hook and line might be less exciting, but appeared to be far more efficient.

There was a great hue and cry once when a couple of sharks swam up to inspect the unsuccessful spear fishers. The swift, streamlined bodies—I got a clear view of the black-tipped dorsal fin of one—came racing in from the edge of the reef and circled round Mike and Johnnie, who hurled their spears like mad and chased after the sharks in a flurry of spray. Once more, all this exertion was in vain, though as nobody particularly cares to have sharks swimming round his ankles it was probably just as well to scare them away.

When we got back to the *Gahleru*, we found a small shark had been hooked on the line which the boys usually kept dangling over the stern. Mike immediately blasted it with his rifle, which thus secured its first and not very creditable kill. The corpse was then disemboweled and hung over the side, in the hope that it would attract an even larger shark which we could hook and use as bait and so on ad infinitum. Any plans for diving we might have had were promptly forgotten as the blood and guts spread through the water, but as a matter of fact the bait was still quite untouched by the morning.

Since the sea was still rough and underwater visibility was very poor, we made no more attempts at diving on this trip. Instead, we headed south toward the Australian mainland, and passed through the entrance of the Torres Straits, with Cape York on our left.

It was high tide, and the beach along this lonely coastline was completely submerged. The thickly packed mangrove trees came right down to the water's edge, and the forest extended unbroken inland as far as the eye could see. This was the fertile, untamed wilderness over which we had flown a week before—the wilderness which stretched for hundreds of miles without a sign of human life.

We made our way slowly along the coast, and presently came to a large bamboo raft anchored half a mile offshore. Since we were now in fairly sheltered waters, the waves had subsided and there was no difficulty in bringing the *Gahleru* alongside the raft. Dave and a couple of the boys scrambled overboard, balancing precariously on the bamboo poles, and pulled up the chains which were dangling from the raft into the water. From these chains hung metal frameworks holding half a dozen parallel slates; the theory was that the embryo oysters—the "spat"—would settle on these plates so that it could be collected.

The old plates were removed for later study in the lab, and new ones installed. As soon as this task was completed, we sailed further along the coast, until a wide, sandy beach appeared. The massed mangroves were still there, but now there was room to walk between them and the sea. Once again the dinghy was lowered and we rowed away from the *Gahleru* to see what we could discover.

Until now all our landings had been on islands—but this was Australia itself, stretching for two thousand miles to the south, and even further to the west. The nearest settlement of any size—Cooktown—was five hundred miles on the other side of this jungle; the nearest city was a thousand miles still further to the south. It was with almost the sensations of explorers landing on an unknown planet that we began to walk along this remote and virtually unvisited shore.

There were occasional gaps in the wall of mangroves where sluggish streams flowed from the interior out to sea. Mike and I went a little way up one of these gloomy creeks, but were glad enough to get back to the beach. At one spot we came across some planks from a wrecked lugger, the rusted exhaust pipe of the engine that had not been able to bring it to safety still protruding through them.

That night, as soon as it became dark, Mike and a couple of the boys went back to the mainland with rifle and torches. Mike was determined to secure a pair of crocodile-skin shoes; we were all asleep by the time he got back, and were disappointed to know next morning that he had had no luck. Several times the hunting party had heard crocs barking in the distance, but the torches had never illumined their red, reptilian eyes.

The *Gahleru* had now completed the mission she had set out to perform, and it was time to go back to T.I. We were glad enough to have a chance of processing the film we had taken—not to mention washing ourselves in fresh water for the first time in almost a week. Though we had not yet seen any pearl shell actually brought up to the surface, the ship was going out again in two days' time. So we left all our gear aboard, hoping that the cockroaches would keep out of the sleeping bags—and that the weather would be kinder to us on the next trip.

XVII

Drifting for Shell

Our second trip on the *Gahleru* was shorter, but much more fruitful. The steady wind which had been blowing continuously for several weeks had abated somewhat, and as we drew away from Thursday Island it seemed to us that the water was clearer. Perhaps it was wishful thinking, but it appeared more blue, and the waves through which we were cutting were no longer that dirty and depressing green which tells the underwater photographer that he will be wasting his time.

On our first voyage we had steered northeast; now we were heading west, toward the Gulf of Carpentaria. It was a short trip this time; only two hours after leaving T.I. we stopped our engine off Crab Island, another typical low, wooded coral island a few miles from the mainland. Horace and Gordon put on their helmets and dropped down to the bottom; a little later, Mike, wearing the Hookah, followed them. With three life lines and three air hoses over the same side the situation was now a little complicated, and the possibilities of entanglement considerable. But the *Gahleru* had no provision for working a diver over the stern, as could be done on a regular pearling lugger, so we had to make the best of it.

A marker buoy carrying a flag had been thrown out to locate the commencement of our drift, and the *Gahleru*, with only the mizzen sail aloft, slowly proceeded down-wind at a couple of knots. Though this seemed slow to us on deck, it meant that the divers on the bottom had to keep moving at a brisk pace, and as each could see only a few feet it was a matter of luck whether they bumped into each other and got their lines crossed. Eventually, after drifting for about a mile, we decided to pull Mike up; he was doing quite nicely, but it was simply asking for trouble to have three divers working simultaneously over the same side, and we were anxious not to worry the regular divers.

Mike had found a couple of shells, but the bottom was rather bare and there was no chance of a good haul.

We drifted two or three miles, until the marker buoy was a mere dot on the horizon. Then we pulled up Horace and Gordon, who between them had found about ten shells—a very poor bag. On a really good drift, a diver may send up several baskets of shell before he ascends himself. Although Crab Island did not seem a very profitable place to work, we decided to stick to it and the *Gahleru* started her engine again and chugged upwind back to the marker buoy while the divers took a rest on deck. Then they went overboard again, and we started another drift.

Working on a flat, sandy bottom, only sixty feet down, and in calm weather, there was little possibility of anything going wrong. A diver's life, I decided, was rather like a private soldier's in time of war—long periods of monotony, punctuated by acute danger. Perhaps even more monotonous was the job of the tender, who had to stand for hours holding the life line, responsive at once to any signal that might come up from the depth. It is very hard to keep alert indefinitely—and many divers have been killed by mistakes on the part of their tenders. There can be few occupations in the world where one man places his life so completely in the hands of another.

We continued drifting, then coming back upwind under power, for most of the afternoon. A modest pile of shell was accumulated, placed in a sack, and hung over the side. The plans we had for our oysters were very different from those of the commercial pearlers, though our ultimate interests were the same. We wanted to keep these specimens alive and healthy.

In the evening, about an hour before sunset, we went ashore in the dinghy. The beach of Crab Island was like none I had ever met before on the Reef; the sand was so soft and fine that it *squeaked* underfoot. What was more, it was covered with countless millions of most beautiful shells. The commonest were auger shells, which I had never encountered at the southern end of the Reef; they were long thin spirals—exact replicas of a unicorn's horn. These fragile shells, bleached white by the sun, lay so thickly that it was sometimes hard to walk without stepping on one of them. Their geometrical perfection was so astonishing that I could not resist picking them up, until my pockets were full of them. Though they were wafer-thin, hardly one had been damaged by the seas and storms that must incessantly attack this beach. They dwindled from a base perhaps a quarter of an inch across the sheerest pin point—their spiral a complete record of the life and growth of the creature whose home they had been.

There was also another curiosity on Crab Island, which I had not seen before but which I recognized at once. Emerging from the water and leading up the beach were what appeared to be tank tracks, two or three feet wide. They would have been a great—and probably disturbing— mystery to anyone who did not know their simple explanation. The turtles had been coming up the beach to lay their eggs, and these were the marks made by their flippers. Usually they ended in a shallow depression in the sand, high above the water line. I dug hopefully in one of these depressions, but not having brought an egg-detector with me failed to hit the exact spot. Stephen, who had come properly equipped with a sack and spike, brought back so many eggs to the dinghy that we had difficulty in finding somewhere to sit on the return journey.

The next morning, after a good night's sleep with the boat rocking gently beneath us, we continued the program of diving and drifting. Slowly the shell accumulated on deck, until there was a pile of eighty or ninety, looking like a heap of dirty dishes that had lain on the bottom of a muddy river for a few years, and had become covered with weeds and barnacles. Nothing could have seemed more remote from the jeweler's window....

After several drifts, I had my first opportunity of going down. As I had never dived before with any equipment which had to be connected to the surface, but had always been a completely mobile and independent marine organism when underwater, I was not very keen on the experiment. However, I knew that it had to be carried out, partly in the cause of science, partly because there was no other way in which I could watch the divers actually at work on the bottom.

Mike fitted me into the Hookah harness—whose only purpose is to provide a firm purchase for the air hose, so that no strain will be placed on the mouthpiece through which air is fed into the lungs. The lead weights were adjusted, I checked to make sure that the face mask was watertight, and then clambered down the ladder. The safety line had been attached around my waist, and I asked Mike to hold me at a depth of ten feet, so that I could clear my ears before going any deeper.

I hung there beneath the shadowy hull of the *Gahleru*, blowing my nose and swallowing until my ears had popped. Then I gave the signal on my life line, and Mike played it out as quickly as he could. I did not know that if one wished to keep upright while descending in this manner, it was necessary to keep back-pedaling with one's legs. I relaxed and let myself fall, with the result that I was soon going down head first, with my legs trailing above me. This didn't matter—but it would have been a different story had I been using a helmet. By this time it would have been full of water, unless I had managed to find the trick of keeping it upright. . . .

I did not enjoy losing my freedom of vertical movement, which I had always taken for granted in all previous dives I had ever made. Now I was weighted down, and had to depend upon someone on the surface when I wanted to move upward. But this could not be helped; a diver who has to walk along the bottom has to be heavily weighted; otherwise he will drift away in the slightest current.

The green gloom deepened around me, and quite suddenly I was on the sea bed. Visibility was no more than about ten feet, but all objects up to five feet away were perfectly clear. There was no time, however, to stop and enjoy the view, such as it was. My air hose and safety line were dragging me along the bottom and I had to keep walking forward as steadily as a man on a treadmill.

The sea bed here was flat and sandy, with occasional clumps of fan-shaped sponges. The only fish I saw were some tiny ones which darted away at my approach; that morning I had seen a manta ray jump out of the water half a mile from the *Gahleru*, and, remembering the one which had approached our anchor line at Heron Island, I hoped that there were none around to get interested in my air hose.

Within a minute of reaching the bottom, I found my first pearl oyster. It was a little fellow ("it" is the only possible pronoun for oysters, which can be male or female not only consecutively, but even simultaneously), and so I decided to leave it there to grow up. In any case, I had no bag with me and did not wish to be encumbered with a shell six inches across. Relying on Probability Theory, I argued that since I had found one shell so quickly, I would fairly soon come across a bigger one, which would be worth carrying back. As it happened, mathematics let me down and that first shell was also my last.

Presently, in my erratic (and largely involuntary) progress along the bottom, I blundered into one of the helmet divers. Now that he was buoyed up by the water around him, he was no longer quite so helpless, but he still seemed a grotesque and clumsy figure. Feeling rather smug and superior with my greater mobility and my wider angle of vision, I waved cheerfully to the diver as he trudged along beneath his geyser of bubbles. Since I could see him so clearly, I decided to go back and get the camera in the hope of securing some photographs, so I gave the standard two tugs on my life line and was pulled back to the surface. It seemed a long time before I broke water, even though I was ascending briskly enough. Yet I had been only sixty feet down; what would it be like coming back from a couple of hundred feet?

When the camera had been hung round my neck, I went down again at once. And this time, through my own carelessness, I ran into trouble. Because I had cleared my ears without much difficulty on the first descent, I had assumed that it would be still easier this time, and had not asked to be held for a while ten feet down. Consequently, Mike lowered me straight to the bottom.

My right ear popped at once with that startling but reassuring "click" that every diver is glad to feel as he descends. My left ear, however, stubbornly refused to do anything of the sort, and very quickly I was in severe pain. I blew madly, and even yelled into my mask in the hope that the resultant muscular movements would do the trick. The one thing I *didn't* do was to jerk twice on the line; I am not sure if I had forgotten the signal, or whether a foolish stubbornness prevented me from using it. Feeling extremely unhappy, I continued to drop toward the bottom, while the pressure in my ear mounted relentlessly. I was very scared, for once or twice in my diving career I had known ear pains so agonizing as to incapacitate me completely until I had risen a few feet and reduced the pressure. The pain had not yet reached that level—but what would happen if it did, now that I was unable to swim upward under my own power? This was just the sort of unnecessary—or at any rate, exaggerated—panic one can easily get into underwater, when something goes wrong. I still had the use of my arms, after all, and even if Mike didn't respond to the "bring me up" signal I could always start climbing back up the life line under my own power. (Though a friend of mine, who once had to do just this in an emergency, barely managed to make it. As he climbed desperately up the line, his resourceful wife, thinking that he needed *more* rope, kept briskly attaching additional lengths and playing them out to him, so that his progress toward the surface resembled that of Sisyphus climbing the mountain.)

Fortunately, my blowing and yelling managed to stop the pain from getting any worse, and soon after I had reached the bottom there was a curious soft explosion inside my ear, which left me slightly dazed but otherwise none the worse. The feeling of pressure vanished immediately and I was able to take notice of my surroundings once more.

My struggles had got me into something of a tangle, and the *Gahleru* was dragging me remorselessly across the sea bed. I had to spend a minute sorting out life line, air hose, lead weights, and camera strap, but eventually I was operational again. None of the divers were in sight, which was just as well for I wanted no audience while I was unraveling myself.

The sea bed was much the same as it had been a quarter of a mile back—quite flat apart from a few knee-high corals and sponges, which were easily avoided. The only representatives of the animal kingdom that I came across were a couple of feathery starfish, and some multiarmed relatives which I could not identify. One of these creatures was a mass of tentacles which, a few inches from the body, split into other tentacles—which again subdivided, so that eventually there were hundreds of them, all writhing in different directions. I wondered how on earth such a beast—whose nervous system could hardly be very elaborate—knew what all its extremities were doing at any moment. The centipede "which fell distracted in the ditch, considering how to walk" had no problem by comparison.

After walking a few minutes, I presently came across our diver again, and shot off a few photographs with very little expectation that they would be any good. (They weren't.) It was hard work keeping my companion in sight, for my life line seemed determined to pull me the other way. Eventually I lost the battle; the diver disappeared into the murk, like another pedestrian swallowed in a London fog, and I was unable to find him again—though I knew perfectly well that he could not be more than twenty or thirty feet away.

There seemed no point in staying down any longer, so I gave the signal to be pulled up. As I came back to the surface, I once again became aware of pain in my ears—and suddenly realized that my face mask was full of blood. I must have been a fairly gory sight when I removed the mask, for Mike promptly dashed a bucket of water in my face (without bothering to warn me first). He then told me, cheerfully enough, that I had probably punctured an eardrum, but I found this hard to believe as I could still hear perfectly. Whatever the trouble had been, there were no aftereffects, possibly because I was careful to wash out both ears thoroughly with fresh water and alcohol.

We were now about to witness the scientific, as opposed to the purely commercial, approach to the pearl oyster. The pile of shell on the deck had been scraped to remove the covering of dirt and weed, so that the oysters looked as clean and scrubbed as their relatives had done when they set out on their ill-fated promenade with the Walrus and the Carpenter. They were then "tagged," by having a small hole drilled clear through the shell near the hinge, well away from the actual body of the animal. The operation looked and sounded just like a drilling session at the dentist's; I wondered if it felt the same to the oyster. Plastic tags, each carrying the letters "C.S.I.R." and a serial number, were then wired to the shell. The oysters were now no longer anonymous; each had an identification number. They were carefully weighed and measured, and the figures logged on already prepared forms.

Then they were thrown back into the sea.

I could not help wondering what Horace and Gordon, who spent arduous and sometimes dangerous hours collecting these shells ten or more fathoms below the surface, thought about this. The pile of shell which had been gathered on this trip was not a particularly valuable one, but it was probably worth $150. That, however, was only part of the story. Any one of these larger shells—which, of course, we could not open without killing the animal inside—might contain a pearl worth thousands of dollars. The probability was small, but it existed. During the course of her scientific career, the *Gahleru* would certainly have thrown back many pearls in the hundreds of shells she had returned to the sea. It was a piquant thought; we were rather like men destroying a pile of lottery tickets, before the draw had been made. We should never know what we *might* have won.

It was true that these shells were not tossed overboard at random. They were dropped carefully at one of several sites, marked only by bearings on the chart—and the skipper had scanned the horizon to check that no luggers were around to watch what we were doing. In a few years' time, the *Gahleru* would return to this spot and the divers would go down again. Many of the tagged shells—but never all—would be recovered, and the scientists at the lab would be able to measure the rate of growth of the shell under natural conditions.

A good many of the marked shells are, of course, picked up by other divers in the course of their normal work. When they first came across the C.S.I.R. tag, the pearlers quickly threw it away under the impression that they might be fined for stealing government property. Needless to say, they only threw away the tag—not the shell. When they discovered that there was a reward for tagged shells, they became much more co-operative, and most of the shells picked up by other crews now probably reach the lab. If the shell has been back in the sea for only a few weeks before it is brought up again, then most of the *Gahleru's* efforts are wasted as far as this particular specimen is concerned—but at least the lab will know what has happened to it. The one thing that the lab will probably never know is whether the shells thrown back into the sea by the *Gahleru* ever contained any pearls.

We remained off Crab Island for three days, making a couple of excursions ashore in search of food. The mainland was barely a mile from our anchorage, but was separated from us by a huge sandbank. We could row as far as this sandbank in the dinghy, but to complete the journey it was necessary to drag the dinghy across the sand and launch it again in the lagoon on the other side. I made one trip across to this natural barrier accompanied by Mike and a couple of the boys—who thought that they had spotted a crocodile resting on one of the sand dunes, and promptly raced off in search of it. When they reached the spot, of course, there was nothing there, and the tide was rising swiftly around our ankles. The mainland and the *Gahleru* were both equally distant and inaccessible, and the dinghy that had brought us was a good half mile away along the sandbank which was being rapidly converted into a series of separate islands. The sun was also on the point of setting. Altogether, it was not the most comfortable of situations to be in, and I was heartily glad when we were safely on the way back to the *Gahleru*.

The next evening, Mike and Horace crossed the sandbank with the dinghy and went right over to the mainland. We heard occasional shots from the mangrove forest, and when we woke up next morning found that stewed ibis was on the menu. (It tasted like rather elderly duck.) Mike had also had a brush with some wild boar, but those crocodile-skin shoes were no nearer reality.

That night, while we were lying at anchor in the last faint afterglow of the sunset, a small ketch hailed us out of the gathering dusk, and sent over its dinghy to collect our deck hand and his belongings. It came from one of the many isolated mission stations scattered along the coast and among the islands of the Torres Straits, and was taking Stephen back to his people. There seemed something romantic and even moving about this rendezvous between two tiny ships off a lonely coast so many miles from any human habitation, yet no doubt our boys regarded it as casually as metropolitan man looks on catching a bus. The mission ship—which having no engine had to rely on sail alone—immediately continued on its way into the now complete darkness, through these dangerous channels and reefs, with a sublime confidence at which this landlubber could only marvel.

The influence of the missionaries, during the past hundred years, on the natives in this whole area has been enormous and would provide a fascinating study for the sociologist or anthropologist. In so far as they have helped to stamp out tribal warfare and check disease, they have certainly made the lives of the natives happier—often enough at the price of their own. But many will argue that there is a debit side to the account, and that inappropriate social patterns have been imposed upon people who would have been better without them. One would also like to know what the natives think when they hear the different missions preaching their often mutually contradictory creeds.

Had we not been engaged on an entirely different project, with two publishers and three taxation departments breathing heavily down the backs of our necks, we would have liked very much to stay in the Torres Straits area for a few months to study the relations between the white and colored races. There were many paradoxes which I was never able to resolve on our brief visit, partly because fear of committing some *gaffe* prevented me from getting involved in close conversations with the boys. (One of them remarked to Mike: "You understand us—Arthur doesn't." There was some truth in this—but Mike had spent months in the area and had worked on boats manned entirely by natives. By this time he *should* have understood them.)

There was nowhere any traces of the subservience, open or implied, that so often characterizes the attitude of the colored people toward the whites in, for example, the southern part of the United States. Everybody called everybody else by his first name; the skipper was "Bill" to all his crew. I sometimes wondered what my friends in Florida would have thought if they could have seen another typical Thursday Island sight—the all-black clientele at a bar being served by a white lady who was obviously a respectable member of the community and not a refugee from a Somerset Maugham story. This sight raised another mystery I never solved. The mainland natives (the aborigines) are not allowed to drink, nor are most of the islanders. As a result, of course, the police have to waste much of their time making out charges against those who break this law by catering to an automatically created demand.

Yet at the same time that part of the colored community which is presumed to have a sufficient sense of responsibility is permitted to drink whenever it pleases. In one bar I was, quite legally, brought a beer by the brother-in-law of our head diver, who was himself not supposed to drink. I could not help reflecting that there must be all sorts of social complications when one section of a family is compulsorily teetotal. No wonder that, all too frequently, a perfectly orderly party may end up with both host and guests in court next morning. . . .

The popular fallacy still exists—even in Australia, where people ought to know better—that the aborigines are a primitive, backward race incapable of higher education. The fact is that there are no intellectually retarded members of the human family, and an aboriginal baby brought up in a white environment would be just as likely—or unlikely—to become a philosopher or a professor of mathematics as his fair-skinned companions.

The Department of Native Affairs, which watches over

the interests of the colored population (both mainland aboriginals and islanders), clearly has a somewhat tricky task to perform, and how well it does it I have no way of telling. Nor can I judge how firmly based was the complaint of one Australian taxpayer that the natives were always given first priority in everything, and that the D.N.A. wouldn't be happy until it had cleared *all* the whites out of the area.

XVIII

Pearls and Politics

During our last weekend on Thursday Island, we suddenly realized that we had been so busy racing round the Torres Straits that we had seen practically nothing of T.I. itself. As it was a beautiful day—and much too hot for walking—we hired a cab and set out into the interior. About ten minutes later, after winding through dusty lanes, we had crossed the island and found ourselves on its unfamiliar, and relatively unpopulated, eastern shore. By good luck, and not by planning, we arrived just in time to witness and entertaining and instructive ceremony.

The natives from Darnley Island—about 120 miles northeast of T.I.—were celebrating the arrival on their shores of the first missionaries in 1871. A group of extremely ferocious savages were dancing round the Church of England priest, their hostility apparently directed not so much toward him as toward each other. They were re-enacting with gusto the intertribal wars which had flourished before the arrival of the London Missionary Society, and the padre was having a tough time disarming them. Eventually he succeeded, the spears and axes were thrown aside, and all concerned sat down amicably together and engaged in a peaceful discussion, with exchange of cigarettes. The whole mime was watched by an interested crowd of islanders, many of whom could not have been more than one generation removed from the cannibals whose pacification we were witnessing.

There is a piquant legend attached to this first landing on Darnley. The islanders were not, in 1871, very hospitable to strangers. It was true that they were welcomed to dinner, but only in a passive role. However, according to the native beliefs, it was prophesied that one day a spirit would land on a certain beach, which was taboo and never used by any boats. Knowing nothing of the legend, the missionaries happened to choose this beach to disembark, and so were spared the fate that would otherwise have immediately befallen them.

It is a touching story, and may even be true. However, one would be ill advised to quote it as an example of the workings of Providence. The cannibal feast was merely postponed for a few years, not canceled altogether. But there was an unfailing supply of missionaries, and in the long run, of course, they had the last word. Though to the best of my knowledge "long pig" has never been proved to lead to any digestive disorders, it came off the Torres Straits menus half a century ago.

After this reminder of the old times, everyone relaxed to enjoy some native dancing, carried out to the rhythmic beat of long, tubular drums. Much of the time the dancers were in the crouching position, swinging their arms and stamping their feet. The dances were interesting, but after

a while the unvarying beat grew somewhat monotonous—
or, possibly, my ear was not sufficiently perceptive to appreciate the subtle variations. Once or twice the music set
echoes of *The Rite of Spring* jangling in my memory, and
I wondered who had influenced whom. In this age of pho-
nographs and universal radio, the obvious answer might
not be the correct one, for the influence of the western
world is everywhere. I shall never forget one evening in a
dusty oriental bazaar, when the heat, the smell, and all the
trappings of a strange civilization were for a few moments
utterly obliterated by the limpid notes of Beethoven's *Für
Elise*, emerging from a music box with more magic than
any genie being released from a bottle.

Though the dancers (and the audience) were obviously
enjoying themselves, there was one respect in which we
felt a little disappointed. Too often, the costumes were an
unfortunate blending of east and west. Most of the men
had concealed their torsos beneath cheap cotton vests, and
some of the women were wearing long black negligees
which seemed even more inappropriate. We wondered
whether the original native costumes had been banned, or
merely forgotten.

The dance was followed by a splendid dinner, which
the most ferocious of the "savages," in excellent English,
kindly invited us to join. Turtle steak was on the menu,
but I was conservative and stuck to roast pork. There was
always a risk, I felt, of inadvertently acquiring a taste for
one of these exotic dishes, and that would make me very
discontented when I got back to London or New York.

It was now dusk, and we were told that the dancing and
singing would continue far into the night. So three hours
later we came back again with flash cameras, and on a

perfect night under an almost full moon we watched the islanders swinging back and forth in the glare of paraffin lamps, and listened to the pounding of the drums. From time to time a soloist would sing a ballad which would produce shrieks of laughter, and there was so much audience participation that sometimes it was difficult to distinguish performers from spectators.

The audience had a curious method of expressing approval of particular dancers. From time to time someone would dash in among the ranks of swaying bodies, and sprinkle talcum powder over a dancer who he considered had given an unusually good performance. Before long not a few of the men were streaked with white from the vigorously shaken tins wielded by their lady friends. Though it may be a little ungallant to say so, honesty compels me to report that most of these dusky maidens were in the 170-pound class—or over.

Tired out merely with watching, we left soon after midnight. As the truck carried us back through the valleys that led to the other side of the island, the throbbing of the drums slowly died out into the darkness behind us. The men whose faith and devotion had brought them to these islands more than eighty years ago would have been pleased, I thought, to know that they were still so well remembered.

It often happens that, just as you are about to leave a place, a whole array of enticing prospects and opportunities suddenly arises. So it proved to be on Thursday Island. Since we had spent so little time ashore, we had failed to present our respects to the Director of Native Affairs, although we had come armed with a letter of introduction to him. Not until two days before we had arranged to leave the island did we finally pay a belated visit to Mr. O'Leary, who for many years has been responsible for administering Government policy in the Torres Straits region.

As we told the Director the reason for our visit, and described our activities on the *Gahleru*, it quickly became obvious that he was intensely interested in the Hookah diving gear we had been using, and we realized that we were getting involved in local politics. For the last year or so the pearling industry had been in a state of considerable turmoil, largely owing to the fact that for more than half a century the best divers were the Japanese. Or even if they were not the best—and many disputed this—there seemed little question that they were willing to take more risks, and to work in deeper waters, than divers of other nationalities.

Now, as might be expected, Japanese divers became even rarer than pearls after December, 1941, and when the war ended the Australians (who have not forgotten the thousands of men who never came back from the prison camps in the short-lived empire of the Rising Sun) did not welcome their reappearance. Yet many of the pearling masters—particularly those at Darwin, in the Northern Territory—maintained that the industry could not carry on without Japanese divers, and applied to the Government for permission to bring them into the country. An export trade worth a million and a half dollars a year was at stake, and it was hard not to feel sorry for the unfortunate politicians caught in the cross fire between the pleas of the pearling masters and the protests of the ex-servicemen's associations.

There was one way out of the dilemma. If proper equipment and training would enable native divers to operate as efficiently as the Japanese, there would be no need to import foreign divers and everyone would be happy—except the Japanese.

We were not particularly surprised, therefore, when Mike was asked to put on another demonstration of our gear, on one of the luggers controlled by the Department. On general principles, we were all in favor of anything that looked like improving the diver's hard and dangerous life. It must also be confessed that the idea of casually revolutionizing an industry that had been static for half a century, as an accidental by-product of our progress along the Great Barrier Reef, made a strong appeal to our sense of the dramatic.

While at the Department of Native Affairs we also had an opportunity of photographing the remarkable "Chalice" pearl, which had been discovered a few years previously and was still waiting for a buyer. It consists of two separate pearls which were found together, one fitted into a perfectly formed socket on the other. When stood upright with the larger pearl underneath, the two form such a perfect inch-high replica of a chalice or goblet that it seems incredible that it is the result of pure chance. Presumably two adjacent centers of irritation in the mantle of the oyster became nacred, and when the pearls met their growth retained its symmetry, one pearl starting to envelop the other.

Mike's demonstration of the Hookah diving gear took place on one of the Department of Native Affairs' luggers, which had been specially called across from the neighboring island of Badu. It was the first time I had been aboard a real pearling lugger, and the contrast with the relative luxury and cleanliness of the *Gahleru* was considerable. I

realized how lucky I had been to have observed the operations of the pearling industry as a first-class passenger
instead of traveling steerage.

We pulled out of T.I. on a dull, wet morning and
dropped anchor in about five fathoms of muddy water. The
crew (islanders this time, not mainlanders like the boys on
the *Gahleru*, gathered round Mike as he explained how the
equipment worked, and one by one they went overboard
to try it out. A couple came up spluttering, unable to keep
water out of face masks which had not been properly fitted,
but most of them managed quite well. Some refused to
remain near the lugger, where Mike could keep an eye on
them, but immediately wandered off on tours of exploration restricted only by the length of hose available. There
was no doubt about their interests; the problem was to keep
them from running before they had learned to walk.

When we got back to Thursday Island, somewhat determined attempts were made to induce Mike to stay behind and take on the job of resident diver-instructor. A
house and a fat salary were waved in front of his face, but
though his palm was obviously itching he remembered certain plans he had made to liven up New York in a few
months' time, and reluctantly turned the offer down.

Another tempting, but dangerous, proposal was also
made to him. Halfway between Thursday Island and Papua
lie the Darnley Deeps, one of the richest areas for shell in
the whole Torres Straits region. It has long been known as
the Divers' Graveyard, for the bottom is forty fathoms
down and is broken up into innumerable canyons and cre-
vasses, so that the diver is in continual danger of having
his air hose fouled. At such a depth it is possible to work
for periods of only about ten minutes; the divers must then

be brought to the surface at a slow and carefully controlled rate if he is to avoid paralysis or death through the "bends." The cemetery on Darnley Island contains scores of Japanese graves, for where great wealth exists—and shell abounds in these waters—men will always take a risk to try and reach it. A few more fathoms—a few more minutes on the bottom—yes, it is easy to understand the temptation, and how many are certain that they could resist it?

While there is no way of avoiding the bends except by careful adherence to the ascent tables—whatever type of diving equipment is used, short of a completely sealed chamber—it looked as if the Hookah units might allow the diver to work more comfortably and efficiently in these dangerous depths, and the pearling masters were anxious to try the experiment. They wanted to give Mike a lugger so that he could go out to Darnley and see how much shell he could pick up at the thirty or forty fathoms mark. Mike, who will stop at nothing if it is sufficiently interesting or exciting, was willing enough to make the attempt, but it could not be fitted into our program.

Once you have watched a pearl diver at work, and have accompanied him as he hunches his slow-motion way along the bottom, you quickly take his occupation for granted and it seems no more dangerous than that of, for example, a building construction worker or a steeplejack. It is not until you hear first-hand accounts of diving accidents, or pay a visit to one of the island graveyards, that you really appreciate the hazards which are always present, even when the weather is calm and the sea bed smooth and unbroken by obstacles. During his relatively short period as a professional pearl diver on a single lugger, Mike had two opportunities of seeing how easily a diver can die.

The first diver, Freddie, had been working on a "flash" bottom—that is, a bottom covered with sand, mud, and occasional coral fans—nineteen fathoms down. He had been at this depth of about 115 feet for half an hour, and the time had come to bring him to the surface by stages. His tender brought him up to nine fathoms (54 feet) and was "hanging" him there until the nitrogen which had been dissolved in his blood and tissues had had time to work its way out again. There are universally accepted tables (due to Professor J. S. Haldane—father of J. B. S. Haldane, with whom he is often confused) which state how long a diver can remain at various depths, and how long he must take to return to the surface. These tables, or simplified versions of them, should be known to all divers, but they are not always implicitly obeyed.

While Freddie was hanging, the lugger was still working the patch of pearl that had been located, and another diver was on the bottom. Since there was considerable wind, the motor had to be kept running to prevent the boat from drifting too fast for the diver. This method of operation, known as "standing up," involves the danger of fouling the air hose in the propeller, but often there is no alternative and the chance has to be taken. Naturally, the tender takes all possible precautions but he cannot always tell what is happening to the hose as it snakes down into the gloomy water.

Freddie was unlucky enough to have his hose cut by the propeller. Serious though this was—for as soon as the air supply to a helmet is cut off, water starts to rise inside it—it might not have been fatal had it not been compounded with other disasters. In the general stampede, one boy jumped overboard to try and untangle the air hose (the propeller had of course been stopped) and another, rushing to help the tender, accidently knocked *him* overboard. The result of this tragicomedy was that, with no one holding his life line, the unfortunate diver was abruptly dropped and fell like a stone to the bottom, sixty feet below him, weighed down by the lead on his helmet and with no air to breathe.

He managed, somewhere during his fall, to throw off his helmet and swim up to the surface—in the circumstances, an astonishing feat. He was pulled on to the boat, coughing up blood, and gasped, "No air" before he collapsed. At once he was placed in a half-suit—that is, a diving suit which extends down to the waist and can therefore be worn by an unconscious man—and was lowered again for half an hour, another diver going down to keep an eye on him. But the attempt to repressure him was in vain; he had died the moment after reaching the deck. The extra two atmospheres' pressure—with no compensating air to resist it—had crushed his lungs to a pulp. Freddie had avoided the obvious danger of drowning, but had been killed by the stupid accident of being dropped.

On another occasion, when a diver who had been staged was finally brought onto deck, he was unable to speak or move. He was at once placed in a half-suit and lowered to ten fathoms, but he was still helpless when brought back to the surface. There was nothing to do but to head for the nearest mission station, and to get him flown to the decompression chamber at Darwin. Though the man survived, his days as a diver were over; indeed, when last heard of he was still in the hospital and will probably never be able to work again. Perhaps, after all, Freddie was the luckier of the two. . . .

Whatever the future may hold for the pearling trade, we could not help thinking, as our launch drew away from Thursday Island, that we had seen it at the end of one era and the beginning of another. It is even conceivable that the market for pearl shell may collapse more or less completely, owing to competition from the far cheaper and steadily improving plastic substitutes. The pearl oyster also has a major rival in the Barrier Reef itself—the coneshaped trochus shell, the production of which now equals that of pearl. (The figures for both are approximately a thousands tons a year.)

Look closely at the "pearl" buttons on your shirt or dress. Turn them over and examine the undersides. If they are white all the way through, they are genuine pearls. If they are red or brown on the back, they are made from trochus shell. These spiral shells, which are four or five inches high and the same distance across the base, are collected by native divers working in shallow water without breathing equipment. It is therefore much cheaper (and safer) to fish for trochus than for pearl, but the resulting shell is worth only about a quarter as much.

Early in 1955, half a dozen young Australian skin divers decided to make their fortune using Aqualungs to collect trochus shell. Mike had introduced this gear to the industry during the previous year, and had found that for 4working in shallow water it had certain advantages, somewhat offset by the need for a compressor which could charge the cylinders to the required ton or so per square inch. Such compressors are scarce and expensive, but Mike had one which he sold to the hopeful crew of the *Barrier Princess*. They set sail for the seldom-visited Swain Reefs, a hundred miles from the coast, and were unlucky enough to be caught in these un-sheltered waters by one of the cyclones moving in from the Pacific. No trace of them or their boat was ever discovered.

Even if competition from other materials makes diving for the genuine shell an uneconomical business, nothing can ever destroy the glamor and magic of the pearls themselves. Men will always marvel that such beauty can be born on the gloomy sea bed as an accidental by-product of a mollusc's irritation.

We were half a mile out of Thursday Island, and had seen our friends on the quayside shrink to indistinguishable dots, when Mike pulled a Kodachrome container out of his pocket and unscrewed the lid.

"Look," he said, rather smugly.

I peered into the little tin, now no longer holding its *cassette* of film. I remembered how Mike had mysteriously disappeared not long before we were due to leave, and so I was not altogether surprised when I saw the constellation of tiny, captive moons. Even if we never saw T.I. again, we had some of its most famous product to refresh our memories. Whenever we look at that handful of pearls, we will see again the dusty streets, the luggers rocking at anchor, and the dark, smiling faces of its people.

XIX

Of Perilous Seas

The floods and rains that had delayed our visit to the Reef could conceivably have saved our lives, since if we had arrived in Queensland earlier we would probably have gone out on the lost *Barrier Princess*. She was only the latest of a long and tragic line; even before Captain Cook crashed into the Endeavour Reef in 1770, more ships than will ever be known were lost in these dangerous waters.*

How dangerous they can be, even under apparently ideal conditions, is demonstrated by what is perhaps the most famous wreck in the history of the Great Barrier Reef, that of the British India Steam Navigation Company's liner *Quetta* in 1890. The *Quetta* was sailing through well charted waters in the eastern entrance to the Torres Straits in perfectly clear weather under a bright moon. The channel through which she was passing was ten fathoms deep—

---

*For much of the information in this chapter, I am indebted to Frank Reid's *The Romance of the Great Barrier Reef*.

but it contained a spike of rock which had been missed by all the hundreds of other ships which had passed this way. This rock ripped the *Quetta* from end to end, though the impact was so slight that at first her passengers—like those on the *Titanic* twenty years later—did not realize that anything serious had happened.

Yet the ship sank in three minutes, and less than half of the three hundred people aboard her were saved. The Quetta Memorial Church, on Thursday Island, still serves as a reminder of this disaster.

Even in this age of echo sounders, such an accident might still happen. And no precautions could protect a ship from the ludicrous fate which overtook the *Blue Bell* in Keppel Bay, at the southern end of the Reef, one night in 1877.

The *Blue Bell* was sailing quietly on her business when her captain was startled—to put it mildly—to discover that she was rising steadily out of the water. There was nothing unusual about a ship going down—but for one to go *up* was a little unprecedented. At first, those aboard assumed that a whale was surfacing beneath them, but in a little while they realized that the ship was wedged in a rock slowly emerging from the waves. The *Blue Bell* rose inexorably as if on an elevator, until she was twenty feet above high-water mark. There was nothing to do but to abandon her to the wind and the waves until she had broken up.

The charts of the Barrier Reef, particularly in its outer fringes, are full of blank spaces and encouraging remarks such as "Dangerous for a stranger to attempt," "Remains of wreck," "Implicit reliance should not be placed on the beacons as they are liable to be washed away," "Awash at high water," and so on. Even if the Reef were stable and unchanging, to prepare a complete chart of it would be a task of appalling magnitude. But it is constantly altering as its sandbanks move and as the living coral grows up toward the surface, so that any chart must sooner or later become out of date. It is not surprising, therefore, that only the main shipping routes are charted in detail, or that the marine insurance companies are not really happy unless large ships passing through the Reef take aboard a local pilot when they enter it. The waters between the Reef and the mainland are the longest stretch of pilotage in the world; a pilot may board a ship at Brisbane and leave her at Thursday Island, almost fifteen hundred miles away.

As if the danger from reefs and shoals were not enough, every year cyclones of varying violence strike the Queensland coast. One of the worst on record was in 1899, when almost the entire pearling fleet from Thursday Island was wiped out, over fifty vessels being destroyed. I have never been in a cyclone, and never wish to be, but Mike was once caught in a "big blow," while anchored off the edge of a reef, with no shelter for a hundred miles.

It had been a still, dull day, hot and sultry—the sort of day that makes sailors look anxiously at the sky. During the afternoon, clouds had built up until by nightfall the sky was completely overcast. There was no breath of wind, and Mike went to sleep on deck in the hope of getting some fresh air. He was to get plenty before the night was out.

About 1 A.M., he was awakened by a sudden sharp puff of wind against his mosquito netting. Within five minutes, the ship was heeling beneath a screaming gale and mountainous seas were sweeping across the deck. The lugger was riding at anchor with the mizzen sail up to keep it headed into the wind, but the sail did not last for long. It was torn away from the rigging, and by the almost continuous lightning flashes that were their only illumination the crew had to cut the wreckage away. To add to their difficulties, some fuel drums which had been lashed on deck broke adrift and started rolling around, crushing one man's foot and smashing the dinghy. The reef was only three hundred yards away, and the roar of the breakers thundering against the coral made an ominous background to the screaming of the gale.

Such was the force of the wind that the anchor began to drag, so that the lugger started to drive onto the reef. Mike collected together his flippers, face mask, and Aqualung, and waited on the pitching deck, while the lightning sliced through the sky and revealed the steadily approaching breakers in its flashes of illumination. If the ship hit, it would be broken up in a matter of minutes, and with his diving gear Mike calculated he would have a slim chance of getting to safety. It would be a very slim one, since even in moderate seas anyone swimming over a reef can be cut to pieces by the jagged corals and the razor-sharp shells embedded in them.

Luckily, he never had to make the attempt. Toward morning, the storm dropped as swiftly as it had risen. The lugger had almost reached the Reef; another few yards and she would have been pounded to pieces. When the anchor was pulled up, it was found that the stock had been broken completely off, so that it was a miracle that it had been able to act at all.

The danger from cyclones, though it will always exist until something drastic is done about the weather, is no longer as great as it was in the old days. In this age of radio, a fair amount of warning is possible, and when we were out on the *Gahleru* it was very reassuring, twice a day, to tune in to the Thursday Island radio and to pick up not only its general weather forecast, but also the messages relayed to individual ships. If there was anything for us, we could send a suitable reply; even if there wasn't, we could report our position so that T.I. knew that all was well with us.

Radio has done much to end the loneliness and isolation of the Reef's inhabited islands, as indeed it has mitigated that of the Australian outback. It is hard for us to imagine, in this era of instantaneous communications, what it must have been like to live on one of the remoter islands, never knowing when the next ship would come along and there would be news of the outer world.

Anyone shipwrecked on the Reef's countless islands— as thousands of sailors must have been during its history— might have to wait a very long time for rescue, even today. While we were in the north, Gillie Sheldon, a friend of Mike's from Mackay, about five hundred miles north of Brisbane, lost his fishing boat on a reef when he was unable to get its motor restarted. He swam for fourteen hours until he reached the nearest island, where he dug a trench for shelter, and kept himself alive on a diet of raw shellfish. Heavy rains added to his discomfort, but saved his life by providing him with drinking water.

The island on which Gillie had landed was far from the main shipping track; probably years had passed since the last human being had walked upon it, and more years might pass before men returned. But the castaway was lucky; after only eighteen days a Royal Australian Navy survey ship, charting these unfrequented waters, arrived on the scene and rescued him—a good deal thinner, and badly sunburned, but otherwise in good health.

Of all the Reef's stories of peril and rescue, of triumph and tragedy, none can compare with the saga of Mary Watson, which took place in 1881 and is still remembered throughout Queensland. Through the courtesy of the Oxley Memorial Library, Brisbane, I was able to examine the original documents and, so far as I know, much of the following material has never before been published.

The story provides an interesting link with Captain Cook, for it begins on the island which he named and from which he first glimpsed the Great Barrier Reef in all its majesty. After he had repaired the *Endeavour* and set sail once more from what is now Cooktown, he proceeded northeast away from the mainland until he came to a large island crowned by a thousand-foot-high mountain. From this peak, Cook hoped, he would be able to survey the sea and find a safe passage for the battered *Endeavour*.

What he saw from the mountain was a view of breathtaking loveliness, but it was not one to encourage a navigator half a world away from home. Around the base of the island was a maze of shoals and sandbanks, washed by waters of every color from emerald-green to the deepest of blues. The darker water revealed the presence of channels; the lighter areas showed where the endless miles of coral grew almost to the surface. But these hazards had already been negotiated; the sight that filled Cook with apprehension lay ten miles further to the east.

Barring him from the open waters of the Pacific lay a line of foaming breakers, stretching north and south as far as vision could reach. It was, in Cook's own words, a "line of dreadful surf," formed when waves which had been gaining momentum for a thousand miles smashed to a halt against the Outer Barrier as it reared abruptly from the ocean depths. Fortunately, there were breaks in the wall of coral, and through one of these, a few miles north of the island, Cook was to sail into history and to complete the circumnavigation of the world.

Just 110 years after Cook's departure in 1770, a newly married British couple landed on the mountainous island which, because of its extensive reptile population, Cook had named Lizard Island. Captain Watson and his young wife Mary must often have thought of the man who had left his mark all along the coast. They could never have guessed that they too would become part of the Reef's history and that their names also would be recorded on its charts.

Robert Watson, Mariner, of Aberdeen, was forty-two when he married Mary Oxnam, a Cornish girl of exactly half his age. Mary had been a schoolteacher in Cooktown; a photograph taken about the time of her marriage shows a woman looking older than her years and with firm, regular features. She was not beautiful, but one would have guessed her to be competent and levelheaded even without knowing her subsequent history.

Captain Watson pursued a trade which flourished until as late as the Second World War, but which is now virtually extinct. He fished for the sausage-shaped *bêche-de-mer* which inhabits every coral pool and which the Chinese gourmets prized so much. It was regarded in the East not only as a table delicacy but also—a claim which most westerners would regard with, if possible, even more skepticism—a restorer of flagging vigor. The sluggish sea cucumbers were collected by hand when in shallow water, or by being impaled on long spears when they were too deep for comfortable free diving. They were then boiled, gutted, dried in the sun, and smoked until they became as hard and wrinkled as dried prunes. In this condition they kept indefinitely, and since the most prized varieties once fetched as much as $1,000 a ton there were small fortunes to be made collecting them.

Shortly before his marriage, Captain Watson had established a *bêche-de-mer* fishery on Lizard Island, with the help of a European partner and some native divers. Working along the Barrier Reef in small boats, they collected *bêche-de-mer* and brought it back to the island to be cured. When enough had been gathered, they would take it in to Cooktown to be sold to the Chinese dealers, then return to Lizard Island with fresh stores, mail, and news of the outer world. It was a hard and lonely life, and not one which many young brides would have welcomed. Mary Watson had been married only three weeks when she joined her husband in the picturesque solitude of the Reef, twenty miles from the mainland and sixty from the nearest human settlement.

The events of the next year are known, at least in outline, since despite all her household duties Mary found time to keep a journal. In a Letts's Australasian Rough Diary for 1881 (price one shilling) she chronicled life on the island, usually filling the eight or nine lines of space available per day with clear, incisive handwriting. The diary itself would be quite commonplace, almost devoid of interest, were it not for its sudden and dramatic climax. Yet it is worthy of study for the light it throws upon a woman who before the year ended was to show not only remarkable energy and

intelligence, but the greatest courage of which human beings are capable.

After some pages of advertisements (will the products
of our age seem as quaint in the year 2030 as "Barnett's
Soda Water Machinery" or "Lampough's Pyretic Saline"
appear to us?) the diary opens with a note on the memo-
randum leaf prior to the first page for January: "Bob and
self left Cooktown 2:30 P.M. Dec. 11 for Lizard. Mr. Green
and Ah Pang crew." The fact that this December, 1880,
entry was made in the diary for the next year suggests that
Mary Watson did not start keeping a journal until she arrived on Lizard Island, and perhaps felt the need for such
a mute confident.

On the first day of the new year, the island was visited
by a French warship, and the diary also indicates that
though she might have been a schoolmistress Mary Watson
was not always sure of her spelling. The entry for January
1 reads:

> Bob went off to the Man of War. One Muscovy duck
> dead. Made a pair of pyjamers. Had a game of whist
> after tea. Mr. Green and dummy, self and Bob.

Mrs. Watson had obviously been unhappy about "py-
jamers," for she had experimented with "pyjamahs" on the
interleaved sheet of blotting paper.

The well-being of her ducks—and, later, of her hens—
was one of the diarist's main preoccupations, which was
natural enough on a remote tropical island where the problem of morale was closely linked with that of food.

An average day on Lizard Island is briskly summed up

in the entry for Wednesday, January 5, given here in its entirety:

> Washed out soiled clothes, dried and put them aside. Finished book "Lamplighter." Fish brought around, boys cutting fish. After dinner all go over to fish, no tide or fish. Mr. Green mending Isabella sail. Returned from work about nine. Thunder lightning and rain. Wind N.W. shifted S.E. about 9. Amused with a cat and frog after tea.

"Fish," it should be explained, here means *bêche-de-mer*, which of course is not really a fish at all. The *Isabella* was one of Captain Watson's boats, named after his mother, Isabella Ferrier, whose maiden name will appear again in this story.

Most of the entries in the diary are as bald and unemotional as this, but from time to time one glimpse something of the strains and stresses of life on the island. On February 14, for instance, we read:

> Bob away at the Barrier. A little over a pot of fish. Some disturbance between Bob and Sandwich Charlie.

Sandwich Charlie, presumably, was one of the native "boys." He appears again on March 5 under the brief and not-very-informative news item: "Sandwich Charlie not working." One would like to know a little more about Charlie, as indeed about all the men on the island—white, black, and yellow—but after this brief appearance he fades away from the scene.

Apart from any quarrels he may have had with the servants, or with his partner, Robert Watson had not a few rows with his wife. We have, of course, only Mary's side of the story, recording the trivial causes of the tiffs with such a dead-pan absence of humor that one cannot help wondering which side was really to blame. For example, on March 9, after Watson had taken a load of *bêche-de-mer* to port:

Bob returned from Cooktown about ten in a great state of mind about putting double postage on my letters.

It was not, however, in the main body of the diary that Mary put down her inner thoughts—as far as she ever did. She tucked them away at the end of the book, on the blank Cash Account pages, between records of chick and duck hatchings and sad little notes like "Discovered delicate chick dead this morning." There was enough space for some of the more revealing entries on the regular diary pages; perhaps Mary deliberately put them at the end of the book so that they would be less likely to be read by anyone else.

Under January 17, for instance, we read: "Bob and Mr. Green a few hasty words over a log of wood and fishing off inner reefs." It is hard to construct the background of the quarrel from this cryptic sentence, but a few days later comes a brief yet vivid cameo. "A slight fright by discovering Sambo standing in my bedroom door. He had been walking in his sleep. Told me it was 'devil devil.' "

Thereafter comes a succession of entries, all the more pathetic through their very naïveté, recording the changing fortunes of married life as a barograph plots the progress of a storm:

> 25 Jan. Bob slightly annoyed. Did not hear me answer him about putting an egg under a sitting hen. Both very silent.
>
> 2 Feb. Bob and self great row. Self half mad all about me not answering him when spoken to.
>
> 24 Feb. Bob and self row again all about the dead ducks. I did not make any answer when he said something about the weather.
>
> 25 Feb. Both very silent.
>
> 26 Feb. More chatty. Nearly all right.
>
> 27 Feb. Things as usual. . . .

But then, after a brief period of harmony:

> 16 March. Myself in the wars again about the bedroom floor.
>
> 17 March. Both very silent. . . .
>
> 18 March. Very miserable. Bob's opinion came out at tea. Very small.
>
> 19 March. Row over. Things as comfortable as of old.

There are no more of these entries at the end of the diary, for a very good reason. A week later, Captain Watson took his young wife back to the mainland, and installed her in his house in Cooktown, where on April 21 she made this comment on the North Queensland weather: "Blowing very hard through the night. Several houses and the national school were blown down. Sat up all night afraid to go to sleep. Never heard such a noise." This must have been a modest precursor of the cyclones which, a few decades later, virtually destroyed the town.

Thereafter the daily entries are short, recording visits to and from friends in Cooktown, and noting so many headaches and transient sicknesses that it is no surprise when finally, on Friday, June 3, one finds written in a firm hand:

Had to send Fanny away about 6 A.M. for Mrs. Bollam. George Ferrier born 10 to 11 P.M. Only Mrs. Bollam and myself in the house. No doctor required.

Three weeks later, Mary Watson and her infant son left the mainland to return to the island. Her sole comment on the nine-hour journey reads: "Ferrier very good the sea did not affect him. Self sick."

Life on Lizard Island resumed its old routine. Captain Watson's partner Green had been replaced by a Mr. Fuller— whether as a result of earlier quarrels one does not know. The boats went out to the Reef when the weather permitted, but the catches they brought back were often disappointingly small. In August, therefore, Watson made a decision he was to regret for the remainder of his life. He would take a trip north in search of richer *bêche-de-mer* grounds.

The diary for September 1 records the departure:

"Petrel" and "Spray" Bob and Mr. F. with crew away (to fish for 2 months) north. "Ah Sam" and "Ah Leung" left here.

So Mary Watson, with her three-months-old baby, saw her husband's two little boats sail away into the north. Did she resent being left on the island for so long, with only the two Chinese servants for company? If so, her journal gives no hint of it. Perhaps she did not feel as lonely as one might think. There was considerable shipping along the coast, and from time to time boats could be expected to call at Lizard Island. Unfortunately for Mary Watson, the wrong boats arrived.

She may have had her first inkling of trouble when she wrote on September 27:

> Blowing gale of wind. Fine day. Ah Leung saw smoke from S. direction. Suppose it to be a natives camp. Steamer bound north passed very close about 6 P.M. ("Corea" I think.)

Thereafter, all our knowledge of events on the island must be deduced from the three final entries in the diary— and from its sequel. The Watsons had been unlucky; perhaps the fact that law and order were only sixty miles away had made them overconfident. There were still many savage tribes among the islands of the Reef, and on the mainland itself. Sometimes these natives behaved toward the whites with perfect courtesy and kindness; at other times they killed and ate them, without any particular malice. Mary Watson could well have been alarmed at the news that there was now a native camp on the south of the island, but the only entry for the next day reads.

> 28 September. Blowing very strong S. E. breeze.

A day later, however, she knew the worst. The hasty entries, with the spelling mistakes which are the only sign of agitation, tell the story eloquently enough:

29 September. Blowing strong breeze S.E. although not so hard as yesterday.

No eggs.

Ah Leung killed by the blacks over at the "farm."

Ah Sam found his hat which was the only proof.

30 September. Natives down on the beach about 7 P.M.

Fired off rifle and revolver they went away.

1 October. Natives 4 speared Ah Sam 4 places in the right side and three in the shoulder. Got three spears from natives. Saw 10 men altogether.

That is the last entry. The diary was found a month later, when a ship put in to Lizard Island at the end of October. The Watsons' little cottage had been ransacked, and the walls and door were covered with blood. There was no sign of mother, child, or Chinese houseboy, and it seemed obvious that the natives had killed them.

The news was swiftly carried back to Cooktown, and punitive expeditions were sent out to deal with those responsible. Some of the mainland natives who appeared implicated in the crime were arrested, and confessed that they had eaten Ah Sam. Mrs. Watson and Ferrier, they reported, had been taken off in a canoe, but the woman had become violent and had been killed and thrown overboard with her baby.

To settle the matter, Her Majesty's schooner *Spitfire* visited several of the Reef islands and brought back, her captain reported, "complete confirmatory evidence of the murder." The case appeared to be closed; Mary Watson and her little son were two more victims of these beautiful and bloodstained waters, and their names would soon be forgotten except by those who had known or loved them.

Yet despite all the evidence, including the confessions of the "murderers," one man was not satisfied. The remorse that Robert Watson must have felt when he returned to his ravaged home does not bear thinking about, nor do his feelings when he read his wife's diary and her account of those little quarrels and reconciliations from which no marriage is wholly free. It was easy for his friends to believe that he had become unbalanced in thinking that Mary had escaped from Lizard Island, and to regard with tolerant sympathy his frantic search among the surrounding reefs and islets. He had only one piece of evidence to support his theory, which was so far-fetched that no one could really take it seriously.

A small iron tank, open at one side and about four feet square by two feet deep, was missing from the island. It was no use Watson's friends telling him that such a valuable source of metal would have been looted by the natives to make weapons and tools. He would not listen; he insisted that Mary had got away in the tank, but for all his searching he could find no trace of her.

The Reef can guard its secrets for years—indeed, forever—among its thousands of shoals and islands, many of which are still uncharted even to this day. It is astonishing, therefore, that only two months passed before the last chapter in the story of Mary Watson was revealed.

On January 18, 1882, the schooner *Kate Kearney*, under Captain Bremmer, anchored off a small and unnamed island in the Howick Group, forty-two miles northwest of Lizard Island. Bremmer had not intended to land here, but strong seas had forced him to abandon his original choice of anchorage, and so he sent his crew ashore to see if they could find food.

They found instead the body of Ah Sam, covered with wounds. Twenty yards away, drawn up above the high-water mark and hidden in the undergrowth, lay the missing tank. Huddled in it, with her baby still in her arms, was Mary Watson. She and her little son had died of thirst; by a heartbreaking irony of fate, their bodies lay in six inches of water from the rains that had come too late to save them.

It was not hard to reconstruct what had happened, for this brave and resourceful woman had kept a log of the journey. She had decided that her position on the island, surrounded by hostile natives and with a mortally wounded man and a four-months-old baby on her hands, was so hopeless that she would be no worse off if she put out to sea. It would give her a better chance of attracting notice, for she would drift toward the mainland and the more frequented shipping routes.

She made her preparations with great care and thoroughness, putting everything in the tank that might be needed for the voyage. Bread, water, rice, spare clothing, revolver, gold watch, station account books—all these things were somehow squeezed into the tiny space available. Two small oars provided some control over the crazy vessel's progress; when it was finally afloat, it could have possessed no more than a few inches of freeboard, and in any sort of sea it would have been swamped at once. Mary Watson was lucky enough to have set out in perfectly calm weather. It was the only good luck she had, and she deserved more.

It seems strange that she did not take her carefully kept

diary with her, but left it in the cottage where the natives might be expected to destroy it. The actual log of the voyage was kept on seven sheets of plain white paper, obviously torn out of a cheap 3" by 5" notebook. The pages are discolored, the writing faded, but because a pencil was used instead of ink the action of the water has done surprisingly little to obliterate the words. All but a few lines are still perfectly legible.

It is impossible to turn the pages of this most pathetic document without feeling an overwhelming pity for the woman whose vain bid for safety it records. In this cramped and tiny cockleshell, with her two helpless charges (for Ah Sam must have been slowly dying throughout the voyage) she had paddled out from Lizard Island, leaving her home and all that she had worked for to be ransacked and perhaps destroyed. But the log contains no hint of despair, no suggestion of self-pity, no appeals to Providence. Even to the end, we learn little about Mary Watson; we can only judge her by her actions, and on these she cannot be faulted. Was she a heroine merely through lack of imagination? It does not matter; heroism is sufficient unto itself.

The first entry in the log shows a curious mistake which Mary Watson never corrected. It is one that everyone must have made when dating a check or letter in a new month. She had left Lizard Island on the second of October, but without the printed dates to guide her she at once went astray and forgot that it was no longer September. In the circumstances, her mistake was understandable. One can only marvel that she found the time and energy to keep the log at all.

The voyage begins:

Left Lizard Island September 3rd Sunday afternoon
in the tank that beache-de-mers are boiled in. Got
about 3 miles or 4 from the Lizard.

If the day was actually a Sunday, which seems probable, it would have been the second, *not* the third. The log
would then follow on without a break from the last entry
in the printed diary; we must assume, therefore, that Mary
Watson was one out in the date as well as the month.
Anyone who has lived for some weeks on a tropical island
will know that there is nothing surprising about this.

The short entry for "September 4" is largely illegible;
apparently the tank grounded on a reef, for the log continues:

September 5. Remained on the reef all day looking
for a boat. Saw none.

   September 6. Very calm morning able to push
the tank up to an islet with three small mountains
on it Ah Sam went ashore to try and get water as
ours was done there were natives camped there so
we were afraid to go far away we had to wait return
of the tide. Anchored under the mangroves, got on
the reef—very calm.

The next entry records, unemotionally enough, what
must have been the most heartbreaking moment of the
voyage—a moment of despair which so many castaways
have known:

September 7th. Made for an island about 4 or 5
miles from the one spoken of yesterday, ashore but

could not get any water. Cooked some rice and clam fish. Moderate S.E. breeze stayed here all night. Saw a steamer bound north hoisted Ferrier's white and pink wrap, but it did not answer us.

It did not answer us. The officer of the watch on that steamer, if it was identified (as it could have been easily enough) would be another man with a burden on his soul. But it is very hard to see a distress signal fluttering in the open sea—even when one is looking for it.

September 8th. Changed the anchorage of the boat as the wind was freshening went down to a kind of little lake on the same island (this done last night) remained there all day looking out for a boat and did not see any very cold night blowing very hard. No water.

September 9th. Brought the tank ashore as far as possible with the morning tide. Made camp all day under the trees. Blowing very hard. (No water). Gave Ferrier a dip in the sea, he is showing symptoms thirst and took a dip myself. Ah Sam and self very parched with thirst.

September 10th Sunday. Ferrier very bad with inflammation, very much alarmed no fresh water and no more milk but condensed. Self very weak really thought I should have died last night.

The refugees had left Lizard Island more than a week ago, and were now at the end of their resources. It seems incredible that Mary Watson had managed to keep her baby alive, yet as the next—and final—entry in the log shows, he was still healthy:

September 11. Still all alive. Ferrier much better this morning, self feeling very weak I think it will rain today clouds very heavy, wind not quite so high.

No rain morning fine weather. Ah Sam preparing to die have not seen him since 9th. Ferrier more cheerful self not feeling at [all] well.

Have not seen any boats of any description (No water nearly dead with thirst).

The log ends there. The final word "thirst" stands out clearly among its faded companions; it may be that the bleaching action of time and water has passed it by, but it almost seems as if the letters have been forced onto the paper by a last effort of the writer.

Mary Watson had finished her diary. She left no parting message to her husband or to the world, but took in her arms the little son who was never to see his first birthday. There was a loaded revolver by her side, but she did not use it. She lay down in the ungainly craft that had brought her forty miles across the sea, delivering her from one peril to another, and waited for the end.

XX

A Chapter of Accidents

Heron Island had been my first introduction to the Great Barrier Reef; it seemed appropriate that here I should say farewell to it. When Mike and I had flown back to Brisbane from Thursday Island, we decided to make another attempt to find the combination of sunshine, clear water, and windless days that was essential for underwater photography. We had visited Heron at the wrong time of the year, so everyone told us; now the weather would be more stable, though we could not expect the water to be so warm in the depths of the winter. Realizing this, Mike promptly acquired a rubber suit which covered him to knees and elbows; I decided to rely on my natural layer of blubber.

By removing the back seat of the car, we were able to stow all our equipment aboard without having to use the trailer. This made it a good deal easier to drive and, as it turned out, probably saved us from getting into serious trouble when we made an ill-fated halt at the little town of Maryborough, two hundred miles north of Brisbane.

We had stopped to refill with gas and to have a chat with a garage proprietor who had been helpful to us each time we had passed this way before. After a five-minute pause, we pulled away and had just reached the end of the block when a small Austin Utility came storming out of the intersection. There was nothing that Mike could do but slam on the brakes; fortunately we were not going fast and at the moment of our impact our speed had probably been reduced to a few miles an hour. The Austin proceeded serenely on straight across the road, making no effort to slow down or deviate. We nudged it nearly amidships, and what followed was in the best tradition of stock-car racing. The Utility rolled over a couple of times, and came to rest upside down, with an ominous tinkling of glass, at the side of the road. It was astonishing that such a gentle impact—we never felt the shock—could have produced such spectacular results.

I am quite sure that, as I climbed out of our car (which had had its nose pushed in but otherwise showed no sign of damage), I was much more worried about the problem of continuing our journey than I was about the fate of the man in the overturned Austin. At any rate, it was Mike who reached him first; he was curled up in the cab, laughing softly. The door seemed a trifle stiff, so Mike pulled it off its hinges and extricated the driver. His first words were, "Where's my other shoe?"

The inevitable crowd (in one of his more sinister stories, Ray Bradbury maintains that it is always the *same* crowd) had now sprung up from nowhere. On the principle that, since this looked like costing us a lot of money, we might at least get some good pictures, I recorded the sorry scene with the Leica. (I have a strong suspicion that I took the first photo immediately after stepping out of the car, before giving a thought to the other driver.) Two very helpful policemen and an ambulance were on the spot within three minutes; luckily the ambulance was not needed, for the only damage to the driver of the Austin, despite his remarkable acrobatics in rather confined quarters, was a grazed arm.

Quite apart from our skid marks, we were able to give the police convincing proof that we had brought our car almost to a halt at the moment of impact. Seven heavy compressed-air bottles, and one oxygen cylinder, had not moved a fraction of an inch from the positions where they had been resting in the back of the car. I could not help thinking what a contribution their ton-to-the-square-inch contents might have made had there been a really severe crash followed by a fire. . . .

Once we had arranged for our car to be towed to the nearest garage, and had given the police all the information they needed, we had to face the problem of transporting ourselves and our several hundredweights of heavy yet delicate equipment to Gladstone in time to catch the *Capre*. It was a Sunday afternoon, and the *Capre* left on Tuesday morning. There was just one train that would get us there in time; we received the news gratefully, though we were not so happy to hear that it left Maryborough at two o'clock on Monday morning. We did look into the possibility of hiring a cab, but that worked out a little expensive as the round trip involved was some 440 miles. . . .

Dusk had fallen when we finally got all our luggage and equipment to the railway station. By further good luck, there was a hotel immediately opposite, so it would not be too far to walk when we staggered out of our beds in the dreariest hour of the night. We borrowed a battered alarm clock, prayed that it would not let us down, and crept beneath the sheets not only in search of sleep but also in search of warmth. I had no idea that it grew so cold in Queensland, even in the winter. And it was to grow a lot colder before the night was out.

When I have to get up early, which fortunately is not often, my helpful subsconscious always makes a point of rousing me every hour, on the hour, all through the night, just to take a time check. I was not very much refreshed, therefore, when the alarm clock went off at 1 A.M. and it was time to creep shivering out of bed. We packed the few effects we had brought across to the hotel with us, and tiptoed downstairs. Had anyone seen us leaving, they would have drawn the worst conclusions. However, we had paid our bills the evening before; the management had seen to that.

We staggered blearily across the station and supervised the loading of our dozens of boxes, air cylinders, spear guns, and all the other equipment which we often wished weighed as little above water as it did below. In response to our anxious inquiries, we were told that no First Class sleepers were available, so we would have to spend the night trying to catch a few winks while propped up against the frugal upholstery. It would not have been so bad could we have obtained a compartment to ourselves, but the train was full and as we each had to share a seat there was no chance of sprawling outright.

It was now extremely cold, and it looked as if we would have a miserable night ahead of us. However, our spirits revived considerably when the guard told us that though the First Class sleeping berths were full, there were still some Second Class ones available. We followed him down the train, noting without much surprise that in one compartment a gang of diggers had lit a spirit stove in the middle of the floor and were brewing the traditional billy of tea.

When we arrived at the sleeping car, the anticlimax was considerable. It was a six-bunk affair, the upper two bunks on either side folding into the wall. The whole atmosphere was so bleak, the standard of comfort so near the irreducible minimum, that it reminded me of a scene from the *Riot in Cell Block 11* kind of film. Yet worse—much worse—was yet to come.

While I unpacked my pajamas for the second time that night, Mike chased after the guard to get sheets and blankets. He came back a few minutes later with devastating news. Only First Class sleeping berths possessed such luxuries.

The shiny leather couches had all the welcoming comfort of a mortuary slab. We wrapped ourselves up in every scrap of warm clothing we could muster—which was not a great deal, since we were heading into the tropics. As I put on my pajamas over my clothes, I felt fairly warm from the knees up, but my exposed extremities soon began to freeze. Wrapping towels around my feet didn't help; I lay on the couch, wracked by frequent uncontrollable shudders, and thought wistfully of our snug sleeping bags, which were safely (and inaccessibly) stowed away in the luggage van at the end of the train.

The train continued to jolt through the night as if it were running along a dirt road, not on a set of metal rails. Every jolt was transferred with high-fidelity realism through the bunks, which before very long felt like leather-covered wooden planks. I tried to hasten the weary miles by picturing what a *Third Class* sleeping berth would be like, but my imagination was unequal to the task.

After about an hour of jolting, freezing misery on this Trans-Siberian Branch of the Queensland Railways, we began to wonder if we would still be alive by morning. Then deliverance came. The train stopped, and a voice shouted out of the night: "Bundaberg—ten minutes for refreshments." It took some time for the import of the message to sink in, and a few more minutes for our stiffened frames to react to it. Then we walked like a pair of badly oiled robots to the refreshment room, where about forty people were trying to get tea and toast from the two girls on duty. After we had stood in line for a while, Mike said: "You grab the tea—I'll see if I can get our sleeping bags." He darted off down the platform, and just as the inspector was shouting "All aboard!" I managed to seize two cups of tea and a plate of fresh toast. I carried this back in triumph to our refrigerated hearse, and never did railway food taste so good. Here at least someone deserves a word of credit; I wonder at how many British railway stations it is possible to get tea at three in the morning.

We unrolled the sleeping bags that Mike had pilfered from the luggage van, and climbed thankfully into them. Soon we were warm again—probably the only people on the train who were. The jolting of the carriage on its saw-toothed rails still prevented us from sleeping, but that was a minor discomfort. The bliss of being warm once more was so great that I wanted to stay awake to enjoy it.

After about three hours of semislumber, we saw the sun rising like a bloodshot eye over the mangrove swamps south of Gladstone. The grass was dusted with frost—

something which I thought could never happen at sea level on the Tropic of Capricorn. But we had arrived safely, with all our belongings, and as the day warmed up around us we soon forgot the anxieties and discomforts of the previous twenty-four hours.

After a quiet day, recuperating from the trip and doing a little shopping, we loaded our gear once more upon the *Capre*. As the launch pulled out of Gladstone harbor, we felt like a couple of old salts who had spent half their lives among these islands, and could tell all the open-mouthed tourists from the South what the Reef was *really* like. It was a fairly rough trip, and some of the passengers were not particularly anxious to have our information; but we gave it just the same.

When we arrived at Heron Island, we had something of a shock. The Research Station was crowded with Fulbright scholars—two, to be exact, but as the place still had very limited accommodation that meant that there was no room for us. A cable had been sent to the mainland warning us of this state of affairs, but it had never reached us. To make matters worse, the tourist settlement was also full, and for a while it looked as if death from exposure and starvation faced us. After some fast talking, however, we persuaded the management of the resort to let us have an unused cabin, and were soon comfortably installed among all our cameras, air cylinders, and processing kits.

The *non*-receipt of that telegram was one of the luckiest accidents of our entire expedition. If it had arrived safely, when we had made all our plans for our return visit to Heron Island, we should have been thrown into vast confusion—though admittedly we should have avoided that unpleasantness at Maryborough. As it was, we went sublimely ahead, and were lucky enough to reach the island just when the long spell of bad weather was coming to its end. It was true that the water was cold—though not so cold that we could not stay in it without protection for an hour at a time. But after the first few days of our second visit, the wind died away to a dead calm, the sun came out in a cloudless sky, and the waves which had seemed to march forever against the reef lost their momentum. There was a stillness which sometimes appeared quite uncanny; over the rocks which were normally submerged by boiling foam, the glassy water lay in motionless sheets, mirroring the low islands on the far horizon. When we rowed out across the reef, we sometimes seemed suspended in mid-air above a fantastic landscape of faery trees, and to speak in more than a whisper verged upon sacrilege.

These were the conditions of which we had always dreamed, but which had eluded us so often that we had begun to imagine that they existed nowhere outside the travel brochures. We were determined to make the best of them before taking our final farewell of the Great Barrier Reef and returning to the world of newspapers and cinemas, of traffic lights and hurrying crowds—the world, above all, of clocks and calendars.

XXI

The Turtle Hunt

During our first visit to Heron Island, we had seldom used our breathing gear because we had only a limited supply of air, and felt that we ought to save it for emergencies. We were so ultra-careful, in fact, that we carried most of our compressed air back to the mainland again—a mistake which we were determined not to make a second time. As soon as weather conditions allowed, we used our Porpoise units to revisit the spots which, until now, we had inspected only on brief dives whose endurance had been limited by the capacity of our lungs.

It was a wonderful sensation to sink slowly, without haste or strain, down the faces of the coral cliffs which we had never before had time to examine at leisure. We could crawl into caves which were alive with the most fantastic colors, so that their walls often seemed covered with exotic tapestries. Some of these colors—the blues and yellows— were visible to the naked eye as soon as it had time to adapt itself to the gloom. The reds and crimsons, however, were revealed only during the momentary explosion of light from the camera flash bulbs, and until we processed the film we had little idea of the hidden beauty that had surrounded us.

With our relative freedom of the deeps, we were also able to help the Heron Island management to cope with a minor emergency. The chains linking the *Capre's* mooring buoys with their heavy anchorages on the sea bed had become entangled in a snarl of metal links sixty feet down, and Mike volunteered to sort matters out. It seemed a fairly simple job, though the powerful current running round the edge of the reef made swimming difficult.

It was late afternoon when Mike put on his rubber suit, switched on his air, and fell over the side into the clear though dimly lit water. We saw his ascending bubbles being swept away by the current, but as he had gone hand-over-hand down the anchor line he was able to stay in position without too much trouble. Once on the bottom, he found a hopeless snarl of heavy chains and forty-gallon oil drums, which had become flooded and were therefore no longer very effective as buoys. The links of the chains were about four inches long, and even working under normal conditions, on the surface, it would have required a good deal of effort to disentangle them. After Mike had been wrestling for ten minutes, pushing and pulling and using the current to its best advantage, the main mooring drum moved ponderously in a tight circle, untangling—except for the lower portion—the whole Gordian knot. When Mike had reached the sea bed, some sixty feet down, he started to unravel the remainder of the tangle, and had partly succeeded when a large wave on the surface struck the ship moored above him and tightened the entire system of chains. This, combined with the force of the current and the weight of the flooded buoy, caused the thick chains to tighten around Mike's wrist, holding him trapped a few feet above the sea bed. The current kept the heavy buoy out of his reach, so that he was unable to pull it toward him and release himself.

He had about thirty minutes of air left in his cylinder; as he looked up along the stream of bubbles rising to the distant surface, he thought to himself: "Well, no one can see me down here—and if they could, there's nothing they could do to help me."

Like all good divers (and unlike me) Mike always carries a knife when he is underwater. Partly by luck and partly by good judgment, he had with him on this dive a big German hunting knife—a diabolical weapon with a massive nine-inch blade. He had taken it down thinking that he might have to saw through some ropes; instead, he found himself using it as a lever. Prying the blade between the twisted links, he managed to open them sufficiently to release his hand. Then he finished the job of untangling the moorings, and joined us back on the surface. It was not until a long time later that anyone discovered just why he had been delayed on the bottom.

That was not the only salvage job we did during our stay on the island—I say *we*, for on the next occasion I became involved as well. Had we been professional divers, our bill for services rendered would have been considerable. As it was, we had the free use of a dinghy during our stay, so everyone was satisfied. It is impossible to do any effective diving around a coral reef without some kind of boat, notwithstanding the solo performance described in the next chapter, which should be regarded as an exception rather than the rule.

Only about a mile from Heron Island, but separated from it by a channel of water whose deeper blue always contrasts vividly with the light green of the shallows around the island, is the Wistari Reef. Completely submerged at high tide, Wistari rises from the waves twice a day, to reveal miles of coral boulders surrounding an extensive lagoon. Only on a very calm day is it safe to make a landing on the reef, and then one has to make sure that one can get away before the tide returns. It would not be a pleasant experience to be marooned on Wistari, with the water rising inexorably and the coral boulders disappearing one by one. This actually happened to one distinguished visitor, when the boat that should have taken him off forgot to return. He was rescued at dusk, standing on the last exposed lump of coral, while sharks circled inquisitively round him.

We were lucky enough to borrow an outboard motor on a day when the sea was exceptionally calm, and soon had put-putted across the channel until we were skirting the now-exposed edge of the reef. On our right, extending like a low, irregular wall almost as far as the eye could reach, was the line of massive boulders which countless storms had tossed on to the edge of Wistari, as upon the weather side of every reef. These blocks of dead coral, often weighing several tons, are known as niggerheads or bommies, and still dot the sea like rows of little islands long after the reef around them has been totally submerged.

Though it was such a calm and almost windless day, there was nevertheless a considerable swell when we reached Wistari, and we followed the edge of the reef for

a mile or so before finding a spot where the coral ledge
was relatively smooth and we could run the dinghy around
without risk. Then we scrambled ashore over the wilderness
of bleached and broken coral and started to explore the
wide rampart surrounding the shallow lagoon which oc-
cupies most of the center of the reef.

At first sight, it was a somewhat depressing spot. We
were standing in the midst of the ocean, and the only permanently dry land was a mile away. If the outboard motor
refused to start again, it would be a long row back. If anything happened to the dinghy, it would be a still longer
swim. . . .

Nowhere was there any sign of life; the coral on this
portion of the reef was completely dead. We wound our
way among scores of small boulders, shaped and smoothed
by the seas which thunder incessantly across Wistari. Every
one of these boulders sheltered a whole universe of marine
creatures, and soon our little party had dispersed in all
directions to see what wonders it could find. It was fascinating to overturn the lumps of dead coral, and to watch
beautifully marked cowries crawl for shelter, ornate crabs
wave their claws bravely in Lilliputian defiance, or feathery
starfish writhe across the sand. You never knew what the
next boulder would hide; it could conceal beauty, or danger, or both. The strangest creature I discovered on Wistari
(strangest to me, that is; no doubt a marine biologist could
identify it at once) was a centipedal beast about a foot long
and half an inch across. It was a beautiful iridescent blue-
black, and its body gleamed in the sun like polished metal.
When discovered, it writhed through the rocks in frantic
speed, and as I dared not pick it up (for I had foolishly not
brought gloves) it soon disappeared. Each segment of its

body sprouted two vicious hooks, so that the creature re-sembled an animated band saw as it scuttled to safety.

Even with gloves, it is not safe to touch some of the reef's denizens. The bristle worm, for example, is covered with hundreds of spines, like the finest of glass fiber. These spines break off at a touch and work their way through thick leather with the greatest of ease, leaving the fingers partially numbed when they penetrate the skin.

We spent over an hour on the exposed reef, being care-ful never to get too far from the dinghy, though as the tide was rising there was no danger of its being swept away even had it not been anchored with particular caution. Soon the sea started to creep in across the stretches of flat coral, and the niggerheads around us began to stand out in isolation on the edge of the reef. Loaded down with the specimens we had collected, we hurried back to the boat, pushed it off into the gentle swell of the waves, and headed out into the channel.

Now was our chance to have a better look at the vast coral plateau surrounding Heron Island itself. During all the time we had been there, we had never been able to visit the eastern fringe of the reef, which lay on the very hori-zon, far beyond the reach of the most agile fossicker. So when we left Wistari, we did not head directly back to Heron Island, but cut across to the eastern portion of the reef.

For almost an hour we skirted the edge of the immense and now submerged plateau, whose limits were still clearly revealed by the broken line of niggerheads. We could ap-proach safely to within a few feet of the reef's edge, for the water was so clear that there was no danger of running aground. Beneath us unfolded a panorama of fascinating canyons, of curious sandy strips cutting almost like roads through the living coral, of grottoes and little hillocks which might one day give birth to new islands. It would have taken weeks to explore properly this one section of a single reef—and there were thousands, if not tens of thousands, of such reefs to visit when this one had no more secrets to reveal.

A few days later, we had a chance of examining more new territory. The *Capre* was going out on a fishing trip, and those who didn't want to fish could be put ashore on one of the neighboring islands while the anglers remained on board. As it was a fine day, though there was a rather cold wind blowing, we decided not to miss this opportunity, and carted our photographic and diving gear out to the *Capre*. We also had with us a surf ski which Mike had managed to borrow; for the benefit of those who have never seen this somewhat hair-raising mode of transportation, a surf ski is a streamlined sliver of wood about fifteen feet long, four inches deep, and just wide enough to sit on. Even when you are lying flat, it requires a nice sense of balance to stay on a surf ski if the water is at all choppy—and to sit upright and paddle is something that requires real skill. Surf skis are very popular among Australian spearmen who have to operate at considerable distances from the shore, since they can be used as places of refuge in an emergency. You can have unwanted gear tied to them while you go spearing, and have the satisfaction of knowing that if the sharks get too interested in the bleeding fish with which you are festooning yourself, you can always put a few inches of wood between your anatomy and the water.

An hour and a half after leaving Heron Island, we

arrived at the edge of the reef surrounding Masthead Island. The rest of the trip had to be made by dinghy, and finally by foot across a hundred yards of exposed coral. As we all piled into the boat, and the *Capre* started her motors and roared away out to sea, some humorist shook his fist at her retreating stern and yelled: "You'll hang for this, you mutinous dogs!"

After a picnic lunch on the beach—I am almost ashamed to admit that it was the first time I had drunk a real brew of tea from a genuine billy—Mike and I started to explore the reef, in company with a pair of charming Fulbright scholars. It was a fact, statistically most improbable, that within two weeks no less than four Fulbrighters from various American universities came to Heron Island. On a pro rata basis, this would imply that there must have been several million of them studying the rest of Australia.

Dorothy was a botanist from Duke University, and set us collecting seaweed ("With holdfasts, please"). Celia was a political economist, so there was little we could do for her except help her over the rougher patches of coral. When we found anything interesting, Dorothy would promptly photograph it with a mortar-sized reflex camera. I am sure that when her lavishly illustrated thesis appears, it will start another wave of Fulbright scholars heading for Heron Island.

You never know what you will find when exploring a reef, and this one kept its biggest excitement until the very end—until, in fact, we were already making our way back to rendezvous with the *Capre* on the other side of the island. The tide was still well out, for we had landed when it was ebbing and it would be some hours yet before the reef was covered. A few hundred yards from the island's sandy beach a number of coral pools formed a complex of little lakes, and in one of these lakes five big turtles had been trapped. And by "big," I mean exactly that. The smallest would have tipped the scales at a hundred pounds, while the largest must have weighed two or three times as much.

At first sight, the pool looked as if it were empty. It was not until the massive boulders lying in it started to move slowly around that one realized that they were not boulders at all.

Mike wasted no time, but promptly plunged into the pool. At once, the water started to boil. The great, ungainly beasts hurtled themselves in all directions, and the surface of the pool was thrown into such convulsions that we could catch only occasional glimpses of the mobile rocks dashing frantically around in its depths. After much shouting and splashing, Mike managed to trap the smallest of the turtles in one corner of the pool, so that it could not retreat and was stranded helplessly on the coral. He grabbed its front flippers and, after a brisk tussle, turned the beast over on its back. We then had no difficulty in dragging it completely out of the pool; it lay pathetically waving its limbs and looking at us with big, sad eyes.

Having successfully tested his turtle-catching technique, Mike decided to be more ambitious. However, a three-hundred-pounder was rather a handful for one person to manage, so he called for reinforcements.

A couple of days before, our expedition had been joined by a full-time volunteer, John Goldsmith. John was a member of the Underwater Research Group of Queensland, and had timed his holiday on Heron Island to coincide with our stay there. Though a three-hundred-pound turtle could probably take a man's hand off with one snap of its beak, he promptly joined Mike in the pool, which erupted again as the remaining beasts paddled frantically in search of non-existent shelter.

Once they had cornered the big boy, Mike and John managed to repeat the maneuver and get him stranded on the coral. It took the rest of us, grabbing a flipper apiece, to heave him completely out of the pool. After all this effort, however, there was nothing we could do with him except take photos of each other sitting on his back—his carapace was about four feet across, so there was plenty of room—and then to let him go. Mike tried to ride him back into the pool, but he was as hard to stay on as a bucking bronco once he had reached water again, and in a couple of seconds Mike was swimming by himself.

We had no intention of letting our more manageable victim go, but were determined to take her back to Heron Island. (It *was* a she, so we could christen her Myrtle without inaccuracy.) We had no very precise idea of what we should do with her, but vague thoughts of turtle soups and steaks did pass through our minds.

After much heaving and puffing, we got Myrtle back to the beach, carried her halfway round the island, and then lugged her out across the reef again to the dinghy which would take us back to the *Capre*. We tried to avoid unnecessary violence, but there were times when it was necessary to skid her like a sled over the coral. She didn't seem to enjoy this, but she made no active objection—not even snapping at our ankles when we rowed out to the *Capre*, now waiting off the edge of the reef.

She continued to lie on her back throughout the homeward voyage, as if resigned to her fate. But there was still plenty of fight in her; before we were to touch land again, she was to make a determined bid for freedom.

When the *Capre* tied up at her mooring off Heron Island, Mike decided to take his prize back on the surf ski, so that he could return in triumph like a successful hunter. So poor Myrtle was lashed securely—though not securely enough—to the ski, and it was lowered into the water. Unfortunately, her weight upset the calculations; no sooner did the ski go over the side than it slipped out of its handlers' grasp. With a mighty splash, Myrtle and ski fell into the water and started to drift away on the powerful current along the edge of the reef.

As soon as it hit the water, the ski promptly turned over, submerging Myrtle, who at once revived. She managed to extricate herself from her bonds sufficiently to start paddling, and the ski doubled its speed of departure. As it passed the stern of the *Capre*, there was a second splash as Mike went in after it; a moment later came a third splash as John went in after him. By the time the two of them had reached the ski, it was a hundred feet away, and details of the resulting three-cornered conflict were somewhat obscured by distance. Mike and John wanted to go west, the ski wanted to go east, and Myrtle, who was still attached to it by one flipper, wanted to go straight down.

After a prolonged tussle, Mike and John managed to get Myrtle more or less under control, and, swimming alongside the ski, tried to push it back to the *Capre*. However, the current was too strong for them, and they steadily lost ground. What made their position extremely precarious was the fact that Myrtle, owing to the bad treatment she had received, was bleeding slightly, and the general commotion could hardly have been improved upon as a means of attracting sharks to the spot.

The motorboat which had met the *Capre* at her mooring was taking on the passengers and their goods, and its skipper refused to be moved by the yells for assistance which were now steadily dwindling into the distance. There was nothing much I could do except help to load the boat as quickly as possible, and it seemed an age before we finally untied from the *Capre* and went to the rescue. When we pulled the three swimmers aboard, Myrtle—despite having been dragged on her back across a quarter of a mile of reef—seemed the least exhausted of the trio.

It was, I think, around about this moment that the project for turning Myrtle into steaks was quietly abandoned. She had put up such a good fight that we did not have the heart to eat her (even if we had the stomach, which was also questionable). There was at the Tourist Center a small pool, holding two turtles and sundry sharks. As Myrtle was a good deal larger than the specimens already in captivity, we added her to the collection and she quickly made herself at home.

At least one occupant of the pool was very pleased to see her. Some weeks before, a couple of remora, or sucker fish, had been caught; the smaller of these had attached itself to one of the sharks, but the larger was too big to find any suitable host. It spent most of its time swimming disconsolately beside the already-occupied shark, looking the picture of frustration.

As soon as Myrtle was dumped into the pool, it had found a home. It wasted no time in latching onto her, though occasionally when the pool was partly drained and most of Myrtle was out of the water it would have to start swimming again.

Sucker fish are remarkable creatures—the straphangers of the sea. They are beautifully streamlined little fish, two or three feet in length, with the tops of their heads modified into suction pads. Though they are quite good swimmers, they have found that they can make a better living by attaching themselves to larger fish, letting them do the hard work. When a large shark is caught on a line and hauled aboard a fishing boat, it is quite usual for several remora to detach themselves and fall back into the sea. Sometimes they leave it too late and are caught themselves.

In many parts of the world, native fishermen have used remora as automatically homing surface-to-underwater guided missiles. The technique is simple; you catch your sucker fish, tie a string securely to its tail, and let it loose when your canoe is close enough to a likely target. The Barrier Reef aborigines are particularly adept at catching turtles in this manner; once the remora has attached itself to the turtle's shell, the native angler plays his line, perhaps for several hours, until the animal is exhausted and can be speared. The grip of the remora's suction pad is so powerful that turtles weighing several hundred pounds cannot break away.

There is a common belief that sucker fish are parasites who actually extract nourishment from the bodies of their hosts—that they are leeches, in fact. This is quite untrue; remora would have a job getting much nourishment out of a turtle shell, and indeed have been known to attach themselves to ships. They are scavengers, and will accompany anything—animate or inanimate—in whose presence they will find scraps of food.

One day when the turtle pool had been drained, and the sharks and remora had all been squeezed rather uncomfortably into a small tank, I was able to seize a chance I had missed two years before on the other side of the world. I had been skin diving over a wreck fifteen miles out from the Florida coast when a small sucker fish, obviously looking for a parking place, had swum up to me and begun a careful survey. As I did not know what it would feel like to have that efficient-looking suction pad pressed against my bare skin, I had offered the fish one of my flippers. It had taken a sniff at this, decided that it did not like the taste of rubber, and promptly departed, leaving me regretting my lack of the true scientific spirit.

I finished the experiment on Heron Island, by getting someone to clamp Myrtle's remora on my back. The fish promptly applied suction, and it was impossible to remove it by pulling—either my skin, or the suction pad, would have come off first. But by this time I knew the trick of dislodging remoras; their pads consist of about twenty back-ward-sloping slats, so arranged that when the host moves through the water, the resulting pressure clamps them even more tightly to its body. Because of this, though it may be very hard to pull a remora off, it is quite easy to *push* it off. If sharks were intelligent enough to swim backward, they could soon dislodge the hitchhikers who, if they do nothing else, must slow them down and impede their hunting ability.

The remora's grip was not exactly pleasant, but I cannot pretend that it was at all painful, though it left a red weal which took a few minutes to vanish. The next time I meet one of these interesting little fish, I will not hesitate to offer it a temporary home if it seems lost. But should I then find myself being towed rapidly backward, I will reverse myself with all possible speed so that the suction pad comes unstuck. I would hate to think of those fishermen throwing their harpoons before they had checked on their catch. . . .

XXII

Aladdin's Cave

The sensible underwater explorer never goes diving alone, but by this definition there are no sensible underwater explorers. There are times when even the most cautious person (and I would be high on such a list) cannot resist temptation.

It was a beautiful, warm afternoon, with the sun shining steadily from a cloudless sky. Not a breath of wind was blowing, and the water beyond the reef lay flat and untroubled by waves. Conditions for diving were perfect, but Mike was not feeling well. Since such a day might not come again, I refused to waste it and set out by myself.

As it was near low tide, most of the reef was uncovered and I had to carry my gear for the first hundred yards. As soon as the water became deep enough to swim in, I put on my flippers and started to paddle out to sea.

I was now in a two-dimensional world, and could easily imagine that I was one of the inhabitants of Flatland. Visibility was so good that I could see sixty or seventy feet horizontally, but the smooth sandy bottom was only a couple of feet from my nose. I was sandwiched between the flat mirror of the surface and the almost equally flat sea bed—two parallel planes that stretched to the limits of vision in every direction.

Presently the water deepened, and the sand gave way to coral. On my left loomed the rusty wreck of the small freighter which some years ago had been stranded on the edge of the Heron reef, and provided a useful windbreak for the boats transferring passengers to the *Capre*. I circled the wreck, and scared a few large fish back into the shelter of the trenches which the tides had scooped along its keel. There was nothing very interesting here, so I continued toward the deeper water.

It is always mysterious on the edge of the reef, when you are swimming along the steeply sloping zone which divides the reef-flat from the open sea. You never know what will come racing swiftly in from deep water, and you can be fairly sure that sharks are not more than a few seconds' cruising time away. As I circled above the living coral, which was so near the surface that I could touch it with my flippers while continuing to breathe through my snorkle tube, I kept a wary eye on the seaward slope.

Suddenly, four most peculiar objects shot past me like rockets. They were traveling in close formation, and as soon as they had passed swung round in a tight curve to have a better look at me. I then saw that they were not some unusual fish, but were a quartet of squid, each a couple of feet in length. They were beautiful little beasts, colored in soft pastel shades, impossible to describe accurately as they changed them at a moment's notice. Their tentacles were tucked tightly together and completed their neat streamlined shape as they shot head-first through the water.

Though they were inquisitive, they would not let me get within twenty feet of them, but darted off again so rapidly that I had no hope of following. As they disappeared into the distance, they looked like translucent parasols squirting themselves through the water. It seemed strange that creatures so closely related to the unprepossessing octopus could be so beautiful and so agile.

I continued my swim along the reef edge, pausing to photograph a small thicket of lavender-tinted staghorn coral. Once I came across a school of fish busily nibbling at some delectable portion of the sea bed, rather like the birds which gather behind a plow to peck for worms in the broken ground. They were much too interested in their own affairs to take any notice of me.

The scenery now became wilder; the underwater landscape was built on a larger scale. Though I was careful not to get more than a few yards from the edge of the reef, so that I could reach shallow water in case of cramp (perhaps the greatest danger facing the lone swimmer), I frequently found myself floating twenty or thirty feet above the coral plates and boulders which now practically covered the sea bed. There were so many fish that sometimes they obscured the view; this may sound like a piece of typical Australian hyperbole, but was literally true. When a school of fifty kingfish, each weighing ten or twenty pounds, closes in to have a good look at you, visibility is slightly restricted.

I spent more than two hours swimming and diving along the edge of the reef—the longest continuous time I had ever stayed in the water—and only the declining sunlight compelled me to leave at last. For that two hours I had had the reef to myself; I had been like a man taking a solitary walk through some lonely forest.

But any such land-based analogy can be no more than a pale reflection of the truth. There is no jungle on the surface of the earth as packed with life as the frozen forest of a coral reef. Nor can there ever be, for the air may give oxygen to the creatures which move through it, but it cannot give them food. Water does both, as the world may one day realize when mankind moves its farms from the desert of the land out into the fertile and inexhaustible sea.

It was in this same area, a few days later, that we met the biggest fish we ever encountered off the Heron reef—and, ironically enough, had a good object lesson in the dangers of solitary diving. Mike, John Goldsmith, and I had gone out in the dinghy on a general photo reconnaissance, and as we were short of compressed air, Mike was diving with oxygen apparatus of the type used by frogmen. There is an important distinction here which very few nondivers realize, as is proved by the number of occasions on which Aqualung-type cylinders are described by reporters and caption writers as being full of compressed oxygen, instead of compressed air.

The pure oxygen equipment is compact, gives greater endurance, and releases no telltale bubbles, since the exhaled gases are not blown out into the water but are purified by removal of carbon dioxide and used again. These features make it ideal for military use—but it has one serious disadvantage. Anyone employing oxygen rebreathers at depths of more than about thirty-five feet is liable, with very little warning, to become unconscious and thus to drown.

The reason for this is complicated; the explanation

usually given is that oxygen breathed under the pressure met thirty-five feet down becomes a poison. Like most simple explanations, this is certainly only part of the truth, and if you know what you are doing it is possible to use pure oxygen sixty or eighty feet down, where the total pressure is more than three atmospheres.

I was in the dinghy, Mike was exploring with the oxygen rebreather, and John was skin diving along the edge of the reef. Suddenly John saw immediately beneath him a huge grouper, five or six feet long, and weighing at least three hundred pounds. It was drifting toward deeper water, apparently in no hurry—but it soon began to accelerate when it saw all the cameras converging upon it. Mike and John were quickly left behind; I was more fortunately placed, being further out from the edge of the reef, and was able to keep the fish in sight. After a few seconds it slowed down, and coasted along the bottom, thirty feet below me, making those disconcerting yawns—or rather gulps—which are so characteristic of the giant cods.

It was swinging out to sea in a great circle which, if continued, would soon bring it back to its starting point. I followed at full boost, yelling to the others and pointing out the grouper's direction of travel every time I came back to the surface for air. To my annoyance, both Mike and John appeared to have lost all interest in the hunt, and had climbed into the dinghy. While I was trying to discover what had happened to them, I lost track of the grouper, which disappeared into the underwater haze.

My temper was not at its best when I reached the dinghy and demanded the reason for this lack of co-operation. However, I soon cooled off when I was given it. The carbon dioxide absorber in Mike's oxygen equipment had become exhausted while he was on the bottom, and he had almost passed out owing to the steady accumulation of CO_2 in his breathing bag. He had barely managed to blow up the bag by turning the oxygen valve full on, thus floating himself to the surface.

After this contretemps, we decided to leave the big grouper alone for the day, but to return later with more serviceable equipment. On this second visit, as it turned out, Mike's gear functioned perfectly, and it was my turn to run into trouble.

The cod lived in a tortuous cave about three feet high, which almost completely surrounded the base of a huge coral plateau. Mike, now wearing the Porpoise compressed-air gear, went into the cave carrying camera and flash bulbs. I waited just outside with another camera, in case the fish emerged in some unexpected direction. For the first time on this trip, I was wearing my old Aqualung, as the cylinder still contained a good deal of air and I wanted to use it up.

Mike disappeared into the cave, stirring up a cloud of sediment as he did so. I crouched outside, wondering if I would shortly be engaged in a tug of war with the grouper—for it was quite capable, if provoked too far, of swallowing Mike's head and shoulders.

Luckily for him, Mike did not need my assistance, for at that moment my breathing tube became flooded and I started to swallow mouthfuls of aerated water. I know that it was possible to clear an Aqualung mouthpiece of water easily enough by rolling over on your right—or left—side, and then blowing. Unfortunately, it had been so long since I had used the unit that I couldn't remember which side to roll on. I tried both, but neither seemed to work, and very soon I had no air left with which to blow. Luckily, I was only thirty feet down, and so I wasted no time in returning to the surface.

I felt very annoyed with myself, for this silly accident could have been serious had I been in deep water. A few days before, I had been using the Porpoise equipment fifty feet down, and in brushing against a rock had knocked the breathing tube out of my mouth. On that occasion, I had hardly given the matter a second thought—it was so easy to slip the mouthpiece back between my teeth and to resume breathing. The much smaller air space exposed to the sea in the Porpoise design made flooding virtually impossible.

It was doubtless my own carelessness which started me breathing water, and my own incompetence which prevented me from curing the trouble. But how much better, I thought as I emerged spluttering on the surface, to stick to equipment where this sort of thing couldn't happen.

No one can swim on the surface with heavy breathing-gear on his back, for the weight of the air cylinder, if he tries to hold his head above water, promptly pushes him back again and he is soon exhausted. For this reason, you should never go diving without a snorkle tube tucked in your belt. Then, if you are forced to swim on the surface with an empty air bottle strapped to your back, you can still breathe comfortably even though your head and body are fully submerged.

I had my snorkle; what I *hadn't* done was check to see that it was working properly. A breathing tube is such a simple device that it seems nothing could go wrong with it, but few things in this world are completely foolproof, as I was now busily demonstrating. At some time I must have given the mouthpiece too hard a bite, for the plastic tube had caved in and the rate of air flow through the construction had been greatly cut down.

Even this would not have mattered had not a third factor then come into play. For the only time during the entire expedition, I had left my own face mask on shore and had been compelled to borrow someone else's. A diver should always stick to his own face mask, not only for hygienic reasons but because it soon molds itself to his features and so ensures a perfect fit. The mask I had borrowed was leaking rather badly; I had not bothered about this when I had plenty of air to blow the water out, but now it was a serious matter. I couldn't get enough air through the snorkle to breathe properly, the mask flooded so that my nose was permanently submerged in a private swimming pool, the heavy air cylinder stopped me from raising my head out of the water—and the powerful current along the reef was sweeping me away from the dinghy.

I struggled for some time to sort matters out, then felt a warning twinge of cramp and decided that even at the risk of losing face I had better shout for help. Luckily, John was in the dinghy—discussing seaweeds and political economy with Dot and Celia, who had come along to watch us in action—and in a few minutes he had pulled up the anchor and rowed across to collect me. I climbed back into the boat, spat out quantities of Australian sea water and Australian adjectives, then grabbed a new snorkle and face mask so that I could find what Mike had been doing all this time. If he had been relying on my help, he was probably inside the grouper by now.

Luckily, he had managed quite well on his own. At first, when he had crawled under the ledge of rock, the general gloom and the sediment stirred up from the sandy bottom had prevented him from seeing anything. Then the fog had cleared, and his eyes swiftly adapted themselves to the low level of illumination. What had seemed to be a Stygian cave began to glow with color; the walls and ceiling were completely covered with living tapestries of blue and yellow and gold, with fiery crimsons bursting forth in surprising gouts of flame. The sight was so unexpectedly beautiful that for a moment Mike forgot his quest, but focused the camera on the painted walls, determined to record a scene which, until that moment, no human eye could ever have witnessed.

The explosion of the flash, lighting up the farthest corners of the cave, gave its colors a briefly enhanced glory which they had never known before. When his eyes had recovered from their momentary shock, Mike saw that the passageway on the left, from floor to ceiling, was completely blocked with a wall of tiny fish. There were hundreds of them, no more than an inch or two in length. It was as if they formed a living screen, preventing him from seeing what lay behind them.

The screen, however, was not continuous. Through its gaps Mike could see a great wall of scaly fish. The giant grouper was lying there, watching him with its bulging eyes as he crawled into its parlor.

It was impossible to photograph it behind its screen; Mike had first to claw away the multitudes of tiny fish that seemed equally unafraid of him and of the giant who could swallow them all at one gulp. They retreated as far as its gills, and the great head emerged into the open, its pugnacious underjaw jutting forward. Still it made no move, and Mike was able to take his time composing the photograph. When the flash blasted forth again, the grouper decided that it had had enough. It shot off along the tapestried tunnel, darted out through the back door of its coral home, and sought seclusion in the open sea.

Despite my troubles, the mission was one of the most successful we ever carried out, for when they were developed Mike's photographs were perfect. The flash had captured every detail of the cave and every spot on the massive, bulldog head protruding from its living smoke screen.

Though we made several later calls, we never found the grouper at home again. I do not imagine that we had scared him away—the giant cod is one of the most unscareable fish in the sea, as many divers have found to their cost. He was probably out hunting when we came looking for him.

In the same cave, however, we did meet what is sometimes considered the most beautiful of all coral fishes—the fire fish or butterfly cod. This little creature has fins which open out so that they resemble a bunch of feathers, and swims daintily to and fro preening itself like a peacock. I had dived into the cave and was admiring the colored walls when I noticed the fire fish orbiting under the roof. Though I longed to capture it, there was nothing I could do, for the fire fish lives up to its name. The beautiful, spiny fins are poison-tipped, for though not as venomous as the stonefish, it belongs to the same family. I tried, in vain, to hook it with my snorkle, but it side-stepped me. Mike was equally unsuccessful with a hastily improvised net. We did not even get a photograph, for this was one of those days when all the cameras went on strike, the flash bulbs fired only when we inserted them in their sockets and not when we pressed the trigger, and in general a bad time was had by all.

Many of these equipment failures were our own fault; sometimes we were so busy diving, processing film, and doing the paper work of the expedition that we simply did not have time to service our gear as thoroughly as we should have done. We learned by our mistakes, and if we had to retrace our footsteps could now obtain the same results with about a quarter of the effort.

Perhaps we were lucky, in that we only made mistakes which gave us a second chance. That is not always the case when you are working underwater; the misadventures I have related in this chapter show how easily quite trivial errors or mishaps can lead to serious consequences. My flooding Aqualung—my ill-fitting face mask—my choked snorkle—any of these might not have mattered had they occurred in isolation. Yet coming all at once, they added up to a situation in which I was very glad that a boat was so near at hand.

However, I will waste no more time in cautionary admonitions. The divers and would-be divers who may read these words will fall into two categories. One group will have already made all these mistakes; the rest will do so in their own good time, despite all the warnings I or any-one else can give. I hope that they will make them in the security of their local swimming pool, instead of out in the lonely and unforgiving sea.

XXIII

The Last Dive

Our time on the Reef was running out; in a few days we should have to return to the mainland and retrace our path to Brisbane, Sydney—and then the northern hemisphere. Every moment now became doubly precious, and I hated to miss any chance of seeing the underwater fairyland which we might never visit again.

I was somewhat annoyed, therefore, when Mike was asked to carry out yet another salvage job, for I had photographic plans already drawn up. This time, the task was to recover a huge anchor, which lay with its two hundred feet of heavy chain in about ten fathoms of water. My annoyance turned out to be misplaced; any kind of dive, even if at first sight it appeared to be completely routine, is likely to provide something of interest, and so it proved to be the case here.

The operation was carried out from the *Capre,* and this time Mike used the Hookah equipment, with its pipe line leading to an air supply on the surface. However, he used it with one drastic modification. We were short of compressed air, being down to our last couple of bottles. As there was a cylinder of commercial oxygen on the *Capre*, Mike decided to use that.

As has already been mentioned in the last chapter, pure oxygen is supposed to be poisonous at depths of more than thirty-five feet, and Mike intended to breathe it at twice that depth. This time, it was true, there would be no danger of any carbon dioxide build-up through failure of the CO_2 absorber which had caused trouble before. All the exhaled gases would be breathed out, and not used again. It was wasteful, but Mike was sure it was safe. In any case, he would be attached to the surface by the air hose, and if something went wrong we could always haul him up. . . .

The hose was coupled to the oxygen cylinder, Mike put on the harness, and slipped over the side. Since it looked like being a fairly long job, he was also wearing a rubber suit as protection against the cold. He dropped quickly to the bottom, taking a wire cable with him, and attached it to the end of the lost chain. That was relatively easy, but now began the tedious part. The chain was so heavy that only a few feet could be lifted onto the *Capre* at a time, and during this operation Mike had to remain in the water, attaching and releasing clamps fixed at intervals to the massive links. It was a dirty job, and if one of the clamps suddenly came loose he was liable to have a quarter of a ton of chain dumped on his head.

The operation was nearly finished when Mike (who was suffering from a bad cold when he started to work) felt too sick to continue. We pulled him back on deck, and I took over. The *Capre's* little windlass could cope with only about fifteen feet of chain at a time, and when I had helped four or five installments aboard, all the slack had been taken up and the chain was tautly vertical from the sea bed to the surface. The great anchor, sixty feet below me, was beginning to move, stirring up little clouds of mud.

Now that I was no longer wanted on the surface, I decided to go down and have a look at the bottom. I gave the necessary instructions to my tender, who lowered me away slowly—for I had not forgotten the trouble my ears had given me the last time I dived too quickly.

Visibility was fantastically good; it was possible to see about a hundred feet in every direction, and the *Capre* looked like a toy boat far above my head. When I reached the bottom, the great anchor had been winched into the vertical position, and stood upright on its flukes. I felt dwarfed as it waved menacingly before me, and I remembered that some of the links in the chain had been very badly worn. Since I was using shoes, not flippers, I had very little mobility, and my tender didn't understand my signals when I asked for more hose so that I could walk away from this tottering mass of iron. If the chain broke, I would hardly have time to shout "Timber!"

There was no way in which I could tell that I was breathing pure oxygen instead of compressed air. There was, perhaps, a slightly metallic taste in my mouth, and my rate of respiration seemed to be a little more rapid than usual. If this was true, I find it surprising, since I should have expected my lungs to work more slowly in a 100 percent oxygen atmosphere than a 20 per cent one.

While I was trying to get away from this Damoclean anchor—which was now quite clear of the bottom, and was suspended about ten feet off the sea bed—a couple of fair-sized cod came to have a look at me. They were far smaller than their big brother a few hundred yards along the reef, probably tipping the scales at a mere twenty or thirty pounds. But they had the same characteristic front view— the downward drooping mouth, the big goo-goo eyes bulging out of the sides of their heads.

A few minutes later, Mike, now recovered from his temporary sickness, arrived on the scene with flash camera and Porpoise unit. We took photographs of each other, standing on the flukes of the anchor and clinging to its stock. As I climbed back to the surface, I felt that glow of satisfaction that comes to all Boy Scouts who have done their Good Turn for the day and can now revert to normal.

This was Mike's last dive on Heron Island. We had both been working too hard, in our anxiety not to waste the good weather, and had become plagued by an accumulation of boils, bruises, and cuts. I had also managed to crack a rib while climbing over the side of the dinghy with the heavy breathing gear on my back. However, to quote Squadron Leader Walter Mitty, it was only a scratch; I set the bone myself.

These ailments had reduced our efficiency and sometimes prevented us from diving altogether. They were not as frustrating as they would once have been, for by this time we had gathered most of the material we needed, and realized that these accumulating ills were Nature's way of warning us that it was time we took a rest.

My own final dive took place, appropriately enough, among our favorite coral hills. It was already midafternoon when, with John Goldsmith and three interested onlookers who had come along on condition that they did the rowing, we took the dinghy out to the edge of the reef. The water was calm, but visibility was rather poor—though not so many months ago I should have thought it marvelous to be able to see thirty feet, as we could do easily enough. We dropped the anchor onto the little mountain below us, and watched it slide down the slope until it lodged in a crevice. Unlike most sailors, we never had to worry about the anchor getting caught. If this happened, we could always go down and release it.

I had mapped out a definite plan of action for this final dive, though when I saw the poor visibility I was not altogether happy about carrying it out. During the whole of this second stay—and we had now been on Heron Island for over three weeks—we had not met a single shark. Perhaps if we speared some fish, that might bring them on the scene and I would be able to get some photographs.

With the last of the Porpoise air cylinders on my back, and the camera slung round my neck, I swam down into the familiar little valley and grottoes. All the usual occupants were there, including one scarred and distrustful cod which we had photographed at least a dozen times, usually when he was making rude faces at us.

A few minutes later, John, wearing a twin-cylinder unit, joined me on the bottom. He was carrying a Lyle Davis gun, and although one can be black-listed from all the best spearfishermen's associations for hunting with the aid of breathing gear, we considered that the circumstances permitted it. After all, we were not hunting ordinary fish—we were hunting sharks, and anything we speared would be merely the bait.

After a certain number of attempts (I will not say how many) John impaled a fine coral trout. He was obviously disappointed when I refused to come in and take a close-up of him and his victim; I was determined not to be caught with a used flash bulb and an uncocked camera if a shark came into view, and kept spinning round in the water to obtain 360 degrees of vision. John got fed up with waiting around for his photograph to be taken—or perhaps he did not care for the idea of sharing these rather misty waters with an injured fish which was sending out distress signals in all directions. He swam back to the boat, and its occupants—who had been observing us through viewing glasses—hauled the trout aboard. This was not at all what I had intended, as I wanted the fish to be left in the water.

However, if sharks were interested in our bait, they would surely have appeared by this time. I decided to wait around no longer, but to go on a last stroll down the reef where it deepened out into the sea.

This was an area which had always fascinated me, but which I had entered only two or three times before, since I felt that we could not afford the air to go exploring so far down. Now that did not matter, for this was my last dive and I might as well empty the last remaining cylinder.

The coral hills from which I had started my leisurely swim stood in about thirty feet of water, and soon faded into the blue mist behind and above me as I went down the long, gentle slope. The bottom here was white sand—quite flat, but not horizontal. When I stopped to survey the view, I seemed to be standing on a limitless plain that had been tilted so that there was something subtly wrong about the entire visible landscape. The stream of bubbles from my exhaust valve, surely, should not go up in *that* direction! I found myself tending to lean forward, in an attempt to bring myself at right angles to the slope and thus to remove the cause of my slight visual disorientation.

The A-bomb-shaped mass of coral which towered thirty

feet from the sea bed loomed up on my right. There had always been a pair of pipefish swimming mournfully around it, and they were there now. I took a few flash shots, and the burned-out bulbs shot skyward like ascending balloons. They would drift past the dinghy, and inform its occupants that I was at work fifty feet below them. Not all our used flash bulbs, incidentally, were jettisoned in this way. We parked some of them with care, and anyone diving into a certain cave will be surprised to find a few clinging to the ceiling above his head. Had we thought of it in time, we might have left our cards as well, sealed up in a water-tight jar ... perhaps inscribed with the slogan we had concocted for the expedition: WRECKS ARRANGED AND SALVAGED.

The great overhanging mushroom faded into the mists behind me, and still the sea bed sloped on downward with no sign of leveling out. A weirdly shaped boulder, like a gnarled and hunch-backed gnome, appeared ahead of me, and I stood admiring it for some time, thinking what an excellent illustration it would have made for a Hans Andersen story. It and I were now the only objects breaking the gray uniformity of the endless, tilted plain.

I was now a considerable distance from the dinghy, and it was unwise to go any further. Indeed, it was probably unwise to have come this far alone. But I knew that another of the big cods lived in this neighborhood, and wanted to take a photograph of him if it were possible. There still seemed to be plenty of air in my cylinder, and I was economically determined to use it to the last breath. That air had cost us a good deal—not in terms of money, but in terms of the effort involved in carrying these steel bottles a total distance of two thousand miles, and manhandling them dozens of times from one vehicle to another.

I swam a little further down the long slope, and presently saw ahead of me a curious rock half-embedded in the sand. At least, that was my first impression; then I realized that here was the cod, lying on the bottom. It was over a yard long, its body a pepper-and-salt color which made it blend rather well against the sandy sea bed. As I approached, it moved slowly away, and refused to turn broadside-on so that I could get a good photograph. I had enough pictures of retreating fish in my collection, and unless I could get my subject to co-operate I was not going to waste any film.

Suddenly, with a graceful flapping of wings, a big leopard ray appeared out of the haze and began to swing round me in a wide circle. I immediately abandoned the cod in favor of this much more interesting creature, with its pointed, almost birdlike head and its beautifully mottled body. Being careful not to swim directly toward it, which might have scared it off, I made a circuitous approach to the ray, and was almost in position when one of those typically frustrating underwater accidents occurred. The flash bulb, apparently even more eager than I was to get a photograph, fired spontaneously.

The explosion of light scared the ray out of its wits; it was the only fish I had ever seen really frightened by a flash bulb. The big manta we had met on our first visit had not been unduly worried even when the flash went off in its face at two yards' range—and the null reaction of the barracuda has already been mentioned. In an instant, the ray seemed to change; its leisurely flapping became a swift and powerful beat. Trailing its long whip behind it, it raced out of sight at a speed which I could not hope to match.

A little belatedly, I decided to make my way back to the dinghy, though I had no intention of surfacing until compelled to. Presently the familiar coral sculptures began to reappear, first as dim silhouettes, then as solid objects with all their wealth of colorful detail and their populations of never-resting fish. As I stood in the sandy amphitheater which I had grown to know so well, I realized that this might be the very last time I would ever dive in the waters of the Great Barrier Reef. The enterprise which had absorbed so much of my time and effort over the last two years had now virtually come to its end. I felt sorry that Mike, who had put even more time into the project, could not be with me on this final dive.

Something made me look up. A phalanx of slim, ghostly shapes was passing overhead—so many of them that they occupied a considerable portion of my "sky." They were too far away for clear vision, but I recognized them at once. The fish that John had wounded had at last brought the hunters onto the scene. The barracuda had taken their time, but they were here.

It did not seem to be as large a pack as the one that Mike and I had encountered before. There were perhaps fifty of the long, lean sea wolves moving slowly above the coral peaks beneath which I was swimming. They kept their distance as I hurried upward, driving toward the dinghy as quickly as I could.

Treading water, I stripped off the Porpoise unit and handed it over the side of the boat. I wanted to have a closer look at those 'cuda, and did not wish to be encumbered with too much equipment in case I had to move quickly. John was already in the dinghy, and looked at me in horrified disbelief when I shouted to him: "Get your gun—there are about fifty 'cuda here. I want you to spear one so that we can see what happens!"

"You've got a hope," he said, or words to that effect. He had seen the photographs we had taken when immersed in the earlier pack of barracuda, and they appeared to have damped his enthusiasm for hunting. Nothing I could do would persuade him to leave the boat, so I set off with camera alone, getting the dinghy to raise anchor and follow me. I felt quite certain that, with this refuge so close at hand, I could always reach safety should the barracuda become too inquisitive.

They were still circling below, but the underwater visibility was becoming poor for the sun was now halfway down the sky. When swimming on the surface, I could no longer see the bottom, but appeared to be poised over an infinite blue abyss. It was a somewhat disturbing sensation, for I now had no sense of scale and when I dived I could no longer tell how far I was either from the sea bed or the surface. I would take a deep breath, then swim vertically downward for what seemed a very long time before the misty outlines of the coral rock would appear far below me. By that time, I would have to start thinking about going back for air.

On two or three of these dives I saw the barracuda again, like pale wraiths patrolling the sea. But I could not get near them, and I very quickly realized that it was not at all sensible to continue swimming under these conditions. Moreover, I was getting tired and cold, and at any moment I might feel the first twinges of cramp. I decided not to press my luck, and with one final glance around the now empty and featureless blue that encompassed me, I climbed back into the boat.

The sad little pipefish, the truculent cod, the nervous leopard rays, and all the other inhabitants of this section of the reef would now be left in peace. But for how long? I wondered. Perhaps we had taken too many people out to the reef; if, when we returned, it was so crowded with underwater explorers that there was no room for the fish, we would have only ourselves to blame.

XXIV

A Walk in the Dark

Like a visitor to London who is halfway through packing when he suddenly realizes that he has never seen the Tower or Westminster Abbey, I remembered one unforgivable oversight while we were preparing to leave Heron Island. I had never been out on the exposed reef at night.

With a few exceptions, the coral animals withdraw into their tiny homes during the hours of daylight, and do not emerge to feed until nightfall. One rather drab green coral—a close-packed honeycomb of minute tubes—does brave exposure to the sun, and may be found during the day beneath a short fuzz of tentacles, so that it resembles a stone covered with moss. If you scratch the stone at any point, the moss promptly disappears as the tentacles retreat, and a bald patch spreads swiftly over the entire face of the coral. Within a few seconds, all the polyps have withdrawn into their little caves, and will not emerge again until they have recovered from their shock. It is amusing to scratch your initials on one of these corals, and to watch the letters rapidly enlarge as a wave of panic sweeps over the colony.

The most colorful corals, however, can be observed only if you go out to the reef after dark with a powerful flashlight. To do this in comfort you need a still, warm night—and of course a favorable tide. We had barely two days left on Heron Island when I finally made the experiment. It was not very successful, but it was certainly unforgettable.

There was no moon, and the clear sky was blazing with the strange southern constellations whose outlines I had never learned. I had persuaded three somewhat reluctant companions to come with me—Norman, an acquaintance from our spear-fishing days in Sydney, and Peter and Harry, two lads who collected everything they could lay their hands on from venomous snakes (live) to aboriginal surgical instruments, which I was surprised to find had reached a high degree of perfection. Pete and Harry were desperately anxious to add a stonefish to their museum, but despite all their efforts they never succeeded in locating any of Spike's surviving relatives.

We gathered on the western beach of the island just before low tide, our torches throwing pools of light upon the sand. It was very dark; the reef was a dimly discernible shadow close at hand, but its distant edge was only a silhouette against the stars. If we strained our eyes into the night, we could just see the outlines of the beached freighter, a quarter of a mile away.

The problem of choosing a path through the difficult territory ahead of us had so engaged my mind that, for once, I scarcely noticed the glory of the tropical sky. Then somebody pointed to the west and said: "What's that light over there?"

I looked up into the stars. The sun had set long before, and no trace of the brief evening's afterglow remained. Yet straddling the western sky, and stretching halfway to the zenith, was a faint cone of light, tilted somewhat toward the south. At first glance, it might have been taken for the Milky Way—but the densely packed star-clouds of the Galaxy arched across a different portion of the heavens.

It was, I knew, the zodiacal light—that pale and mysterious apparition that stretches outward from the sun like a millionfold-greater enlargement of the corona. I was seeing it for the first time in my life, and was surprised at its extent and the ease with which it could be observed in these clear and unpolluted skies, far from the glare of any cities. We stood looking up at it for several minutes, our torches extinguished, before we started to move out across the reef.

It was soon obvious that we had chosen a bad night. Though the tide was out as far as it would go, it was unusually high and the entire reef was still covered with at least a foot of water. I tried to encourage the party by telling them that further out toward the reef edge there might still be large areas of exposed coral on which we could walk, and that we had plenty of time to get there and back before the tide turned. So we took a bearing on the zodiacal light and headed out from shore.

It was eerie wading through the still pools, not knowing what the beams of our torches might suddenly reveal. There were thousands of small crabs out foraging; some of them would scuttle away at our approach, but others would bravely stand their ground and wave threatening claws. We had traveled no more than a dozen yards when we came across a small shark resting on the bottom; our torches did not disturb it, and it let us walk up to it before swimming slowly away.

We had soon lost all sense of distance, and although we knew we were traveling in a more or less straight line it was impossible to tell how far from the island we were— or how much further we had to go before we would come to the edge of the reef. Our progress over the dead and often treacherous coral, which was not easy to walk upon even in the daylight, became painfully slow.

Quite abruptly we came to an area of phosphorescence; with every step, stars burst out beneath our feet. Even if we stood in one spot, the slightest movement produced sparkles of light as the ripples spread out across the pool. When we switched on our torches, the beams destroyed the magic and gave no clue as to its cause—they revealed nothing but empty water and a lifeless, sandy bottom. Yet as soon as out lights were turned off, the constellations flashed out again, twinkling all around our feet and matching those in the sky above, so that we seemed to be walking upon stars.

The water was deepening; it was now up to our knees, and my promise of finding any exposed coral seemed unlikely to be fulfilled. We were a long way from the beach, and by this time the tide had begun to turn. My companions did not seem to be enjoying themselves as much as I had hoped. They knew that when the tide came in, sharks were likely to come with it. Once we heard, in the darkness far ahead of us, a distant, muffled crash, as of a great body falling back into the water. The whales were moving north to their breeding grounds, so that the calves would be born in the warm equatorial waters. One of them must have jumped out there in the night—or perhaps a big ray was trying to dislodge the parasites that worried it.

I was leading the party, because I knew the way (or thought I did; though by this time I was becoming a little doubtful) and because it was my idea in the first place. According to my calculations, at any moment now we should find ourselves on a firm, flat rampart of living coral, where walking would be much easier and safer and we would have a chance of seeing the exposed polyps to the best advantage. It was highly disconcerting, therefore, when the ground suddenly fell away beneath me and I found myself standing at the very brink of a deep pool, full of strange and mysterious shapes which the beams of our torches were quite unable to elucidate. In the bright light of day, a coral pool is a place of beauty, but when darkness falls it becomes as sinister as the enchanted garden of any demon king. Here might Kastcheï have imprisoned the Firebird and concealed the magic egg which held the secret of his power.

The companions joined me at the side of the pool, and I had to confess that my navigation had proved unequal to the task. True, I had got them safely to the edge of the reef, but not in the place I had expected. Instead of a nice, solid rampart we were confronted with six feet of water, and the tide was now swiftly rising. We could, of course, get to the place I was aiming at by working along the margin of the reef, but I was not quite sure whether we should aim to the right or the left. And whichever way we went, except backward, we were likely to come across more of these unexpected and ominous pools.

The decision as to what to do next was quickly made

for us. From the darkness beyond the reef came a sudden steady splashing. It was quite near at hand, and had an indescribably *purposeful* suggestion about it, as if something was determined to waste no time, but had made up its mind to reach us as quickly as it could.

As far as the boys were concerned, this was the last straw. For some time Harry had expressed an urgent desire to return to more solid ground, and now the others added their pleas to his. Faced with this regrettable lack of support, I was compelled to start the retreat. Naturally, since I had to lead the way, this implied placing Harry, Peter, and Norman between me and whatever it was that seemed so eager to reach the reef.

We retired in fairly good order, though Harry twice jumped out of the water shouting, "Something hit me!" and was only slightly relieved to discover that it had been Norman's spear. And Peter, misjudging his footing in the darkness, immersed himself several times in his haste to get back to the island. We all breathed a little more freely when the water level dropped to below our knees, and we knew that we were now unlikely to meet any sharks more than five or six feet long.

At last the rocks bordering the shore loomed up ahead of us, and we shook the rising waters from our feet. As we scrambled across the flat but treacherous stone, I expressed my regret that our mission had been a failure, and that none of us had actually seen the corals in their nocturnal beauty. "Now tomorrow night," I said, "the tide will be a bit better, and if we time it right—"

I had to move quickly to get away.

XXV

The Reef is Waiting

It was a dismal and cloudy morning when we went aboard the *Capre* for the last time. After several days of calm, a gusty wind had come up and it almost seemed as if the weather, which had been so good to us, had waited until we were leaving before letting itself go again. We did not look forward to the five-hour trip back to the mainland.

Luckily, our fears were groundless. As we watched Heron Island sink astern and gradually merge itself into the Wistari Reef, the clouds began to break. Vast spokes of light from the high but still-hidden sun slowly cartwheeled across the horizon, then merged together in one blaze as the sun at last burst through. It was a spectacular farewell, and as I caught my last glimpse of the island I felt sad, but wholly content.

The sea was calmer than we had ever known it. As smoothly as if traveling on rails, the *Capre* roared into the west, without the slightest trace of rolling or pitching. It was almost uncanny; could they have seen us now, those

Heron Islanders who had gleefully commiserated with us for the rough crossing we were going to have would be most surprised—and disappointed.

Since there was now nothing to see, I settled down to do some quiet reading. We were halfway to the mainland when, several miles away, a column of smoke suddenly materialized out of the water, then slowly dispersed. A moment later there was another—then a third. A school of whales was moving up the coast, running the gantlet of the long, narrow lagoon formed by the Great Barrier Reef and the Australian mainland. Many of their companions must have been taken by the whaling ships operating further south; others would be destroyed by their natural enemies before they could return with their newborn calves to the rich pastures of the Antarctic seas.

It was awe-inspiring to watch the huge, dark bodies sliding through the water. Ever and anon there would be a sudden flash of white, as the great flukes emerged and smashed against the surface with a crack which we could sometimes hear even above the noise of our engines. There was no way of telling whether the whales were merely playing, or whether they were being attacked. Often one would rear completely out of the water, its whole incredible body momentarily balanced upon its flukes. Then it would fall back into the sea with a slow-motion leisureliness which, from our distant vantage point, was the clearest and most striking proof of its real size.

No one, I thought, could watch these gigantic beasts— the largest creatures that have ever moved on the surface of this planet since time began—without a sense of wonder. I knew now how Herman Melville felt when for the first time he saw the sea furrowed by a glistening back as large as an overturned ship, and conceived in the image of Moby Dick a symbol of the dark forces that lie behind the Universe.

Soon the whales were astern, the clear blue water over which we had been sailing turned to a muddy green, and we were skirting the mangrove-covered island which guards the port of Gladstone from the sea. Then came the long and tedious business of getting all our equipment from the dock-side to the station—and Round Two of our bout with the Queensland Government Railways.

Our car, now repaired, was still in Maryborough, two hundred miles to the south. We had booked tickets on the Gladstone-Maryborough train, and when we had transported our small mountain of baggage to the station we were assured that there was plenty of time to have a meal before weighing in. We had just ordered a large lunch at a near-by café when we received the devastating news that the train was already here, and would be leaving in ten minutes.

Throwing our steak and eggs into a cardboard box, we raced to the station. But there was nothing we could do; it was impossible to get some twenty items of assorted baggage weighed and ticketed in the time available. We had to sit like evicted tenants on our boxes of air cylinders while we watched the train pull out.

Then followed much recrimination and an indignant interview with the stationmaster. Fortunately, there were several southbound trains that afternoon, and it was not difficult to book seats on the next one out. What *was* difficult to discover was the time the train was expected to leave; every porter gave a different estimate, so we decided to take no chances but to check in our baggage immediately and thereafter to keep a continuous watch on the station. The next train wasn't going to get away without us.

So in the late afternoon we finally left the Tropic of Capricorn, and in little more than seven hours' traveling arrived at our destination, a whole two hundred miles away. It was now midnight, and when the train halted under the stars at the junction outside Maryborough the baggage van was very out in the no man's land beyond the station. While I tried to arrange transport into town, Mike walked down the line to see that all our luggage had been safely unloaded.

Despite the late hour, there was a good deal of local activity, and when our train had pulled out, shunting engines started moving around us on mysterious errands. Presently one of them began to approach along the main line, and at that moment I heard, unmistakably if somewhat unintelligibly, Mike yelling at the top of his voice out there in the darkness beyond the station. His exact words were not audible, but his intonation conveyed his general feelings quite clearly. It was easy to detect the frequent appearance of the Great Australian Adjective, as well as the remaining triad comprising what Sidney Baker, in his scholarly work *The Australian Language,* has called "the four Indispensable B's."

The violence of his verbal reaction assured me that, whatever might have happened, Mike was none the worse. He was still slightly incandescent when I arrived, and it was some time before I could extract a coherent account from him.

The porters, it seemed, had unloaded the contents of the baggage van not by, but *on* the railway track. Mike had managed to move almost all our property out of the way when the next train arrived, but was unable to cope with the large wooden crate containing six Porpoise air cylinders. The train had smashed the box and tossed it off the track, but its contents—which were made of high-quality steel and so could stand up to rather rough treatment—were none the worse. As I surveyed the wreckage, I wondered what would have happened if the train wheels had hit, fair and square, one of those cylinders with a full charge of air in it—and thus carrying a total pressure of almost a thousand tons.

The rest of our gear had been missed by inches. The complete photographic record of the expedition, containing some hundreds of color slides, would have been lost if Mike had not arrived on the scene in time. Even now, I do not like to recall how narrowly all our months of work escaped being destroyed. It was a strange coincidence that, in several thousand miles of travel, we should twice have skirted disaster in the small Queensland town.

We quickly checked our property for damage, and then started to breathe again. Other goods consigned to Maryborough had not been so fortunate as ours; I fancied that the local cinema would be feeling the pinch, as a large container of 35-millimeter film was lying in a somewhat battered condition beside the line. Mike had been much too busy safeguarding our belongings to rescue anyone else's.

When the porters returned to the scene of the crime, they did not appear to be at all upset, but put the blame on the engine driver. We learned, with some incredulity, that this kind of thing happened quite often. If we needed proof of this, it lay close enough at hand. There in the bushes beside the track were two large and shattered trunks—casualties of the previous night, which had not yet been removed from the battlefield.

We did not feel really safe until, early the next morning, we were once more driving south in the now-repaired Chevy, the scene of our misfortunes receding behind us. It was true that, when one considered all the things that *might* have happened to our expedition, we had little to grumble about, but I have never had much sympathy for the "Well-it-might-have-been-a-lot-worse" school of optimism.

As I glance back over this account of our adventures, I wish that I could have been a little kinder to the Queensland roads and railways. There *are* some excellent trains, but we had to take the ones forced upon us by circumstances outside our control. And as far as the roads are concerned, here the State faces a problem which is virtually insoluble. A small population scattered over vast distances cannot possibly finance the sort of road network which the Englishman or American takes for granted, and the annual heavy rains, with their accompanying floods and washouts, aggravate the problem.

Australia is a country which is by-passing the age of surface transport. Its internal air system is probably the best in the world; DC-4's put down at small country towns, and turbo-prop Viscounts are slicing schedules in all directions. Against this sort of competition, the railways have not got a chance, and perhaps they know it. When we go to Heron Island again, as one day we hope to do, we shall fly to the new airfield that has been opened at Gladstone. And later still, no doubt, there will be a helicopter service over to the island, leaving the *Capre* to concentrate on fishing trips around the neighboring reefs.

As we drove south to Brisbane, through now familiar scenes warmed by the gentle sun of early spring, we tried to marshal our thoughts and to put into some sort of order the impressions and experiences we had gained. It was hard to find any patterns; we had gone to the Reef with no preconceived ideas and had brought back from it no far-reaching conclusions. We were conscious of all that we might have done, had we the time and the equipment. One omission I would have given much to rectify. I had never been to the Outer Barrier itself, and seen the surf beating against the great submerged ramparts through which Cook and Bligh sailed into history two centuries ago. Out there, facing the Pacific, is virgin territory which few divers indeed can ever have plumbed. It can be a dangerous place to visit, except during certain seasons, and even then one may have to wait for weeks for the right conditions. But I think that the wait would be worth it.

In an age which is seeking new frontiers, the Great Barrier Reef provides one of the few unexploited—indeed, largely unexplored—regions still remaining on this planet. In at least three major fields of human activity—commerce, science, and recreation—it offers opportunities which it would be hard to match elsewhere.

The unromantic but vital battle to feed an explosively increasing population can never cease, and must be intensified in the years that lie ahead. Though it may not be as rich as the cold waters round the poles, the great lagoon within the thousand-mile-long coral wall of the Reef must hold prodigious quantities of fish, and could be an inexhaustible source of shark and whale by-products. Inexhaustible, that is, if its exploitation is properly controlled. At present the waters of the Reef yield fish and shell to the value of over a million pounds a year, and this output could certainly be much increased without risk of over-fishing.

To the scientist—whether his interest lies in geology, biology, oceanography, or even anthropology—the Great Barrier Reef presents a challenge which, largely because of the difficulty of transport over such distances, has not yet been properly met. There has been only one major expedition to the Reef—and that was almost forty years ago. In 1928 a group of eighteen scientists spent a year on Low Isles, about forty-five miles north of Cairns, and the reports of this expedition were later issued in many volumes by the British Museum. It is surely time that, with the new resources and equipment now available, the Reef was made the subject of another comprehensive survey. Of course, such a project would cost at least ten times as much as in 1928, but as some corrective to that the general interest in the sea and matters pertaining to it has enormously increased in the last decade.

When it is complete, the Great Barrier Reef Committee's laboratory on Heron Island will undoubtedly be the spearhead of such research. It has already been used by many students, both from Australia and other parts of the world. When the aquarium now planned is operating, it will also be a major attraction to the tourists.

Every year, several thousand visitors take their holidays at the Reef's resort islands, and many more travel out by launch on brief excursions from the mainland. But this is barely a beginning; in the foreseeable future, the Reef could become one of the great playgrounds of the world. This is not a prospect that I view with unmixed pleasure, though I hope and believe that the Reef is too big to be spoiled by man. It could absorb a million tourists, and they would be lost in its immensity.

Mike and I often indulge in a pleasant daydream where we try to picture what we would do with one of the more romantic outer islands and a syndicate of complacent millionaires. With its own helicopter service, the Reef Hotel would be within an hour of the mainland, yet it would be so far from the coast that it would be washed by the unsullied waters of the open Pacific. Part of the hotel would be sunk into the reef; there would be wide-windowed corridors below the water line, through which all the life and beauty of the coral world outside could be observed. By day or night, this would provide an entertainment which only those who have seen it can ever really imagine.

By night? Yes, for when there was neither sun nor moon, many of the creatures of the reef would glow with their own phosphorescence, providing a luminous background against which the great sharks might be seen gliding as sinister silhouettes. From time to time submerged searchlights could be switched on, attracting fish like moths around a lamp, and showing the coral polyps fully extended from their tiny limestone cells.

This display would appeal to all, but for the more adventurous there could be the unique and unforgettable opportunity of underwater tours along the reef. They would emerge, with breathing gear and short-range communication sets of the type already in existence, from a chamber just below the water line, and follow a guide who would introduce them to his pet grouper, show them round the coral glades, answer all their questions, and gently discourage them from collecting specimens or swimming off by themselves. No fishing of any kind, either by spear or line, would be allowed around the hotel. There would be opportunities for that on reefs some miles away, but here would be a sanctuary where men and fish could share the water in peace, each studying the other's peculiar ways.

There is nothing fantastic about this dream, though I do not know if it would survive the cold scrutiny of the cost accountant's eye. Today's underwater observatories are but the beginning; it can be only a matter of time before there are not merely underwater hotels, but even underwater homes. . . .

Whatever the future may bring, the Reef can wait. As I leave—for how long I cannot guess—the world of coral and sun and rainbow-rivaling fish, I remember the Reef in one of the moods of fury which have put terror into the hearts of so many sailors, in so many diverse craft. I think of a day when a gale was howling northward along the Queensland coast, tossing the branches of the pisonia trees above my head. Looking across toward the hidden mainland, forty miles away, I could see the breakers foaming over the neighboring reef. It seemed as if, every few seconds, a line of white cliffs formed magically upon the horizon, then as suddenly disappeared as the wall of spray fell back into the sea.

The storm was destroying billions of the coral animals, shattering their tiny homes around them. But even before it had passed and the seas were calm again, the mindless architects who built this twelve-hundred-mile-long range of sunken mountains would be at work repairing the damage. They laid the foundations of the Reef ages before Man appeared upon this planet; and theirs is a monument which may still endure when all the creations of his brain and hand have passed away.

COMING IN JULY 2002

THE REEFS OF TAPROBANE
by Arthur C. Clarke
ISBN: 0-7434-4502-3

THE SECOND VOLUME IN THE "BLUE PLANET TRILOGY"

Looking for new underwater worlds to conquer, Arthur Clarke and Mike Wilson followed up their expedition to Australia's Great Barrier Reef (described in *The Coast of Coral*) by exploring the romantic seas surrounding Ceylon.

Meetings with dangerous and beautiful marine creatures were only one side of the expedition's activities. Their adventures included the discovery of a 3,000-year-old Hindu temple lying one the ocean bed. Clarke and Wilson lived among the Ceylonese natives, their contact with Europeans virtually limited to the dozen members of the Ceylonese Reefcombers Club, who shared many of their underwater adventures.

Clarke and Wilson's experiences provide vivid impressions of old and new Ceylon, one of the key countries of the Far East.

With 16 pages of stunning black-and-white photographs by Mike Wilson!

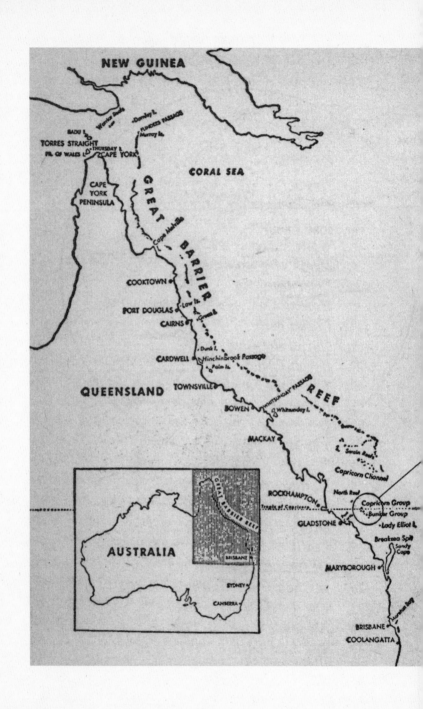

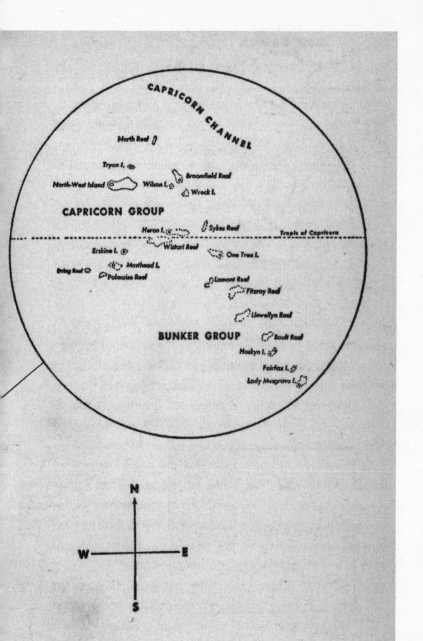

ALSO BY ARTHUR C. CLARKE

THE SENTINEL
ISBN: 0-7434-0721-0

Few masters of science fiction have brought us glimpses of the near future as vividly as Arthur C. Clarke. It is the startling realism of his vision that has made classics of his *Childhood's End* and *2001: A Space Odyssey*—and Clarke himself one of the genre's most successful writers.

To commemorate one of the most notable dates in science fiction history comes this special anniversary edition of *The Sentinel*, a brilliant collection of Clarke's highest caliber short fiction. Among the ten stories included in this volume are:

"The Sentinel": The story that inspired *2001: A Space Odyssey*, one of the most famous SF movies of all time

"Guardian Angel": The rarely-glimpsed work that gave birth to *Childhood's End*

"The Songs of Distant Earth": A fantastic tale of first contact with an alien world, which became the basis for one of Clarke's most successful novels

"Breaking Strain": The inspiration for the popular book series *Arthur C. Clarke's Venus Prime*

with an introduction and notes by the author

TALES FROM PLANET EARTH
ISBN: 0-7434-2379-8

The fiction of Arthur C. Clarke has spanned the universe. He has carried us across unimaginable distances to alien times and places. Yet he has not lost sight of his home. Many of his greatest stories are set—or have their roots—right here on Planet Earth.

For Arthur C. Clarke, more than any other science fiction writer, "home" is the entire Earth, through all of space and time. In this book, he shows us around his home to share his wonder. He invites us to share his vision and his dream.

Includes "On Golden Seas"—never before collected in any Clarke book!

**With a Preface by science fiction Grand Master
Isaac Asimov,
and notes by the author**